NOV 0 0 2021

Praise for

KILLER CONTENT

"Odessa has an unconventional, appealing voice, and she's no shrinking violet. I laughed out loud in places. *Killer Content* is a killer read!" —*New York Times* bestselling author Sofie Kelly

"Blacke pens a delightful main character in boots-wearing Odessa Dean, a rural Louisiana transplant to Brooklyn. I loved this immersive whodunnit, with its diverse cast and unique social media theme. #killermystery."

—Jennifer J. Chow, author of *Mimi Lee Gets a Clue*

WITHDRAWN

"Sparkling with delightful dry wit, this tale of a small-town Southern girl taking on the big city is a debut that satisfies from beginning to end."

—Laurie Cass, national bestselling author of *Gone with the Whisker*

"Cowboy boot–wearing Odessa Dean brings Southern sensibility to the Big Apple. Quirky characters, viral videos, books, beer, and murder! An entertaining Millennial tale."

—Abby Collette, author of *A Deadly Inside Scoop*

"In lieu of the standard cute cop vs. talented amateur standoff, Blacke's quirky characters and offbeat plot twists allow her debut to work some pleasing variations on the theme. Refreshing fare." —*Kirkus Reviews*

D0424284

"Cozy fans will enjoy seeing Brooklyn (and Brooklynites) through spunky outsider Odessa's eyes as she gathers the evidence. Distinctive characters enhance the lively plot. Blacke is off to a promising start."
——*Publishers Weekly*

WITHDRAWN

TITLES BY OLIVIA BLACKE

Killer Content

No Memes of Escape

NO MEMES OF ESCAPE

A Brooklyn Murder Mystery

Olivia Blacke

BERKLEY PRIME CRIME
NEW YORK

BERKLEY PRIME CRIME
Published by Berkley
An imprint of Penguin Random House LLC
penguinrandomhouse.com

Copyright © 2021 by Olivia Blacke
Penguin Random House supports copyright. Copyright fuels creativity, encourages
diverse voices, promotes free speech, and creates a vibrant culture. Thank you for buying
an authorized edition of this book and for complying with copyright laws by not
reproducing, scanning, or distributing any part of it in any form without permission.
You are supporting writers and allowing Penguin Random House to
continue to publish books for every reader.

BERKLEY and the BERKLEY & B colophon are registered trademarks and
BERKLEY PRIME CRIME is a trademark of Penguin Random House LLC.

Library of Congress Cataloging-in-Publication Data

Names: Blacke, Olivia, author.
Title: No memes of escape / Olivia Blacke.
Description: First Edition. | New York: Berkley Prime Crime, 2021. |
Series: Brooklyn murder mysteries; 2
Identifiers: LCCN 2021012455 (print) | LCCN 2021012456 (ebook) |
ISBN 9780593197905 (trade paperback) | ISBN 9780593197912 (ebook)
Subjects: GSAFD: Mystery fiction.
Classification: LCC PS3602.L325293 N6 2021 (print) |
LCC PS3602.L325293 (ebook) | DDC 813/.6—dc23
LC record available at https://lccn.loc.gov/2021012455
LC ebook record available at https://lccn.loc.gov/2021012456

First Edition: October 2021

Printed in the United States of America
1st Printing

Book design by Alison Cnockaert

This is a work of fiction. Names, characters, places, and incidents either are the product
of the author's imagination or are used fictitiously, and any resemblance to actual persons,
living or dead, business establishments, events, or locales is entirely coincidental.

Do kindness

1

Odessa Dean @OdessaWaiting · July 12
Look who's back, y'all. #NYC #Williamsburg

WE WON!

I wasn't used to winning, or even being on the winning team. In high school, back in Louisiana, they used to make everyone play volleyball in the old echoey gym and without fail, whatever team I was on lost. They even had a special nickname for me, Odessa the Jinx. If only they could see me now—the undisputed champion of the Williamsburg—Brooklyn, not Colonial—Summer Cornhole Tournament.

There was a big, heavy trophy and everything.

I know, I know, there's a common misconception that my generation was raised on trophies, but before today I'd never won a single trophy in my entire life. I was starting to realize that I had a gigantic competitive streak I'd never discovered before.

Then again, ever since moving—albeit temporarily—from the sleepy little town of Piney Island, Louisiana, to the trendy Brooklyn neighborhood of Williamsburg, I'd discovered a whole

OLIVIA BLACKE

lot about myself. I used to think of myself as Odessa, the perki-
est waitress at the Crawdad Shack, who was friendly, decent
with a sewing machine, and unfailingly polite to the elderly.
Now I was still all those things—except substitute Untapped
Books & Café for the Crawdad Shack—but now I'd learned to
cook a few simple meals, could navigate the confusing New York
City subway system (as long as I had the MTA app up on my
phone), and apparently, reigned supreme at cornhole.

Talk about self-improvement!

Cornhole was similar to horseshoes, except instead of throwing iron horseshoes at a pole, contestants took turns tossing
weighted beanbags at a hole in a short wooden wedge. I'd never
played cornhole before today, but beginner's luck must have
been on my side because my partner and I beat all the other
teams. Winning was a new sensation for me, and I loved it.

Before coming to Williamsburg for three months to apartment-
and cat-sit for my aunt Melanie while she toured Europe, there
were a lot of things I'd never experienced. Food trucks. Ubers.
Street tacos. Craft beer. Avocado toast. Since moving here, I'd
also found out I was adept at solving murders, but I didn't plan
on doing that again anytime soon. No, siree. One was more than
enough for me.

One and done.

I was out of the murder solving business.

My best-friend-slash-roommate, Izzy, threw her arm around
my shoulders. "We did it, Odessa!" She stretched out her other
arm to get a selfie of the two of us cradling the massive trophy.

"I know, right?" I agreed.

Izzy Wilson was one of the first people I'd met in Williamsburg. As the spunky cashier at Untapped Books & Café, where I served an ever-revolving menu of savory dishes, artisanal sandwiches, and a wide selection of cold craft beers to our eclectic customers, we clicked instantly. She appointed herself my personal guide to all things Brooklyn, so when she needed a place to crash for a few days, I let her stay with me. That had been three weeks ago, and she was still there.

Izzy was taller than me, and had longer arms, which gave her a better angle for taking the picture. "Hashtag squad goals!" she said, making a goofy grin. The light caught her hair—which was only a few inches long. This week it was a shade of aquamarine that I imagined the ocean around the Bahamas must look, and it made her look like an ecstatic pixie.

"Send that to me, will ya?" I asked.

"I'll post it to Insta," she replied.

"Perfect," I agreed. Since moving to Williamsburg, I'd seriously upped my social media game. I went from only updating my status when something interesting happened to posting to multiple sites a day, several times a day. Plus, I was in charge of the social media accounts for the bookstore-slash-café where Izzy and I worked.

Izzy swiped around on her phone. "Done." She checked the screen. "Plans?"

"None," I admitted. "It's a good thing I'm working the late shift. I never expected to make it past the first round of the competition, much less win the tournament."

"Me, too. Evening shift, I mean. I never doubted we'd come out on top. The two of us together? Unstoppable." Undoubtably filled with the same pride I was, she grinned again at the trophy as I wedged it into my messenger bag. "This totes calls for a celebration."

I checked my bank account balance on my phone. It wasn't pretty. Williamsburg had an awful lot to offer. A fabulous range of live indie music. Mind-blowing street art. Delicious, flavorful dishes served from an ever-rotating fleet of food trucks. A unique and constantly changing selection of funky craft beers.

And none of it was cheap.

Despite working as many hours as the café would allow and staying at my aunt's for free in exchange for keeping an eye on her adorable cat, Rufus, I was perpetually broke. "As long as your idea of a celebration doesn't cost much more than a lemonade at that new handcart in Domino Park, I'm in."

Izzy hooked her arm around mine. "I know a little place where the beers are cold, the service is great, and we always get a discount." We spent enough time at Untapped Books & Café working, and still found ourselves there off the clock more often than not. In addition to the *very* handy employee discount, pretty much everyone I knew in Williamsburg either worked there or ate there every day.

Food at Untapped was half-price for us, but we paid full price for beer unless we were overstocked. "The way we're pushing Pursuit of Hoppiness, they'd probably pay us to take it off their hands," I suggested.

"Sounds good. After that tournament I'm starving and Parker's been working on a vegan mock-egg salad I'm dying to taste test."

Izzy, like approximately half of Williamsburg as far as I could tell, was vegan. Parker Reed, the enthusiastic day chef at the café, was always inventing new recipes for our eclectic custom-ers. He was a genius in the kitchen and made sure to have op-tions for multiple dietary restrictions from vegan to gluten-free. I used to think vegan food sounded gross, but the more dishes I tried, the more I liked it. I wasn't giving up delicious fried shrimp po' boy sandwiches anytime soon, but a vegan egg salad sounded intriguing. "Deal," I agreed.

We turned the corner and almost smacked into a clump of women who were giggling in that high-pitched tone that usually indicated one too many mimosas with brunch.

The white woman in the center of the cluster wore a light pink silk blouse. Her long nails were painted almost the exact same shade of pink. She had on little jewelry save for a diamond that was too big and shiny to be real that dangled from a simple gold necklace. She literally looked down at me over a hawkish nose, and said, "Excuse you," in a haughty voice, as if she and her gaggle of friends weren't the ones hogging the entire sidewalk.

"Vickie?" Izzy asked. "Victoria Marsh?"

The woman's head swiveled toward her. "Izzy? Isabelle Wil-son? Wow, it *is* you. What a surprise."

"Oh em gee!" another woman said, pushing her way to the front of the cluster of women. They made enough noise and took up the space of a dozen people, but when they weren't all chat-ting away, I realized there were just four of them.

She was a Black woman, dressed in a casual button-down, comfortable-looking shirt with wide-legged pants. Instead of a purse or backpack, she carried a colorful bag that was stuffed to the brim. Judging by the rubber ducky, penguin, and teddy bear pattern, I guessed it was a diaper bag. She had piercing holes in both earlobes but no visible earrings, and wore her hair super short. "Izzy!" she squealed.

Izzy closed the distance between us and the other women and threw her arms around her waist. "Gennifer!" she squealed, rocking back and forth in a hug. "It's been . . . what, forever!"

"Three years, at least," she responded, wheezing as she pried herself free of Izzy's embrace. Having been on the receiving end of an enthusiastic hug from Izzy before, I sympathized with her for being out of breath. She turned to me. "Hi! I'm Gennifer-with-a-G Buckley. You are?"

"Odessa Dean," I replied. "Take it you know our Izzy?"

"Know her? Only since we were both in diapers." She turned her attention back to Izzy. "What are you doing in Brooklyn? Last I heard, you moved to Minnesota or some place with cows."

I turned my attention to Izzy. I had a hard time picturing Izzy surviving in the Midwest. I wasn't even sure that vegans were welcome in Minnesota, and her short blue hair might raise a few eyebrows.

Izzy laughed. "Where'd you hear that? Me, leave New York? Not hardly. How's Pete? And little Penny?"

Gennifer flashed a dazzling wedding ring in a subconscious gesture. "All good. Pete just got a promotion, and Penny's growing like a weed. She's with her grandma today."

"I must admit, I never expected to bump into you in Brooklyn," Izzy said. "I thought the ferry gave you hives."

"Ferry?" I asked.

"Staten Island Ferry," Gennifer clarified. "Izzy, Vickie, and I grew up together on Staten Island."

Vickie interrupted, fluttering perfectly shaped pink fingernails near her throat. "Gosh, we've known each other since, what, sixth grade?"

"Fifth," Gennifer supplied. "Vickie, Izzy, and I all lived on the same block."

"You did?" I asked, shooting Izzy a sideways glance. I was still getting the hang of New York. The city was made up of five boroughs—including the most well-known, Manhattan, and my borough of Brooklyn. Inside each of the boroughs were individual neighborhoods, like Williamsburg. There was a certain hierarchy of desirability and panache that came with location, along with quite a few stereotypes. I never would have imagined that Izzy had started out in Staten Island, the most suburban of all the boroughs.

"Sure did. Dongan Hills pride!" Gennifer said, slapping Izzy on the back.

"Of course, some of us got out of Staten Island as soon as possible and never looked back," Vickie added with a self-satisfied grin on her face.

"Of course," Izzy agreed, while rolling her eyes. "What brings you across the bridge?" One of the things that confused me to no end was how New Yorkers not only rarely ventured out of New York City, they hardly ever left their own neighborhood, much less their borough, especially if it meant taking a bridge or tunnel. Manhattanites rarely visited Brooklyn, Queens, or the Bronx if they could help it, and liked to pretend that Staten Island and New Jersey didn't exist at all.

"We're celebrating," Vickie replied, straightening her shoulders. "We have a reservation for an escape room over on Fifth.

I'd love to stay and chat, but if we don't hurry, we're gonna be late."

I doubted she'd ever been late for anything in her entire life. She was like those customers who showed up five minutes before opening and then acted huffy when we didn't unlock the doors early to accommodate them. Considering no one on the staff—myself included—was ever on time, opening at the posted time was challenging enough without the early bird knocking on the door demanding their turn at the proverbial worm.

"Izzy, why don't you guys join us?" Gennifer suggested. "Becks and Nadia dropped out at the last minute, so we've got spare tickets. Come along. It's already paid for, so it wouldn't cost a cent."

Vickie's smile twitched but was back in place so quickly I might have imagined it. "Oh, I'm sure Izzy and her little friend have plans." She didn't glance in my direction, but as it was the first time she'd acknowledged my presence since she'd almost trampled me, I'd assumed she had forgotten that I existed.

"Nope," I interjected. "Free as a bird." Izzy jabbed me with her elbow, but I ignored her. "We'd love to join you, right?"

Izzy glared at me, and I suppressed the urge to giggle. I couldn't remember seeing her grumpy before. She was perpetually cheery. I should know. As her roomie, I'd seen her wake up with a smile on her face. She whistled to herself when she did dishes. She volunteered to do laundry because she thought it was fun. I'd even caught her singing in her sleep. "Um, yeah, sure," Izzy said.

"Then it's settled!" Gennifer said brightly.

"The more the merrier," Vickie agreed, but her dry voice said otherwise. I was starting to wonder if inviting myself along was such a good idea.

"Yup," Izzy agreed. "Only, you said you were going to that escape room on Fifth? 'Cause you're headed in the wrong direction." She pointed back to the way they'd come. "It's behind you."

"Yeah, sure, of course. You know how it is. I get turned around every time I leave the city," Vickie said.

"Sure you do," Izzy muttered.

New York City might be comprised of multiple boroughs covering over three hundred miles, but "the city" usually referred to the blocks of Manhattan below 110th Street. No matter that Williamsburg was hipper than any place in Manhattan, it might as well have been as backwater as Piney Island, Louisiana, as far as Manhattanites were concerned.

In the six weeks I'd been here, I'd only ventured into Manhattan a few times. I'd done a few of the touristy things like touring the Statue of Liberty, Times Square, and the Chrysler Building. Izzy had taken me to see a band called Jimber Timber play in the Village. Mostly I'd stayed in Williamsburg, because even if I lived here for the next hundred years, I would never be able to sample more than a sliver of all that my new neighborhood had to offer. If women like Vickie never wanted to cross the bridge into Brooklyn, I was all right with that. It was crowded enough without her.

As soon as there was a little bit of breathing room between us and the rest of the women—Vickie, Gennifer, and two others I hadn't officially met yet—I asked Izzy, "What's the deal?"

She glanced up and judged the distance between us and the

others, who had gone back to their boisterous tittering. "I don't much like Vickie," she confessed.

"I picked up on the tension, but I've never done an escape room before." There was a lot about Williamsburg I still hadn't experienced. At the beginning of summer, three months seemed like a lifetime, but once I got here, I realized that it wasn't nearly enough time to take advantage of everything New York had to offer. Already, half of that time had flown by and I hadn't even seen a play on Broadway yet.

"We could do one anytime, just you and me."

"I already checked. They're expensive." Maybe to a New Yorker it wasn't much, but to me, on waitress wages? Anything that cost more than a Happy Meal was a stretch. "I should have checked with you first, but . . ." I let my voice trail off.

"You're right," she said with a nod and a bright grin. "I mean, it would be silly to pass up a free escape room, wouldn't it? Plus, you'll like Gennifer. She's a trip. We used to get into so much trouble back in school."

"That I can imagine." Izzy was a free spirit, to say the least. It wasn't hard to envision her as a child, running around Staten Island, breaking all the rules.

"Come on, then," she said. I'd gotten better at walking fast since coming to Brooklyn, but with my shorter legs, I don't think I'd ever be able to keep up with a native New Yorker on a mission. "Hurry it up or they'll start without us."

2

Dizzy Izzy @IsabelleWilliamsburg · July 12
what did @odessawaiting drag me into this time? how can
i escape an escape? #escape #puzzles #williamsburg

WE ARRIVED AT a building that, like most of Williamsburg, had
once been an industrial warehouse. The sign over the door said,
"Verrazzano-Narrows Escape!" Real punny. And also ironic considering the Verrazzano-Narrows Bridge was the only direct
route from Brooklyn to Staten Island without getting wet, and
half of our party was from Staten Island originally.

After checking in at the front desk, a sleepy-looking guy gave
each of us a clipboard with a stack of release forms to sign, a list
of the dos and don'ts, and a coupon for 10 percent off our next
exciting escape room experience.

Their words, not mine.

Before I could sit down, Gennifer came over. She reminded
me of Izzy—friendly and cheerful—but with half her energy.
"I'm so sorry, I already forgot your name."

"Odessa Dean," I said, offering my hand.

"What'd she say her name was?" Vickie asked in a stage whisper to the woman closest to her.

"Who knows?" the woman replied. "I can't hardly understand a word she says."

I liked to think my backwoods Louisiana accent, thick and lazy as the stifling bayou, had improved in the last few weeks. I sounded less like a southern-fried unicorn—as Izzy had once labeled me—these days, but sometimes when I spoke, people still got a confused look on their face. I reminded myself to slow down and enunciate, as I repeated my name. Personally, I didn't think I had an accent, but every time I opened my mouth, New Yorkers stared at me like I was speaking a foreign language. If they thought I was bad, they should hear my cousins or some of my customers back home at the Crawdad Shack. Now *they* had accents so thick sometimes even I couldn't understand them.

Gennifer indicated a woman who was several years older than anyone else in the group, if the gray streaks around her temples and the elaborate necklace of purple glass baubles were any indication. The necklace reminded me of the fake grapes that adorned my grandmother's living room coffee table. Her clothes were neatly pressed, but her outfit—a short red jacket-like blouse with big black buttons and an even bigger black collar paired with straight-legged black pants—looked like something that came out of the professional section of a catalog in the nineties, or my mother's closet. "This is Marlie. She works with Vickie."

Her face twitched as if she'd been holding a fake smile too long. That was a sensation I was intimately familiar with, as my job required me to be bright and friendly at all times, even when

I wasn't feeling it. It was exhausting sometimes. Marlie and I nodded at each other before Gennifer continued. "And this is Amanda, never Mandy. She and Vickie went to NYU together."

Amanda gave me a hard head-to-toe assessment, her sharp green eyes taking in the slightly frayed collar of my long, ribbed tank top that did an amazing job of flattering my curves, a flouncy purple, green, and blue tie-dyed homemade skirt, and my practical-but-ugly-as-sin orthopedic loafers. Don't knock 'em until you've spent a double on your feet. "Nice to meet you," she said.

"Vickie said something about celebrating?" I asked. "What's the big occasion?"

"Vickie won the heckin' good broker of the month prize at her office, for the twelfth month in a row, which makes her the best broker in New York City."

"*Earned*, Gennifer," Vickie corrected her. "*Won* makes it sound like I was the tenth caller or something."

"Congratulations," I said. Behind me, Izzy echoed the sentiment. She didn't sound quite as enthusiastic as I did, but if Vickie noticed, she didn't react.

"Ladies, I'm gonna need those forms," the guy behind the desk called out.

Vickie handed him her clipboard. "I know you," she said, staring at him.

"You rented me an apartment last year," he said.

"That's right! Park Slope?"

"Flatbush," he corrected her.

"I knew it." She turned her attention back to our little group. "See? That's why I earned the real estate broker of the month prize every single month for a full year. It's not about big sales, Marlie, it's about consistent sales. Although, I made a killer commission off that Flatbush deal."

Izzy rolled her eyes so hard I thought she might fall out of her chair. Beside her, I continued to skim the rules. We had sixty minutes to solve a series of increasingly difficult puzzles to get through each room. Seemed simple enough. I was good with puzzles, from jigsaws to crosswords.

After signing what frankly seemed like an obscene amount of waivers and returning the forms to the front desk, I shoved my messenger bag into a cubby on the wall. "Whatcha doing?" Izzy asked.

"It's not like I'm gonna lug this with me. Our cornhole trophy alone weighs a ton."

She pulled my bag out of the cubicle and slung it over her neck and one arm so it hung cross-body. "Anytime you see a sign that says management isn't responsible for personal items left in lockers, it's pretty much guaranteed that the second you turn your back, some creep is going through your purse." She glared pointedly at the pimpled guy behind the front desk.

"Like I care about your cheapo drugstore makeup and half-chewed pack of gum," he grumbled, tugging on the bow tie of his ill-fitting tux. I felt sorry for him. I didn't always love my work uniform—neon green wasn't flattering on anyone—but at least I didn't have to wear a cheap tuxedo.

"See?" Izzy said.

"You can keep your bags if you want," he said in the same tired tone, "but you have to turn off your phones." He spun the monitor on his desk around so we could see the black-and-white image on the screen. "No cheating. I'll be watching from here, and if I see anyone on their cell phones, you're all banned for life."

Izzy grinned. "I'm all out of data for the month, so joke's on you, Sparky."

He rotated the screen back toward himself and stood, his antiquated office chair letting out a protesting squeal. "If your paperwork is complete, stack your clipboards here and follow me." We did as requested, following him in a single-file line through a swinging door down a bland hallway with five num- bered doors.

"Welcome to Verrazzano-Narrows Escape!, Williamsburg's premier escape room experience," he intoned, and I had to won- der how many times he'd repeated this speech. "In a minute, your exciting experience will begin." He pointed at a digital clock over the door that flashed "60" in red numbers. I noticed that two of the other rooms were in various points of their own countdowns. "I'm Brandon Reaves, and I'll be your Game Mas- ter for your attempt at Clueless. If you find yourself at an im- passe, you can call out for hints, but each one'll cost you ninety seconds off the game clock. Due to New York City health and safety regulations, I'm required to inform you that this door will remain unlocked at all times. You're free to exit for any reason but doing so results in immediate disqualification for the entire team without a refund. I'll see you in sixty minutes."

He tugged on an absurdly crowded key ring that was sus- pended from his belt by a retractable cord and flipped through a jangle of keys until he came to a large, shiny one and inserted it into the lock of Door Three. He unlocked the door and pulled it open, revealing a black-painted room without any visible illumination. We squeezed in, one by one, with barely enough room to stand. "Good luck!" he called, and closed the door with a heavy thud.

I took a deep breath, trying to adjust to the darkness. It was a good thing I wasn't claustrophobic, but even so, I felt panic welling up from the pit of my stomach.

"There should be an opening here somewhere," someone said. I couldn't place the voice other than to know it wasn't Izzy's. "Everyone check around you for a switch or a knob."

I felt the wall behind me and it was solid. There was no sign of the doorknob that the Game Master had unlocked, just a vast smooth surface. I knelt and ran my hand along the baseboard and then flinched as someone stepped on my hand. "Ow! Watch it!" I said, snatching my hand back.

"Sorry," a disembodied voice said.

"Hey, check it out," someone else said, and there was a click as the tiny confined space flooded with light. "Let there be light," Gennifer said.

The side wall was now illuminated, covered in nine squares, each with one to twenty dots on them. Each block of dots glowed a different color. We all stared at the illuminated dots. Well, most of us stared. Amanda pulled out her phone and posed for an extreme-angle selfie.

"What now?" Vickie asked.

"Maybe we should just start trying them," Amanda suggested. She pressed the middle square, the thirteen. The button buzzed, the dots all flashed three times, and then the middle square turned dark. "Okay, not that one." She tried the top-right button. It buzzed. The dots all flashed twice, and then it went dark.

"Wait a second," I said. "I think we only have one more chance. Look. The squares look like dice, right?"

"Except there's no such thing as dice that goes up to twenty," Vickie replied in a superior tone.

"Unless it's a twenty-sided die," I said.

"A what?" Vickie asked.

"Never mind," I replied. Tabletop games were making a comeback. Games my parents used to play in the basement, like Dungeons & Dragons, were now trending in a big way. I was surprised that Vickie hadn't gotten on board—no pun intended—yet. Then again, Williamsburg was ahead of the curve. Maybe the D&D revival hadn't made it to Manhattan yet. "We're in Room Three, right?"

"Right," Vickie said. "But there's no three up there."

"True." I'd noticed that, too. "But on dice, four is on the other side of the three, right? There is a four. We should push that one."

"Are you sure?" Vickie asked. "You said we only have one more shot at it."

Izzy pushed the square with four dots. "She's sure," she said. While I was pleased with her faith in me, I wasn't so certain. What if I'd guessed wrong and the game was over before it even began? Then a bell chimed. There was a click as the far wall swung open to reveal another room. "Told ya!"

We surged forward, everyone eager to pour out of the tiny foyer. Or maybe that was just me. We spilled into a room decorated like a private library, complete with high shelves on the walls lined with books. There was a sliding ladder mounted to the wall like I wished we had back at Untapped Books & Café. I didn't work the bookstore side often, but when I did, I spent more time lugging a stepladder around than I did checking out customers.

The room was lit with electric candles. Comfy-looking leather armchairs were strategically placed in front of faux windows. At the far end of the room was a sturdy oak desk stacked high with dusty old books and scattered papers with illegible notes scrawled across them. I plucked a book off the nearest shelf and ran my hand down the cheap imitation leather cover that was glued to a solid block of balsa wood instead of being bound to actual pages.

"What next?" Vickie asked.

"Game Master, can we have a hint?" Marlie asked loudly. In response, a disembodied voice came over the speaker and said, "Find the secret passage to advance."

"Well, that was helpful," Izzy said, passing by me as she plucked books off the shelf at random. Like the one I'd examined, they were all fake.

I glanced at the wall. There were hundreds of books. Hundreds of hundreds, maybe. "It would take all day to check them all," I said. "We need to be methodical."

Ignoring the shelves, I moved over to the desk. Hanging on the wall behind it, on one of the few spaces not covered by shelves of fake books, was a picture of an old-fashioned whaling ship being tossed about by dark waves as the deckhands leaned over the edge, spears at the ready as they concentrated on an enormous shadowy shape under the water's surface.

" 'Scuse me." Gennifer slid between me and the desk, and

dropped to her knees. She craned her neck to see under the desk. "Last time I did one of these escape rooms, all the important clues were underneath furniture or in hard-to-reach spots. There was even one room where I had to crawl into a coffin and close the lid for the answer to appear." She shuddered. "Def not worth it."

I grinned as I hopped over her outstretched legs. Despite Gennifer's more tailored style, I could see similarities to Izzy in her attitude and speech patterns. Izzy often talked the same way she texted. Once I'd caught her saying "El oh el" instead of actually laughing. "Anything?" I asked.

"Nope." She jumped up and brushed off her pants. They looked expensive, with their clean lines and utter lack of wrinkles. But I'd be willing to bet my right ear they didn't have pockets. Sure, it took effort to make my own clothes, but they had a flattering fit for my body shape, were unique, and *always* had pockets. Go me!

Unaware that I was mentally retailoring her outfit—for starters, I would take out the side seam and replace it with a wide triangle piece of cloth in a funky pattern, maybe something in a nice wide plaid, to achieve a flowy effect that would be more comfortable and flattering—Gennifer had brushed past me and was now trying to remove the enormous painting from the wall. "A hand?" she asked, and I happily obliged.

"It's not budging," I said, tugging on the corners. "I don't think we're supposed to move it."

"Nonsense," Gennifer said. "Everything in here is a potential clue. Some of 'em just take a little more work than others. You see a screwdriver or something lying around?"

"Nope, but I'll keep an eye out for one," I said. I admired her initiative. If she was this focused outside of escape rooms, she could do anything she set her sights on. At the same time, I was a little awed by her. Gennifer seemed to know exactly what she was doing, and I had no idea.

"Everything is a clue," I muttered to myself, repeating Gennifer's advice. I looked up at the enormous painting of the boat hunting the whale. "Look for a copy of *Moby-Dick*," I hollered at Izzy, who was still examining all the books on the walls one by one, as I began to rifle through the desk.

"Game Master, where is *Moby-Dick*?" Marlie called out.

The pimply guy's voice replied immediately, "In the water, right where Ishmael left him."

"Marlie, stop it!" Gennifer said, annoyance making her voice sharp. "Those 'hints' aren't ever going to be helpful, and every time you ask, he takes more time off the clock."

"I was just tryin' to . . ."

Before she could finish, Izzy called out, "Found it!" I turned to see her reach into a ten-gallon fish tank—complete with colored pebbles, a tiny castle, and pink plastic plants, but without water or, thankfully, fish—and pull out an oversized copy of *Moby-Dick*. "What now?"

"Open it, obviously," Vickie suggested. As far as I could tell, it was her first contribution. It was her celebration, so I assumed she'd wanted to do an escape room. For someone who had set the day's agenda, she didn't seem all that invested in the outcome.

Izzy opened the book. "It's just a book." She turned it around so we could all see. Even from halfway across the room, I recognized the familiar opening lines of the classic, due to the large-print font.

"If there's nothing hidden inside, maybe it's not about what's in the book and all about where you found it," Gennifer suggested. She hurried over and dug around with both hands. The colorful rocks at the bottom of the aquarium and the decorations were glued into place.

"Or maybe the fact that it's out of place is the clue," I suggested. "Izzy, while you were searching, did you find any open spots on the shelves?"

"Plenty, but nothing big enough for a book this size." She paused and looked over her shoulder at the wall of books. "Nothing on the first couple of rows, at least, but look up there." She pointed at the second-to-top shelf. It was at least seven feet off the floor. Right next to the tall sliding ladder that I'd coveted earlier, on a shelf crammed with oversized books, was an opening the exact same dimensions as the copy of *Moby-Dick* she held.

We both saw it at the same time, because she called out, "On it!" at almost the same time as I spotted the gap. If it had been at eye level instead of so high up, the difference in the shelf would have been immediately obvious, as all of the shelves below it were spaced a standard twelve inches or so apart, but this shelf was at least two feet below the row above it.

She had to jog around Amanda, who, despite the warning we'd received with our game briefing, was busy taking selfies of herself posed in front of the wall of books. "I can't get these to upload to Instagram," she whined. "Does anyone get a signal in here?"

"Amanda! You can't have your phone out like that. If you get caught, we all get banned and if I can't complete practically the only escape room within fifty miles I haven't beat yet, I'll make you wish you never woke up this morning. Put it away. Pronto," Gennifer chided her.

Ignoring their drama, I hurried toward Izzy and steadied the ladder as she scrambled up its rungs, the oversized book held awkwardly under one arm. She reached the second-to-top shelf. "Careful," I warned her, even as the ladder shimmied in my grip.

"I used to live in an apartment that I could only access via a fire escape that was missing half its rungs and didn't have a handrail." Izzy's adventures in apartments never ceased to amaze me. She was completely nonchalant about her ever-revolving living situation. One day she was living in a condemned schoolhouse, and the next she was sharing my aunt's chic apartment in a bougie building that came complete with a concierge and a rooftop pool.

To her, it was all the same as long as she had someplace safe and relatively dry to sleep at night.

"Next to that, this is a walk in Domino Park," she concluded, stretching out her arm. "A tad to the right, please?"

I obliged, pushing the ladder closer to the opening between two other large books.

Izzy slid the giant copy of *Moby-Dick* into the space, and we heard a loud click. In front of me, a section of bookshelf swung open, revealing a hidden passageway.

3

Realtor Vickie @VictoriaMarshNYCRealtor · July 12
WINNING! #1 #LikeABoss #BestNYCRealtor
#12MonthsInARow #Blessed #CallForAnAppointment

THE SECRET PASSAGE was maybe two feet off the floor, and was three feet high and about the same wide. "This is so extra," I said, unable to contain my excitement. I spent a lot of time listening to true crime podcasts, and to be completely honest, discovering a hidden passage in a library bookshelf was number one or two on my bucket list.

"That can't be right," Gennifer said, sidling up next to me and staring into the darkness. "The conservatory is supposed to have a secret passage, not the library."

"What's a conservatory?" Amanda asked, leaning in to use the flashlight app on her phone to illuminate the narrow tunnel leading out of the room.

"It's a greenhouse," I told her. Like the first room we'd entered, the walls of the passageway were painted black. It was hard to tell with her flashlight ruining the effect, but the light bounced off one side, as if the tunnel had a sharp bend in it.

"I thought it was a music room," Izzy said, sliding down the ladder with ease.

"Do you mean a concert hall? A conservatory is where you set up a telescope," Marlie said with authority.

"You're thinking of an *observatory*," Vickie corrected her.

"I'm pretty sure you're wrong," Marlie replied. "Game Master, what's a conservatory?"

"A greenhouse," came the voice over the speaker. The timer on the wall plummeted by ninety seconds.

"Stop doing that," Gennifer growled. She snatched Amanda's phone out of her hand. "Gimme that." Without waiting for a consensus from the rest of us, she climbed into the passageway.

"I'm not going in there," Vickie said. "If I'd known there would be crawling, I would never have worn silk pants."

"Knock yourself out," Izzy said, and hopped into the tunnel. "You coming, Odessa?"

"Right behind you!" No offense to the Debbie Downers back there, but between Vickie's seeming inability to lift a finger, Marlie's constant abuse of the useless hints, and Amanda putting us all in jeopardy with her constant selfies, we would be better without any of them. Just as I was hoping that we were on our own, there was a thump behind me as one of the remaining players joined us in the tunnel.

We emerged into another room. Izzy smoothed the side of her jumpsuit, which had gotten wrinkled crawling through the secret passage. Izzy had the energy of a bunny rabbit addicted to coffee and never sat still long enough to gain an ounce of fat. As a result, everything she wore hung off her frame like she was a high-fashion model. I'd been teaching her how to sew on our off time, and today she was wearing her latest creation—a blue and white jumpsuit that would have looked like a circus tent on anyone else. But on Izzy, it was adorable.

The second room was lit by two stained glass light fixtures mounted to the ceiling, each centered over a green-felted pool table. Two pool sticks leaned against one table, and several more were mounted to the wall. There were four balls—all solids—on one table and just an empty rack on the other.

One of the walls was made of wood panels, adorned with posters advertising different national beer brands and a framed print of dogs playing poker. There was also a clock mounted on the plain beige wall, but its hands were missing.

At the far end of the room was a large red door with a punch-code lock. The timer over the door ticked down, with only twenty minutes remaining. Where had the time gone? I could have sworn we'd only been in the first room for five minutes, but between all of the bickering and confusion, and Marlie shaving off time with her requests for hints, it had been much more.

"I can't believe we've wasted most of our time already," Gennifer commented, running her fingers along the walls, feeling them for invisible clues. Finding none, she gave up and turned her attention to the door. "What are the numbers on the balls?" she asked, studying the lock.

"One, five, seven, and eight," I told her. I bent down to check the ball return, but a glance at the window confirmed there were no more balls for either table.

"Rats. We need a five-digit code. Look around, and don't forget that the clues could be anywhere."

I looked up. The ceiling was made up of old-fashioned drop tiles, and was shorter than it had been in the previous room. I couldn't reach it, of course, but I grabbed one of the pool sticks and methodically poked at the tiles. "Don't do that," a voice boomed from a speaker built into the wall, which I hadn't noticed before.

I dropped the stick and it clattered to the floor. "Yikes, sorry!" I told the faceless voice.

"Hey, look at this," Izzy said. She tugged on the classic dogs-playing-poker frame and it swung away from the wall on a hinge, revealing a clockface printed out on a round piece of paper. She pulled on it, and it came loose with the distinctive sound of two strips of Velcro being torn apart.

"There's another clock over here," I pointed out.

Izzy aligned the clockface in the center of the blank clock, securing it with another strip of Velcro that was already attached to the wall. I hadn't noticed the Velcro before, because it was the same color beige as the wall.

I was starting to wonder if I wasn't quite as observant as I'd always thought I was.

"Nothing is happening," Izzy said.

"Huh," Gennifer replied, coming over to look over our shoulders. Both of the hands pointed straight down. "Do the hands move?"

I reached out and spun the hands, which were flimsy black plastic arrows attached by a metal paper fastener. They moved freely before both settled back to point at the six. "Looks like it."

"Maybe we need to set it to a specific time?" Izzy suggested.

Gennifer shook her head. "To what end? It's not connected to anything and we need a five-digit number to get out of this room. It might be a red herring."

"A what?" Amanda asked. She'd been busy taking selfies, and this was the first time she'd actively shown interest in solving a puzzle.

"You know, a red herring. A false trail that doesn't lead anywhere. But there's no way they'd build a red herring into an escape room, would they?" I looked to Gennifer for confirmation. "Not when we're already against a clock."

"You'd think, right? It's all part of the challenge. Don't waste too much time trying to figure it out. It may come in handy to solve another puzzle later, or not at all. Keep looking around."

I ducked under the closest pool table and rolled onto my back, hoping that Gennifer was right about major clues being hidden underneath furniture, but I didn't see anything. I wiggled out from under the table and repeated the motion for the other table, with similar disappointing results.

"I already checked down there," Izzy said, and I caught a glimpse of her shoes from my awkward position under the table.

"Whatcha doing?" Amanda asked, squatting down beside me.

"Looking for clues," I said.

"And?"

"Nothing."

"Well, it is pretty dark under there. Maybe this will help." She rolled a flashlight toward me.

"Where'd you get this?" I asked, although I was pretty sure I knew the answer. Since cell phones were forbidden, it had likely been left in the library to make our journey through the dark passage easier. We were probably already disqualified because she'd used her phone, but we had to be close to the end and I wasn't giving up now.

"It was next to the aquarium in the last room," she said, confirming my suspicion. "I thought it might come in handy. But it didn't work."

I fumbled the flashlight switch on, but like Amanda said, nothing happened. I shook it and tried again. This time, even though I still didn't see a beam of light, I caught a glimpse of a set of glowing green numbers and grinned. The numbers were written in invisible ink that showed up only with the help of an ultraviolet flashlight. "One, seven, one, two, nine!" I yelled.

I heard a series of beeps as I shimmied out from under the table, and Gennifer swung the door open. According to the overhead clock, we had almost a full minute to spare.

Amanda gave me a hand up. "Good job, picking up that flashlight," I told her.

Together, we hurried for the exit. On the other side of the door, instead of the waiting room, we found ourselves in a huge industrial kitchen. "You have got to be kidding me," Amanda said.

The clock mounted above the range counted down to zero. A loud buzzer sounded.

I couldn't believe we'd wasted the entire hour already. It felt like we'd been in the room for half that, at most.

The refrigerator door swung open, and the pimply Game Master stepped into the room. "Sorry, folks, but you failed to escape from Clueless. Please come back and try your luck another day." He paused and gave us a tight grin. "Maybe you would be better off in one of the less challenging rooms, like Doors of Our Lives."

"Maybe you'd be better off . . ." Gennifer started, but Izzy grabbed her arm.

"It's just a game," she reminded her. I thought *I* was driven, but apparently that was nothing compared to Gennifer's competitive streak.

Gennifer mumbled something under her breath.

"Now, if you will all just follow me," the Game Master started, then he paused. "Wait a sec. Weren't there six in your party?"

I looked around. Amanda was next to me. Marlie was right behind us, hovering around the open door leading to the billiard room. Izzy and Gennifer were standing in the middle of the kitchen. Gennifer looked annoyed, but as usual, Izzy was enjoying herself. "This was great. We should do this more often!" she said, her eyes roaming the room, still searching for possible clues. She was the only one who didn't seem to care that we'd lost.

"Where's Vickie?" Gennifer asked.

"Last I saw her, she was in the library, complaining about not wanting to crawl through the secret passage," Izzy said.

The Game Master blinked slowly as if he was internally counting to five. "Everyone stay here but *don't touch anything*. Even if you solved any more puzzles, they don't count. Time's up." As soon as he backtracked through the open door behind us, Izzy started flinging cabinets open.

"What are you doing?" I asked. "Game's over."

"Who knows? Maybe this is all a part of the game."

I pointed at the clock, which now blinked all zeros. "I'm pretty sure it's over."

As if to punctuate my statement, there was a faint scream in the distance.

Izzy's head whipped toward the door to the billiard room. "You hear that?"

"Yeah," I answered, and we practically tripped over each other to get through the door. As we wove between the two pool tables, I could hear a voice I didn't quite recognize repeating something over and over again.

I reached the secret passageway first, but then I hesitated. Without Amanda's phone to light the way, it was awful dark.

"Make way," Izzy said, gently prodding me to one side as she climbed up into the tunnel and crawled forward with no hesitation. "There was one place I used to crash at out near Coney Island that didn't have any electricity. We had blackout curtains on the windows so the neighbors wouldn't find out that anyone was living there . . ." Her voice faded as she reached the end of the tunnel and stepped into the library.

I followed her lead, crawling through the passage. I rounded the sharp bend and blinked at the bright light at the end of the tunnel.

From my vantage point, on my hands and knees, ducking so my head didn't hit the low ceiling, I couldn't see anything. Izzy was blocking the exit. "Psst," I hissed, and she stepped to one side.

That's when I saw her.

Vickie lay facedown on the library carpet. I could only see

part of her from my position, but I instantly knew that something wasn't right. She was still. Too still.

As if there were any question remaining, the Game Master stood over her, rocking back and forth, repeating in a monotone voice on a loop, "She's dead. She's dead. She's dead."

4

Odessa Dean @OdessaWaiting · July 12
Oof. Déjà vu all over again #mystery #mayhem #murder

SIX WEEKS AGO, I'd never eaten avocado toast. I didn't have an Instagram account. I had never tried craft beer. I'd never ridden mass transit or ordered an Uber, much less had my very own well-used New York City MetroCard.

And I'd never seen a dead body up close.

I hadn't even known anyone who had died before one of my fellow waitresses at Untapped was murdered last month. And now, for the second time in as many months, I was sitting inside of a police station waiting to be questioned. There were several differences from my last experience, on top of my newly found familiarity with the inside of a cop shop. This time, there was no question that the victim's death had been the result of foul play. Also, instead of being a concerned coworker, I was a material witness.

But most importantly, now I knew the plainclothes officer sitting across from me in the narrow interrogation room.

Detective Vincent Castillo wore dark tailored pants and a shiny black vest over a cream-colored, long-sleeved, button-down shirt. His tie was a narrow strip of blue chevrons, the only pattern in his outfit that I could see. His hair was buzzed short and his eyes were bright and observant. His now-familiar Puerto Rican accent was missing his usual sense of humor. Instead, he was all business.

"This is getting to be a habit, Odessa," he said, not looking up as he bent over a chunky tablet. Like most of the equipment I'd seen so far at the Brooklyn police station, it was woefully out of date, built in the early days when tablets weighed a ton.

I shrugged, then realizing he still wasn't looking at me, said, "It wasn't like . . ."

He cut me off with a wave of his hand, then aimed a remote control at a box on the wall. A red light came on. "This conversation is being recorded. Detective Vincent Castillo, NYPD. Please state your name for the record."

"Odessa Dean," I replied, being careful to enunciate. Maybe I have a teensy bit of a Southern drawl, especially when I'm stressed. Whatever. Castillo was used to it by now.

"Address?" he asked.

I frowned at him. "You know my address, Vincent . . ."

He cut me off again. "Detective Castillo," he corrected me, and I realized that Vincent, the laid-back coulda-been television heartthrob who had been dating my roommate, Izzy, for the last three weeks had been replaced with this more professional doppelgänger. If he could be all business, I could, too.

I rattled off my aunt's address in an old turn-of-the-century warehouse that had been converted into high-end Williamsburg apartments in the late nineties. Then I added, for the record, "At least, that's where I'm staying while Aunt Melanie's out of town. In a few weeks, I'll be back in Louisiana."

Castillo continued, "And what is your relationship with the deceased?"

"Vickie?" I asked, then realized that was an unnecessary question. It wasn't as if I knew multiple people who had died today. "I just met her an hour or two ago. She used to go to school with my roomie, Izzy Wilson." I tilted my head and stared at him, wondering if he was going to acknowledge his relationship with Izzy.

Last night, he'd brought over pizza and beer. The three of us had watched a movie on my laptop. He'd left long after midnight. And now he was interrogating me like we were total strangers.

"You'd never met the vic before today?"

"Nope," I replied, struck by the irony. When her parents had named her, I doubted they ever thought that their daughter Vickie would one day be called a "vic" by the NYPD. I shook my head to clear it of such inappropriate thoughts. "Has anyone talked to her parents yet?"

"You let us handle that, Ms. Dean." Castillo pursed his lips. "Where were you when Ms. Marsh was killed?"

I paused, thinking about Vickie. I didn't know anything about her, other than she wore expensive clothes and struck me as haughty. I had no idea if she was a dog or a cat person, or if she liked punk rock or opera. She could be a philanthropist or a serial killer for all I knew.

Could have been, I mentally corrected myself.

"I'm not exactly sure."

Castillo paused with his stylus poised over the tablet he scribbled on as I talked. "You don't know where you were? There were only six of you, and you were all locked inside an escape room together. How could you not know where you were?"

"It's not like I *saw* her die," I told him. I shuddered at the thought. "Anyway, it wasn't one single room. It was a bunch of rooms with doors and passageways connecting them, so there's that. There was the lobby, and then the little tiny entrance with the light-up numbers on the wall, which led to the library, the tunnel behind the fake bookshelf that fed into the billiard room, then the big padlocked door to the kitchen. I was in the kitchen when the Game Master—the pimply-faced kid in the cheap tuxedo—found Vickie dead back in the library."

"Who else was in the kitchen with you? Did anyone see you there?"

"As in, do I have an alibi?" I would have laughed if it weren't for the expression on his face. "Are you serious?" I shook my head. "It was a game. We were all running around trying to figure out the different clues. I think that girl Amanda was already in the kitchen when I got there, but she might have been behind me. Vickie's coworker Marlie was ahead of us. Wait, no, she was still in doorway to the billiard room. Izzy and Gennifer were in the kitchen though, I think. Maybe."

I closed my eyes and tried to rewind the hour we'd spent in the escape room. It wasn't like I was paying attention to who was where at all times. I was concentrating on solving the puzzles. Vickie must have followed us into the billiard room. Or had she? Had she backtracked to the library for some reason without telling anyone, or had she never left?

We'd all been running around, doing our own thing. Come to think about it, that was probably why we'd had such an abysmal performance. If we'd communicated better, maybe we could have solved the puzzles quicker. We might have stuck closer together.

Vickie might still be alive.

"I just don't know, Vincent," I said. He cleared his throat and stared daggers at me, but I no longer cared whether or not I addressed Castillo properly. "I'm trying to remember if I saw Vickie in the billiard room or not. I don't think so. I wasn't trying to keep track of everyone."

Castillo leaned forward. "Come on, Odessa, give me something."

I couldn't help but notice he'd dropped the formalities, too. "I should have paid less attention to the game and more attention to what was happening around me. Maybe if I'd tried a little harder to get our little group to work together, Vickie might not have gotten herself killed." I folded my hands on the table in front of me and leaned forward, mirroring Castillo's behavior. "It was chaos. There were these clocks counting down and everyone was talking at once and, well, I don't really know what happened. At the time, all I cared about was solving the next puzzle."

Castillo straightened and focused on his tablet for a second before asking, "Did you hear anything out of the ordinary?"

I had to think about that. "Everyone was talking over each other. Plus the walls were kinda thin. I could hear laughter and voices, maybe coming from one of the other escape rooms. I didn't hear anyone crying for help though, if that's what you're asking. We heard a scream when the proctor found her, and that's when Izzy and I came running."

"Where were you this morning, before the escape room?" he asked, changing gears.

I breathed a sigh of relief. "That's easy. Izzy and I were at a cornhole tournament in Domino Park. We came in first place, if you can believe it."

"You won?" he prompted.

"Right? I'd never even played before." I relaxed. It was easier reliving the cornhole tournament than thinking about the escape room. "But it was really fun and I guess we got lucky, because the next thing I know, we were the last team standing. Got a big trophy and everything." I grinned. "Never won a trophy before today."

"Uh-huh." He rotated the tablet and turned it to face me so I could see the photo on the screen. "Is this your trophy?"

I nodded. "Yeah, that's it. Why does that matter?"

"Because this trophy was used to bludgeon Ms. Marsh to death." He paused and studied my expression as a dozen different emotions went to war in the pit of my stomach. "Did you hear me? Professor Plum wasn't killed in the study with a candlestick. Your cornhole trophy was the murder weapon."

When I was in sixth grade, my parents drove me all the way to Dallas to visit Six Flags Over Texas. I was small for my age. I dutifully posed next to the measuring stick for all the big roller coasters. The Texas Giant. Judge Roy Scream. The Shock Wave. I was too short to be allowed on any of them. But there was this one ride I could get on, a big round room that spun around in a circle until the floor disappeared, pinning the riders to the side with centrifugal force.

Or was it centripetal force? I never could remember the difference.

For a moment, I was transported back to that day when little twelve-year-old me felt the floor drop out from under myself. Like today, I was dizzy and confused, but that was a whole lot more fun. Or at least, it would have been if I hadn't eaten that Texas-sized serving of chili cheese fries immediately before stepping into a human blender.

I didn't know why I could remember a ride that made me puke when I was twelve, but couldn't for the life of me recall whether or not Vickie was in the billiard room when I was climbing under the pool table an hour ago. The human brain was a weird machine.

"Ms. Dean? Odessa?" Castillo's voice sounded like it was coming from far away. "Can you answer the question?"

"Huh?" I hadn't heard him ask a question. Just like that day in the Texas heat, I felt queasy and disoriented. "Can I get a glass of water?"

"In a minute. Am I going to find your fingerprints on the murder weapon?"

I swallowed hard. It felt like I was breathing through sand. Fingerprints. Murder weapon. "Well, sure. I mean, it was my trophy."

"And why exactly was your cornhole trophy in the library?"

"I have no idea! I mean, it wasn't supposed to be in the library. It was in my bag."

"Your messenger bag was also in the library," Castillo said. "Why?" His voice was gentler now, but still without the slightest trace of his usual humor. Maybe it was because of all the horrible things he saw on a daily basis at work, but when he took off his tie at the end of his shift, he never missed a chance to smile and joke. That was why he and Izzy fit so well together. She saw the humor in every situation. She would probably think even this was funny, if she'd been in here with us.

But she wasn't. They'd separated us so they could interview us individually.

"I don't know. I musta put it down . . ." But no, that wasn't right. I'd stuffed my bag in one of the cubbyholes in the lobby so I didn't have to lug it around with me. "Wait a second. Izzy had my bag."

"Izzy had your bag," he repeated, his voice gone cold again. "Why did Ms. Wilson have your purse?"

I shrugged. "She offered to carry it. I guess she set it down somewhere while we were looking for clues. You'll have to ask her."

He gave me a terse nod. "We will. Thank you for your cooperation, Ms. Dean. If we have any additional questions . . ."

"You know where to find me."

Castillo pointed the remote control at the camera again, clicked the button, and the red light went out. "What on earth have you dragged Izzy into, Odessa?"

"Nothing!" I glanced at the camera, silent and dark now, and then at the door behind my shoulder. "It wasn't even my idea." But it kinda was, wasn't it? I'd all but begged Izzy to tag along to the escape room. I couldn't have possibly known what was going to happen, but I couldn't help feeling like I was somehow to blame. I should have kept my mouth shut when Gennifer invited us to join them.

Shoulda, woulda, coulda, as my Gammie loved to say.

"Can I go now?"

Castillo nodded. "Try to stay out of trouble. Please."

"I will," I promised. I stood and half turned toward the door before turning back to ask, "You still coming over for dinner tonight?"

He gave me an irritated look, not unlike the one I was tempted to give to customers who asked if our avocado toast contained real avocado, or if our "locally bottled" beer came in a can or a bottle. "I'm gonna take a rain check."

I let myself out of the interview room.

Izzy was sitting on a long wooden bench, like something that belonged in a public park. "Well?" Izzy asked. "How'd it go?"

Before I could answer her, Castillo stuck his head out of the interview room. He crooked a finger at Izzy and she stood up. "I'll wait for you," I offered.

"Thanks," she said. She glanced over at Castillo and held up one finger, telling him she'd be there in just a minute. I wondered if he was going to be as serious in his interview with Izzy as he'd been with me. Would he go easier on her just because they were dating? For that matter, was he even allowed to interview his own girlfriend? Seemed like a conflict of interest to me.

"Back in a sec," Izzy promised. Then she headed for the interrogation room.

Castillo was tall. Trim. Well dressed. Intelligent. A perfect match for Izzy, and nice, to boot. Outside of work, at least.

I was confused why he seemed so frustrated with me. He had to know I didn't have anything to do with Vickie Marsh's death. I didn't even know her a few hours ago. Sure, my fingerprints were on the trophy someone had used to bludgeon her with, but it was my trophy. My fingerprints should be on it! Obviously, I was innocent. I had no reason to hurt anyone, much less a stranger.

I plopped down on the chair to wait and realized I didn't even have my phone to use to pass the time surfing the internet. My phone, like my wallet and keys, had been in my bag along with the trophy. The murder weapon. Which meant it was probably all sitting in evidence somewhere.

That wouldn't do.

I stood and hurried back to the interview room. I knocked and opened the door without waiting for an answer. Castillo looked up, and when he realized it was me, frowned. "Ms. Dean, I'm right in the middle of . . ."

"I know," I said. "Can I get my phone back? And my keys?"

"Front desk. Close the door behind you."

5

Odessa Dean @OdessaWaiting · July 12
U wake up in jail next to ur bestie. In 3 words, what
happened? #fingerprints #on #murder #weapon
#thatsfourwords

THE LINE FOR the front desk wasn't long, but it moved at a snail's pace. My personal effects—my wallet, my phone, a half-used lip balm, three sticks of gum, and my apartment key on a Statue of Liberty key chain, along with the assorted miscellany that tended to accumulate in a woman's purse—were returned to me in a gallon-sized clear plastic bag, along with my now-empty messenger bag and a folded-up uniform shirt for the bookstore-slash-café where I worked. "What about my trophy?" I asked.

"Evidence," the bored clerk explained.

I dumped the contents of the plastic bag into my messenger bag. A wadded-up candy bar wrapper fell onto the floor. I bent over to scoop it up. The bag was heavy on my shoulder. I'd probably never see the cornhole trophy again, but at least I had the rest of my stuff back, which was more than I had a few minutes ago. "Thanks," I told the clerk, signing the final form and handing it back.

"Hey! There you are!" I turned and saw Izzy hurrying toward me. Her face was red and even from halfway across the crowded lobby, I could see her eyes were puffy.

"You all right?"

"Let's go," she said with a quick glance behind her.

"Are you sure you're all right?"

"Hundred percent. Just ready to get out of here," she said with a quick glance behind her.

"Did Vincent . . ." I wasn't sure how to phrase it, but if my boyfriend had interrogated me, I'd probably be in a foul mood, too.

"I can't even." She flapped her hand in a dismissive gesture. "It's beer o'clock," she announced as she led the way out of the station.

"Actually, we've got to get to work. And I'm pretty sure we're late."

She checked the time. "Yowza. Todd's gonna throw a fit."

Our boss, Todd, was the manager at Untapped Books & Café. Technically we worked for the owner but I'd never actually met him. Todd signed the checks and wrote the schedule, and he liked to yell at the employees. Scratch that. He *loved* to yell at the employees. A lot.

He wasn't the easiest person to work for, but he wasn't the worst, either. He was old and out of touch, but acted like he was still the cool football jock he'd probably been in the good ol' days. Then again, he'd graduated from high school way back in the eighties, a decade before I was born.

At twenty-three, I was at the tail end of the Millennial generation, Gen Y, the Oregon Trail Generation, or whatever they were calling us now. For all that the Gen Xers and baby boomers tended to think of Millennials as teenagers, we're old enough to have advanced degrees and kids of our own and mortgages by now. Although, between overwhelming student loans, the skyrocketing cost of health care, and lack of affordable housing, most of us were lucky to own a cactus and a clean pair of underwear.

I don't even have that much. The cactus, that is. I've got several pair of clean underwear, thank you very much.

There's a tiny washer and dryer unit in my aunt's apartment, along with full-sized laundry facilities in the basement, which made laundry a snap. I just didn't have what they call a green thumb. I could kill a plastic ficus tree. I'd already managed to maim all my aunt's houseplants.

And technically she hadn't even left me instructions on how to water the plants, much less how much or how often. How was I supposed to know that root rot was a thing?

It's a good thing I had better luck with pets because her cat, Rufus—all ten adorable pounds of him—was healthy, happy, and very much alive. Rufus wouldn't be quite as happy if I managed to lose my waitressing job and had to go back to feeding him generic-brand cat food because I wouldn't be able to afford the high-quality ingredients Izzy made into homemade food for him.

"We better get going. You know how Todd gets."

"We are in so much trouble," she agreed. Todd reigned supreme like a middle-aged dictator, and I doubted he would let us off the hook for being late just because we were detained by the police.

That might even make things worse.

No, scratch that. It would *definitely* make things worse.

A few blocks later, we reached the bookstore. Untapped Books & Café wasn't much to look at from the street. It had a big window overlooking the sidewalk, and a recessed door up a few chipped concrete steps. There was a faded awning over the window, framing a display that featured employee picks instead of this month's best sellers. There was a neon light hung in the corner that simply said "Beer." The hours-of-operation sign was flipped to "Open."

I pushed open the front door. We were greeted by the familiar tinkle of the bell mounted over the doorframe. Huckleberry, the official shop dog, lifted his big yellow head off the floor and gave us a halfhearted woof of welcome. His lack of enthusiasm was a result of his advanced age—he was born sometime between nineteen years ago and the last ice age—along with an apparently busted air conditioner in the store. Again. It had to be ninety degrees outside, and wasn't much cooler inside.

I squatted down to show Huckleberry some love. He looked like a cross between a golden retriever and a couch cushion that had been left out in the rain. A recent bath and haircut improved his appearance enormously, but when he melted against the atrocious carpet of the bookstore, it was hard to tell if he was a dog or a Muppet. "Aww, it's my favorite doggo," I told him. "Looks like you need a boop." I lightly tapped his nose and he gave me a big doggy grin in return.

"Well, well, well. If it isn't our reigning cornhole champions,"

Andre said, rising up from the stool behind the cash register to give Izzy and me a slow clap.

Unlike Todd, the assistant manager, Andre Gibson, was flexible. Friendly. Fun to work with. He was that in-between age that wasn't yet old enough to have gray in his thick black hair but was too old to stay out all night partying. He was a snappy dresser and always had a smile on his face, and a kind word for everyone. Even when his employees were horribly late for their shifts. "Any chance I can get an autograph from the cornhole queens of Williamsburg?"

I rose from my crouch on the floor. The cornhole tournament felt like it had been a decade ago, not just a few hours. "How did you . . . ?"

Andre chuckled. "Izzy posted that cute pic of you two on Instagram. Let me guess, you guys have been out 'celebrating,'"—he made actual air quotes around the word—"and that's why you're so late to work?"

"Actually . . ." I started to say, but Izzy interrupted.

"Oh, you know us," she said with a giggle. She leaned against the counter. "Surprised to see you here so early." Not that it was early, not really. It might have been if we'd gotten to work on time, but it was nearing the switchover from morning shift to night shift, when Andre normally took over. Since there were only two managers, they worked pretty much seven days a week. I had no idea how they managed it. "Where's Todd?"

Andre grinned. "He had to run an errand, so I came in early to cover for him." I glanced at Izzy, but she was concentrating on Andre. It wasn't like Todd to leave early. In the short time I'd worked there, I hadn't even known him to take a single day off.

"But you two were already late by the time he left, and he's hella mad."

"He'll get over it," Izzy said. "You want me on the register or do you have another job in mind for me?"

It was a legit question. We all had our job descriptions, but then we had our *real* job descriptions, which pretty much entailed doing whatever odd chores Todd or Andre needed. When I was the newest employee, I was always the one to walk Huckleberry, haul out the constant stream of trash, or clean the disorganized stockroom. It usually fell to me to inventory the toilet paper rolls or coax the ancient office computer to run faster. Now that I was handling the social media accounts, Todd generally left me alone to wait tables as long as the Instagram and Twitter accounts were updated daily, even on my days off.

"You're so late, it would serve you right if I sent you both home," Andre said.

"But you won't," Izzy said promptly. If I hadn't been right by her side the entire time, I never would have guessed that Izzy's afternoon had been traumatic. She was her normal self—spunky and sociable.

"I could use some help arranging the stockroom. Inventory's coming up and that place is a wreck."

"On it, boss," Izzy said, tipping an imaginary hat at him.

"And get into uniform," he said sternly. "Both of you. Oh, and, Odessa? Before I forget, Todd asked me to see if you could boost Untapped's social media presence."

"How so?" I asked. I actually enjoyed updating the store's accounts, but full-on advertising was above my pay grade. Seeing a twinkle in Andre's eyes, I braced myself for the worst. "Are we talking Facebook ads or does he want me out on the sidewalk in a humiliating costume handing out flyers?" I'd done that once, and I'd promised myself never again. There were few things worse than wearing a crawdad costume in the middle of a broiling Louisiana summer, but if anyone could top that, it would be Todd.

"No biggie. He just wants you to come up with a meme and make it go viral."

"What?" I shook my head. "That's not how it works."

"I know, I know. And I tried explaining that to him. He doesn't believe me that the best memes are organic. Just do me a favor, and the next couple of pictures you take, slap a cute caption on them before posting. Then you can say you tried."

"Aye, aye," I said, and hurried off to the small—but clean—bathroom off the hallway that separated the public areas of the bookstore and café from the employees-only area. Not that people respected the distinction. More often than not, we had to wait for the employee bathroom because a customer was using it but today, I got lucky.

Izzy was checking her hair in the mirror as I changed into my uniform, which just meant swapping my tank top for a neon green polo with the Untapped Books & Café logo stitched on it. Beyond that, they didn't care what we wore—shorts, jeans, a skirt, even pajama bottoms—it was all fair game. Nine times out of ten, I chose a long, flowy skirt—usually one of my own creation—and a pair of sensible but ugly secondhand orthopedic loafers.

"Don't you think it's weird that Todd's not here? That's not like him. He'll disappear into the office in the back on occasion, but he prefers to lurk over everyone's shoulders rather than trust that we know how to do our jobs," I said.

"Don't look a gift donkey in the mouth, Odessa," Izzy said.

"It's horse," I corrected her.

"I'm not so sure about that. I've always considered him more of an . . ."

"Gotta run," I told her. I tucked my tank top into my bag, washed my hands, and left the bathroom. On my way to the café floor, I grabbed my apron off the hook it hung on along the hall-way wall.

I tied the apron around my waist and headed into the café, pausing to stash my bag in the designated cabinet in the kitchen when Parker, the day chef, appeared. As usual, his shaggy blond hair strained the limits of his hairnet. He bopped his head to the music that was piped in over cheap Bluetooth speakers mounted up near the ceiling. He flashed me a giant, toothy grin as he lined up plates along the pass-thru and tapped an old-fashioned bell to indicate an order was up.

Scanning the tables, I noted only half of the seats were oc-cupied. That would change as people started getting off work and began trickling in for the Friday night rush. A server I didn't recognize was waiting on a group of regulars. It wasn't uncom-mon to see unfamiliar faces on staff. Between low wages, Todd's micromanaging, and the sheer number of restaurants in New York City to choose among, the waitstaff was a constantly revolv-ing merry-go-round of temporary name tags.

"Hi, I'm Odessa," I introduced myself to the new waitress. She towered over me even though she wore the sensible, flat-soled shoes of an experienced server. Her head was shaved bald,

NO MEMES OF ESCAPE

with the faded lines of a tattoo against her dark skin forming the shape of an intricate mandala—a geometric shape resembling a flower. Peeking out of the neon green polos all the Untapped Books & Café employees wore were arm muscles that could only come from hours at the gym.

Waitressing was enough of a workout for me. Then again, even with all the walking I did now, I might have actually gained a few pounds since moving to Williamsburg. The food was just too good, and there were so many options to choose from. From deep-fried falafel to homemade ice cream, everything just tasted a little better in Brooklyn than it ever had in Louisiana.

"Nan," she replied. " 'Scuse me." She shuffled past me, heading toward the kitchen to pick up her order.

"Can I get a refill?" someone called, and I hurried over to their table. A redheaded woman I sort of recognized sat at the table nearest the kitchen. This one used to have sudoku puzzles underneath the plastic table topper, but after spending who knows how many hours scrubbing various markers off the plastic at the end of every shift, we swapped the puzzles out for a world map.

The woman's plate, which rested near Australia, was so clean I couldn't even guess what she'd ordered. I picked it up. "I'll take that for you." Her glass was also empty. "What are we drinking?"

"Just iced tea," she said. "You're Odessa, right? We met, briefly, at Bethany's wake a few weeks ago."

Now I placed her. She'd spent the whole time flirting with my friend Parker. He hadn't mentioned that he was seeing anyone, but by the way she kept glancing toward the kitchen window, I assumed she was at the café for more than a delicious local meal. "Oh yeah, I remember you." I racked my brain for a minute before coming up with a name. "Hazel?"

She smiled. She had a pretty smile. "That's me."

"One tea, coming right up, Hazel," I said, heading for the drink station. I dropped off her plate and returned with her re-fill. "Holler if you need anything else."

A piercing laugh drew my attention, and I plastered my best customer service smile on my face before turning to face the boisterous table in the back corner of the cramped café. The café had been decorated before influencers and Pinterest, from yard sale rejects that had never gotten around to being refur-bished. The owner had been going for quirky, but between garish orange carnation wallpaper and squeaky vinyl seat cushions, at best, we'd accomplished tacky.

Although, to be fair, I liked it. I wouldn't decorate my own kitchen like this anytime soon—I gravitated toward shiny steel appliances and subway tile backsplashes—but I doubted I would ever own a house; much less be able to afford a designer. Even back in Louisiana, where prices made at least renting my own apartment somewhat obtainable, I lived with my parents and ate my meals in a kitchen with lime green appliances that hadn't been refreshed since the seventies. Now that I was staying at my aunt's, I couldn't even control where the plates were stored, much less the decor.

I might not own my own place, but the thought of all the money I was saving by living at home buoyed my spirits as I straightened my shoulders and got to work.

"What can I get y'all?" I asked as I approached the gaggle of women seated around a table with random yearbook pages laid out under the plastic table topper. They had just started on their meals, so it was probably too early to sell them on dessert. "Refills? More beer?" There were several bottles on the table, and I recognized the labels as some of our most popular local brews, including Bad Hudson Stout and Pour Williamsburg.

Before moving to Williamsburg, I'd only ever tried the big-name, mass-produced brands that came out of aluminum cans. Those same beers were also available in Brooklyn, but hardly anyone ever ordered them. The locals preferred craft beer, small batch brews with simple ingredients and complex tastes. I made a point of learning everything I could about our wide and ever-changing selection of brews.

This week, we were pushing a locally crafted beer served in a dark brown glass bottle with a red, white, and blue label. It had been a big seller over the Fourth of July weekend, but now cases of it were taking up space in our already cramped stockroom. "Have you tried Pursuit of Hoppiness?" I asked them. "It's light and refreshing, but at nine and a half percent, it's one of our strongest IPAs. Guaranteed to give you a buzz, with a nice, slightly sour flavor."

The woman nursing one of the Bad Hudson Stouts gave me a dismissive wave. "Another one of these, please," she requested without making eye contact. "And water," another woman at the table added.

"Coming right up."

Out of the corner of my eye, I caught Nan the waitress glancing in my direction before returning her attention to the table of button-down-shirt-clad men near the front. At least she wasn't jumping down my throat and accusing me of trying to poach her tip. Besides, I recognized her other table from a bank down the street and knew they always left at least 20 percent, after tax.

I took care of the refills. As I passed the open kitchen window to return the water pitcher, there was a break in the music—today we were playing a mixture of commercially popular folk music and the smoky voice of a local lounge singer—and I noticed Izzy leaning against the counter where a few high-topped stools were lined up diner-style. The stools had to have been designed by a sadist, and were rarely occupied except on our busiest nights. "Aren't you supposed to be organizing the stockroom or something?"

"I was. I am. But then I realized I haven't eaten all day."

Parker poked his head out the pass-thru window. "Izzy, order up." He slid a bowl of what looked like egg salad on a bed of lettuce with a garnish of spiral-cut carrots and radishes. I knew it wasn't really egg salad because vegans like Izzy didn't eat any kind of animal product, not even eggs or dairy.

"Mind if I try?" I asked. Without waiting for a response, I scooped up some of the faux egg salad on a piece of radish. It was good, surprisingly so. "If I didn't know this was vegan, I would think it was the real thing," I said.

Parker, who had been hovering around the open window to hear the verdict, beamed. "Really?"

"Yup," I confirmed, dipping another serving onto a slice of cucumber. "I bet you'd fool half of the biddies down at the Sunday social with this."

"Good to know." He disappeared into the kitchen. At least Parker and Izzy understood my accent. Most of the time. Then again, I wasn't sure they even had Sunday socials up here in Williamsburg, so he might have just been being polite.

"Hey, Parker, you gonna be serving that 'egg' salad all weekend or just today?"

He stuck his head back through the pass-thru. "Depends on if people like it or not."

"They'll like it, trust me. Mind plating one up for me for Instagram?" I hadn't updated the café's page yet today, and if I didn't come up with something soon, Todd would have even more ammunition against me. "Don't worry, I'll pay for it. I didn't realize how hungry I was until I tasted it."

He arranged two big scoops on a bright green piece of lettuce, added the garnishes, and sprinkled some cherry tomatoes on top. He slid it onto a blue glass plate, next to a thick slab of fresh, locally made multigrain bread and a dollop of spicy mustard before passing me the plate. "On the house. Least they can do for free advertising."

"You should have been an artist," I told him.

"He *is* an artist," Izzy corrected me as I snapped a picture and posted it as the daily special. Remembering Andre's request, I tried to think of something cutesy to say about it, but while the dish was delicious, it wasn't very meme-worthy. I sat next to Izzy and dug in with gusto.

"Wow, you really do like the egg-less salad!"

"Told ya," I assured him, my mouth full. "It'll be a hit. I promise. Is that what you served Hazel?"

Parker blushed, and I resisted the urge to pump my fist in the air. I knew it. He and Hazel were an item.

I liked Parker. He was my friend, and I liked seeing him happy. He was a phenomenal cook and quite a catch. "She seems nice."

As much as I hated to abandon my meal, there were tables to be waited on and new diners to seat. I grabbed a bite or two every time I swung by the window to drop off or pick up orders, and by the time we got really busy, I'd managed to polish off the plate.

6

Untapped Books & Café @untappedwilliamsburg · July 12
What's your favorite Williamsburg institution, and why is it
Untapped Books & Café? #Williamsburg

BY THE TIME the night shift crew arrived, the café was full. Even
the stools at the long bar were all claimed, and groups had started
pushing tables together. As a waitress, the only thing that bothered me more than people swapping tables—thus making keeping track of checks nearly impossible—were people who dragged
chairs between tables or pushed two tables together. At the end
of the night, there was enough cleanup to be done without also
having to rearrange all the furniture back to the way it was.

Because I'd been so late, I only got to work a few hours, but
it had been a productive shift. My pockets were padded with
small bills from tips. I turned over my tables to the next server,
told Parker—who was finishing up his shift, too—to have a good
evening, and hung up my apron. Izzy had likewise finished in the
stockroom and was waiting for me. "Good to go?" I asked, and
she nodded.

We left together, heading toward my aunt's building. As usual, I took a moment to appreciate Williamsburg. I enjoyed the walk home. I could take in more of the city at my admittedly slow pace, but right now I had to hurry to keep up with Izzy's long-legged stride. When she first moved in with me, I was afraid that between working together and living together, Izzy and I would get sick of each other but so far it hadn't happened. We got along like peanut butter and jelly, and spent our free time together as well, when she wasn't out with Castillo.

My bag was a lot lighter without the trophy weighing it down. What with it being a murder weapon and all, I doubted we'd ever get it back. I still wasn't clear how that had happened. "Hey, Izzy, why did you leave my messenger bag in the library of the escape room?"

She glanced at me. The light changed and we stepped off the curb. She yelled an inventive obscenity at a cabby that barreled through the intersection, ignoring the red light and crosswalk, and got an angry horn in response. Only in New York. "I'd rather not talk about that right now."

"Sure." Alrighty then, sore subject. Not that I blamed her. I hoped Castillo hadn't been too rough on her. I guessed asking her what exactly happened in the interview room, and how Castillo was going to continue heading an investigation that his girlfriend was at the center of, was off-limits, too, even thought I was dying to know. Maybe it was time to change the subject. "I wonder why Todd wasn't at work today. That's not like him. Come to think of it, the last time I saw him, he didn't yell at me or tell me to go scrub the front steps with a toothbrush first. Didn't even have a snarky comment. Is he feeling all right?"

"Better than," Izzy said with a knowing grin, scooting over to let a jogger pushing one of those speed baby strollers pass. She took a breath and held it for a dramatic pause before revealing, "Todd's dating."

"Oh." Words failed me. What kind of woman would date a guy like Todd? He was just so . . . peculiar. Then again, there was someone for everyone, wasn't there? Even my great-aunt Maude met the love of her life at the ripe age of eighty-two after a lifetime of knitting orange sweater vests out of her cat's fur. "What's she like?"

"I haven't *met* any of them yet," Izzy said.

"Any? Them?" My mind boggled that Todd might have more than one date. It wasn't that Todd was repulsive or a swamp monster or something. Everyone deserved to be happy. I'd just never seen the human side of him before and it was going to take a minute to adjust my mindset.

Izzy nodded. "Todd asked for my help to set up an online dating profile and he's had his head in his phone ever since. Been on a couple of dates already, and supposedly been texting someone special."

"I didn't know that Todd could text," I admitted. Todd liked to call people. And leave voicemails. I had never even set up my voicemail before taking the job at Untapped. Even my own parents eventually learned I responded quicker to texts.

"I taught him that, too. You know what would be fun? I could set up a Tinder profile for you, too. It would be nice, having someone to double date with. You, me, Vince, and your internet love match. Won't that be a blast?"

"No thank you," I said emphatically. "I already meet enough

weirdos on the internet without actively looking for them. Besides, I'm only in town for another six weeks," I continued. "Once Aunt Melanie gets back from Europe, I'm on the next Greyhound back to Louisiana. What's the sense in getting involved with someone knowing I'm leaving soon?"

"I'm not talking about getting *involved*," she said with a light-hearted laugh. "Just a date. What would it hurt?"

"I'm happy being single," I told her, and I meant it. My last serious boyfriend had dumped me when he went off to college and I stayed in Piney Island. According to Facebook, he was clerking for a law office in Oklahoma City and was married to a tall, leggy blonde. They had a chubby little toddler and another baby on the way now.

I was still slinging plates and lived with my parents.

We paused at a busy intersection and I glanced down the wide sidewalk. A girl was walking seven dogs of varying sizes on a tangle of leashes. A trio of au pairs were pushing double strollers. An older woman sat on a lawn chair on her stoop, reading a worn novel in the flickering light of the porch lamp mounted over her head. An oversized pigeon swooped down to pick up something one of the stroller parade babies dropped, but was beaten to the prize by a brown rat twice its size. All around us, horns blared, bicycles whirred, and a siren wailed. Over the constant cars and hundreds of disjointed conversations, I could almost make out the faint sound of the East River crashing against its rocky banks.

I grinned and shifted my messenger bag so it was out of the reach of a man who stood a little too close to me on the sidewalk. Tired of waiting for the crosswalk light to go green, he spotted a break in traffic and dashed across the intersection.

"What's up with that smile?" Izzy asked. "You reconsidering my offer to set you up?"

"Nah, I'm just glad I'm not raising a bunch of kids in Oklahoma City on a clerk's salary," I admitted.

"Random," Izzy responded with a questioning look. We'd been walking faster than normal. I was out of breath, but at least I wasn't dwelling on the scene back at the escape room as long as I was struggling to keep up with Izzy.

She did everything quickly. She talked quickly. She walked quickly. And apparently, she recovered quickly. Izzy had been a hot mess when she left the interview room, but by the time we got to work, she was fine. Better than fine, to be honest. She was practically giddy. "I get it, Odessa, you're old-fashioned. You don't like dating apps? Why don't we go out and meet people? Hit a couple of bars. Pick up a guy or two."

"I don't know about that. Seems unsafe."

"Come on, live a little." She hooked her arm through mine. "We're young and live in the greatest city in the world. We might as well enjoy it!"

She had a point.

"Can we at least go home and change first?" I looked down at myself. I'd changed back into my tank top, so I wasn't wearing the bright neon polo shirt anymore. My outfit was comfortable, but even though I meant it when I told Izzy I wasn't interested in dating anyone, if we were going out, I might as well put on something a little fancier.

"Of course."

We let ourselves into my aunt's apartment building. Up until a decade or two ago, Williamsburg had been a wasteland of defunct industrial factories and warehouses overlooking the Manhattan skyline. Then some forward-thinking developers had come in, gentrified everything, and turned it into the hottest neighborhood in New York City. The streets were lined with electric car charging stations and valet stands. Abandoned warehouses were transformed into multimillion-dollar condo buildings. Graffiti was covered up with murals commissioned by the city council.

Unlike Manhattan, my neighborhood still supported mom-and-pop shops, although chain stores were slowly encroaching and leaching away some of the local flavor. Williamsburg had been such a success that the developers were pushing their way farther into Brooklyn, taking over one neighborhood at a time. As a result, affordable housing within biking distance of the Williamsburg Bridge was getting scarcer by the day.

I was lucky. When my aunt Melanie needed someone to watch her place for a few months, she called me. Sure, she could have boarded her cat at some fancy pet spa and asked the building concierge to keep an eye on her unit, but she'd asked me instead and I was incredibly grateful. I never would have had an opportunity to explore the magnificent city without her offering a place to stay, rent-free, for the summer.

And Izzy? When I met her, she was living in a classroom in an abandoned schoolhouse with a junkie and half a dozen feral cats that more or less kept the rats at bay. When the schoolhouse had been temporarily closed for fumigation, she'd had nowhere else to go and ended up crashing with me. She got free room and board for a few weeks, and I got a roomie and friend who knew her way around Williamsburg.

Win-win.

As we waited for the elevator—a luxury in itself—in the well-lit, air-conditioned lobby, I thanked my lucky stars. There was nothing like stumbling across a murder victim and spending half the day in a police station to remind me how good I really had it. And the icing on the cake was that Earl, the elderly concierge who normally manned the front desk, wasn't at his post.

Earl didn't like me much and never bothered to hide that fact. I had no idea what I'd done to get on his bad side—I went out of my way to be nice to everyone—but it seemed like nothing I did could change his mind. On a good day, he glared at me without getting up. On a bad day, he'd call my aunt and tattle on me about something he disapproved of me doing. He was one of the few things in New York I would *not* miss when I left.

The elevator door dinged, and when it opened, Earl was standing inside. "Good evening, Miss Izzy!" he said, beaming at her. Whatever grudge he held against me apparently did not extend to my roomie. "Miss Odessa," he deadpanned.

"Evening, Mr. Earl," I said as brightly as possible.

He stepped forward, holding the door open for us. "Have fun," he smirked.

"I wonder what he meant by that?" I asked as the doors closed behind us and the elevator lurched upward.

Aunt Melanie's apartment was on the top floor. We got out

of the elevator and stepped into the carpeted hallway. Unlike some apartment buildings, this one always smelled faintly of lavender and cleaning products, and the lightbulbs all worked. The floors were clean and even the walls were free of hand-prints. Between the security door downstairs and the concierge, it was a relatively safe building in the nice part of a pricey neigh-borhood.

But when I saw my apartment door ajar, my heart thrummed in my chest.

"Did you leave the door unlocked?" I asked Izzy in a whisper.

She rolled her eyes at me. "I'm a New Yorker. I don't even leave the *bathroom* door unlocked." She stepped in front of me, reached into her pocket, and pulled out a little metal rod. It was a self-defense thing. Even though she'd shown me how it worked, I was still skeptical that something that small could do any dam-age against an attacker, much less an intruder.

I grabbed her arm. "Let's just call the cops. Or at least go downstairs and get Earl."

Izzy grinned. "Oh, please. The cops got their hands full. I've got this."

"Seriously . . ." I pled with her, but it was too little, too late.

Ignoring me, Izzy took three steps forward and flung the door open, screaming like a banshee.

Then there was a high-pitched woman's yelp, followed by the sound of something crashing and breaking. My aunt's cat, a tri-colored orange, white, and gray curly-haired cat, streaked through the open door, hissed, and dashed down the hall away from us. "Rufie!" I yelled after him, but he ignored me.

"Odessa?" a familiar voice called.

I dashed toward the open door. Inside the apartment, Izzy was pinned against the wall by the end of a crutch. I knew the older woman leaning against the underarm brace of the medical crutch well. "Aunt Melanie? What on earth are you doing home?"

7

Odessa Dean @OdessaWaiting · July 12
Tweeps! Settle an argument—how many pillows is 2 many
pillows? Also, anyone wanna loan me a pillow? & maybe a
bed? &, like, an apartment? #surprise #familydrama
#imseriousaboutthatpillow

IZZY DROPPED HER self-defense wand, and Aunt Melanie rocked backward. Seeing that she was about to lose her balance, I rushed past the kitchen island and helped steady my aunt, noticing for the first time that one of her feet was encased in a chunky walking boot. Once she was no longer in any danger of toppling over, I helped her hobble over to the couch.

She slid down onto the couch cushions and rested the crutches on the armrest where my pillow lay. When Izzy moved in, I'd decided to take the couch and gave her the bedroom. She'd offered to swap out every week, but it had seemed like too much of a hassle. Besides, Aunt Melanie's couch was comfortable.

And now that Aunt Melanie was here, in the flesh, sitting on *her* couch in *her* apartment, I realized that I had no idea where me *or* Izzy would be sleeping tonight.

But there was a more pressing problem I needed to deal with first. "I'll be right back," I said to the room in general. I dashed out to the hallway after Rufus the cat. I needn't have worried.

The hallway to my aunt's floor was long and lined with doors on both sides. It stretched down the length of a city block before doubling back to access the apartments on the other side of the narrow courtyard. It continued past two sets of emergency stairs before winding back to the elevator. My aunt's cat, officially Rufus, but more often Rufie, was sitting in the middle of the hallway just a few doors down. He was industriously licking his paws, occasionally looking up to glare at me as if it was my fault that he was reduced to the indignity of being "outside" like a common, well, cat.

Rufus was on the small side for a cat. Half of his face had brown fur and the other half orange with a patch of white fur running up over his chin, nose, and forehead. His multicolored hair had a hint of curl as if he'd stuck one of his adorable toe beans in a light socket. He was a quiet cat and the absolute perfect pet for a New Yorker, even if sometimes a little switch flipped in his kitty brain that made him momentarily act like a dog.

"Come on, little buddy," I said, scooping him up into my arms. Sometimes he wanted to be picked up, and loved cuddling. Other times, he would hiss if I so much as looked in his direction. When he was in one of his doggy phases, he would follow at my heels as well as any puppy on a leash. Today, he was all about the snuggle, despite the drama that had forced him out into the hall. Or maybe because of it.

I cradled him as I carried him back to the apartment, and nudged the door shut behind me with my foot. Rufus immediately sprang out of my arms and launched himself at my aunt, who was as happy to see him as he was to be seen.

"Aunt Melanie, I guess you've met Izzy Wilson."

"Yes, dear," my aunt said. "We were introducing ourselves while you went to fetch the cat. He looks amazing, by the way. I was afraid he would refuse to eat while I was gone. He's such a picky eater and gets depressed when I'm away."

"Actually, I've been making him some of my own blend," Izzy said, looking proud of herself.

The bodega on the corner stocked Rufus's normal cat food. That wasn't good enough for Izzy, or her creativity in the kitchen. This week, Rufus got fresh chicken mixed with celery and carrots. Last week was beef, eggs, and spinach. For a vegan, Izzy really enjoyed experimenting with meaty cat food recipes. She was a pretty good cook for human food, too, but it leaned more toward tofu and quinoa—two foods I had never even tried before leaving Louisiana but I was now firmly pro.

Aunt Melanie picked Rufie up and blew out a huff as if she strained herself. "He must be liking it. He's put on a pound." I hadn't noticed, but then again, I wasn't exactly weighing him every day.

"Homemade cat food is a little extra work," Izzy explained, "but the ingredients are healthier. It's nice to know what he's eating, don't you think?"

"Not to mention he's using the litter box less," I added. Not that I was complaining. Cleaning a litter box was a small price to pay for living in a bougie building like this free of charge. The apartment itself was enormous, with wide windows and a floor-to-ceiling glass door that led out to a balcony large enough to hold a small table and two chairs, overlooking a narrow court-yard. The inside was decorated with enormous bookshelves crammed with more books than an average school library, along with unique knickknacks ranging from the size of a quarter to a seven-foot-tall giraffe statue.

Aunt Melanie collected local art, along with being an artist herself. Not that her apartment displayed any of her paintings, but she had her share of renown in art circles. Personally, I wished I'd inherited even a pinch of her talent. Sure, I could make a gorgeous ball gown out of an old burlap sack, but the last time I tried drawing a stick figure, it was mistaken for a carrot.

I sat on the other end of the couch and studied my aunt. My mother's sister was only a few years younger than her, but seemed closer to my age than hers at first glance. While my mom's hair was a short, silver bob, my aunt's hair was long enough to reach the middle of her back, with a hint of wave as it transitioned from blonde to reddish brown to purple at the tips. Unlike my mother, and myself, Aunt Melanie was rail-thin. She never looked old before today, but there were new thin lines on her forehead and dark bags under her eyes, in addition to the enor-mous contraption on her foot. "But enough about Rufus. What on earth happened to your leg?"

"Long, rambling story," she said, sitting back and closing her eyes. "It's good to be home."

Izzy was busy pulling dishes out of the drying rack and put-ting them in the cupboards where they belonged. Unlike the rest of the eclectically decorated apartment, the kitchen was bland by comparison with beige cabinets and gray countertops. I wasn't even sure anyone had ever cooked in it before Izzy moved in, if the collection of takeout menus and standard cookware still in the original packaging was any indication. If it weren't for the assortment of complementary but unmatched homemade plates, bowls, and glasses, I wouldn't believe that the kitchen was part of my aunt's space at all.

Izzy slid a stack of plates onto the shelf and ran a dish towel over the counters. Even knowing she desperately needed a place to stay, I'd been apprehensive about inviting her to move in, and only partially because it wasn't my apartment. Growing up with no siblings and still living in my parents' house meant I'd never had to share my personal space before. But it turned out that Izzy was the perfect roommate. She loved to cook, but even more important, she loved to clean. Dishes. Laundry. Vacuuming. Even cleaning litter boxes. She said it was her jam, and I was more than happy to indulge her.

Izzy carefully folded the towel over one of the drawer handles. When she moved in, one of the first things she did was put away the paper towels and napkins, replacing them with colorful reusable towels she made herself with a little help from me and my faithful sewing machine. "Well, I can see you two have a lot of catching up to do. Gimme a sec, and I'll be outta your hair." With a curt nod, she disappeared into the bedroom and I could hear the crinkly sound of clothes being hastily shoved into plastic garbage bags.

I followed her and stood in the doorway. I knew this day was coming, but didn't expect it for another month and a half. When Izzy first showed up on the doorstep, a pile of mismatched boxes,

.a suitcase held together with hope and duct tape, and laundry bags bursting at the seams with her meager possessions, I'd been reluctant to let her inside. But now I couldn't bear to see her leave. "Where are you gonna go?"

"I'll figure something out," she said brightly. "I'll probably crash with Vince for a day or two until I come up with something more permanent."

Izzy didn't seem concerned, but I was. She hadn't opened up about what happened in the interrogation room, but if Castillo's interview with her had been half as uncomfortable as it had been with me, they were in for an awkward evening. Besides, with him working long shifts to solve Vickie's murder, I doubted that he would be interested in playing house tonight. "At least call him and let him know you're coming," I urged her, although I couldn't think of an alternative place for her to stay off the top of my head.

"Nah. Never give them a chance to say no. Worked for you, didn't it?" She flashed me a toothy grin. She was right about that much. I never would have agreed to taking on a roomie in my aunt's apartment if Izzy hadn't shown up with a bunch of bags and nowhere else to go. "Have you seen my purple hat?"

"It's in the bathroom," I told her.

"Thanks!" She slid past me and headed to the bathroom, dragging her makeshift luggage behind her.

"Can I at least call you an Uber?" I offered. I made just a fraction of minimum wage at the café, but between a sunny smile and Untapped's collection of local craft beer, I earned a decent haul in tips. Even with free rent, I'd barely been able to make ends meet before Izzy moved in and showed me how to stretch every dime even further. As a result, I could afford a few little luxuries in life, like a pair of shoes at the local consignment shop that I had my eyes on, but I'd much rather use my meager savings to help Izzy.

"Odessa, haven't you learned anything from me?" she asked, shaking her head. "Don't waste money on silly things." She stuck out one leg and wiggled her foot. "What's the point in having feet if you don't use 'em?" Without missing a beat, she scooped her belongings on the bathroom counter into her hat and crammed it all into the aptly named hobo bag slung across her body.

She leaned in for a quick hug. "See ya at work," she said. She dropped her set of keys on the counter.

Then she was gone.

"Your friend Izzy seems nice," Aunt Melanie said, stifling a yawn, as soon as the door shut behind my friend. "It's such a comfort being back in my own home after so many weeks of hotel rooms and train sleeper cars."

"I'm sure," I replied, perching on the low coffee table in front of the couch. "And I'd love to hear all about your adventures. Starting with what happened to your foot."

"It's silly. We were walking around Stonehenge right before sunrise, and I took a bad step. The doctor said it's just a hairline fracture, but I'd rather see my own physician and get a second opinion."

"Personally, considering England's socialized health care, I would have stayed there." Then again, if my aunt could afford this enormous apartment in an upscale building, paying insurance premiums and huge co-pays was probably the least of her worries. "I'm sorry you got hurt. Can I get you anything? Something for the pain maybe?"

"I wouldn't turn down an aspirin. Oh, and a package arrived for you." She gestured at a box on the coffee table. It had the familiar logo of a retail giant emblazoned across the cardboard, but I didn't remember ordering anything.

I jumped up and prepared a glass of water, disappointed in my poor manners for not offering it sooner. I handed it to her, along with a bottle of aspirin. "I wish you'd given me a heads-up that you were coming home early. It would have caused less . . ." I tried to think of the best word for my aunt hobbling around on a walking cast, pinning my best friend to the wall with her crutch. ". . . drama."

"What do you mean? I texted you last night. Or was it today? I've never been good with time zones."

"I didn't get a text," I replied.

She dug her phone out of her carry-on bag, which rested beside me on the coffee table, and tapped through the screens. "Huh, look at that, I never pressed send. Sorry. Then again, the painkillers they gave me at the hospital were quite a wonder. I wouldn't have been surprised if I'd gotten on the wrong plane and ended up in Queensland or something."

Aunt Melanie shifted slightly so she was lying across the couch cushions. "A little help, please?"

I got up and helped her arrange the heavy boot on a stack of pillows at the end of the couch. "Can I get you something to eat? We've got some leftover vegan pizza on cauliflower crust in the fridge, and I've got a flyer for a new Thai place that just opened down the street." When she didn't answer, I glanced at my aunt. She was already sound asleep.

At the end of her bed there was an antique wooden trunk

that held extra linens. I pulled out a thin blanket and spread it across her, careful not to wake her before turning off the lights and retreating to her bedroom.

Now what was I supposed to do? I wasn't sure if I should sleep in her bed while my aunt, my elder at that, snored softly on her couch, but if she'd wanted the bedroom she would have crashed there instead. Besides, no matter that my aunt had lived in New York since fleeing Louisiana a few days after high school graduation, she still had Southern manners instilled in her. By that logic, I was a guest and guests don't sleep on the couch. It was the same reason that Izzy had stayed in the bedroom while she was here.

I grabbed the package off the coffee table and went to the bedroom, closing the door as softly as I could. I kicked off my shoes and sat cross-legged in the middle of her soft mattress, where I could examine the box. The original packing tape had been cut and resealed with clear plastic tape, and the return address was Piney Island, Louisiana.

My mom hadn't been quite as enthusiastic as I was about me coming to New York. She was afraid the big city would chew me up and spit me out. Or, more likely, she was afraid it would seduce me like it had her sister Melanie and I'd never come home again. We talked on the phone or Skype at least once a week. But even when I'd first arrived, and I was nervous and homesick, she hadn't sent any care packages.

Until now.

I peeled back the tape and opened the box. Inside a Walmart bag was a disposable food container, which held the broken remains of what looked like a dozen snickerdoodle cookies. I picked up one of the larger crumbs and popped it into my mouth. It was still soft and delicious.

Besides the container of cookies, there was a local Piney Island newspaper. I flipped through it, wondering if there was a story she wanted me to read, or if she just wanted me to get nostalgic. In the back, she'd circled several Help Wanted ads in red. That's my mom for you, real subtle. She knew as well as I did that my old job at the Crawdad Shack was still waiting for me, but she thought I was wasting my potential. Sure, waiting tables didn't pay all that well, but I enjoyed it, and shouldn't that matter, too?

Underneath the paper was a shoebox. It wasn't any old shoebox, though. It was at least twice as big as a sneaker box, and was well-worn around the edges. I peeled the box open and nearly squealed in delight. Cowboy boots! One of my own pair, black and silver leather, perfectly broken in, and as comfortable as they got.

Ever since I'd lost my boots—the only pair of shoes I'd brought to Brooklyn—in an unfortunate seagull incident a few weeks ago, I'd been trying to convince myself that a pair of secondhand orthopedic loafers was a fair substitute. Sure, they were comfy, but they weren't my style. Cowboy boots were. I hugged my boots to my chest.

Then a thought struck me. I'd always known that my adventure in the big city had an expiration date, but I'd planned on being in Williamsburg for another six weeks. How would that work now that Aunt Melanie was back early? I couldn't stay on her sofa indefinitely. She didn't need an apartment sitter or cat sitter anymore, and sooner or later she was going to want her privacy back.

Unlike Izzy, I didn't have an alternate place to stay.

How many things had I not done yet, thinking I had plenty of time in Brooklyn? I'd eaten at almost every food truck, but there was a new one every day. I'd spent a day at the Met and had a picnic lunch in Central Park. I'd toured the observation deck of the Empire State Building. I'd eaten real knishes at Katz's, ordered New York–style pizza by the slice, and even had an authentic Coney Island hot dog on the boardwalk. I got to experience outdoor concerts, went to gallery openings, and spent Saturdays at the Brooklyn Flea. I'd even faced my fears and ridden my aunt's bike across the Williamsburg Bridge and back.

But that was just the tip of the iceberg that New York had to offer.

Just thinking about leaving my friends at the café, a lump formed in my throat. Sure, I'd been a little homesick when I first arrived. It hadn't helped that I was a complete fish out of water. But now I had friends and, to my surprise, I didn't want to leave.

I didn't want to go back to living with my parents.

I didn't want to go back to the tiny town I'd grown up in, only to watch my friends move away and start lives elsewhere.

I didn't want to go back to slinging jambalaya and Coors Light at the Crawdad Shack.

I didn't want to go back.

Period.

8

....

Melanie Tuckerman
60 Min

Guess who's home? Long story, but I'm back in NYC early.
Amazing trip, can't wait to catch up with everyone. Got lots of
pix (will post later!) and inspiration. Gained at least 10 pounds
in Paris—OMG the bread! The cheese! THE WINE! Oh, and
broke my foot, so there's that.

....

I'D NEVER PERSONALLY experienced jet lag. I'd always wanted to
travel the world, but until a few months ago when my aunt had
called and invited me to apartment-sit for her in Brooklyn, the
farthest I'd ever gotten from Piney Island, Louisiana, was a little
over two hundred miles to Dallas. Whether it was from the jet
lag, painkillers, or sheer exhaustion, Aunt Melanie was still
sound asleep on the couch when the sun streaming in through
the bedroom curtains woke me.

Sunrises and sunsets in New York were my favorite, when
the vivid colors reflected off literal miles of glass and steel. Don't
get me wrong, Manhattan at night was spectacular, especially

from the Williamsburg side of the river, but all the man-made light shows in the world couldn't hold a candle to nature.

Change my mind.

Not that I was a huge fan of being up this early, but as long as I was awake, I might as well appreciate it.

Normally, I would brew a cup of coffee and take it to the balcony, enjoying a rare moment of peace and quiet before the rest of the city woke up and resumed the constant cacophony. This morning, I didn't want to disturb my aunt, so I slipped in and out of the bathroom, fed the cat, and headed out without waking her.

On weekends, Untapped Books & Café opened at eight but I wasn't scheduled until eleven, so I had time to kill. Sure, I could go into the café and sweet-talk myself into a free plate of Parker's cinnamon apple French toast, but the moment I stepped foot inside, Todd would likely put me to work rewiring the kitchen or scrubbing the dumpsters out back or something. Unpaid, of course.

Instead, I bought a cup of coffee at the corner bodega and took my time strolling in the shadow of graffiti-covered buildings. Although in Williamsburg, graffiti was street art, and some of it was spectacular.

The day was going to be a scorcher. The sun beat down on dirty sidewalks without so much as a hint of a breeze. Overhead, the whir of dozens of air-conditioning units hanging from windows sounded like a chorus of drones. A bicyclist whizzed past, fearlessly weaving in between traffic and cars parked along the curb. Horns beeped and somewhere in the distance an ambulance siren whined. The cowboy boots my mom had mailed me made satisfying clunks on the pavement as I walked.

New York was dirty. Loud. Dirty. Crowded. Dirty. Expensive. Did I mention dirty?

But there was nowhere on Earth I would rather be.

I paused at the corner long enough to gauge a break in traffic and then dashed across the street. The light turned red, and a blue and white NYPD car blurted its horn and sped through the intersection anyway. Then the cruiser made an illegal U-turn in the middle of the street and angled over to the curb several feet in front of me.

The passenger-side window slid down and I heard someone say, "Odessa, jump in."

I bent down to look through the open window and recognized Detective Castillo behind the wheel. "Vincent, what's going on?" I asked.

He made a vague gesture at the window. "The AC in this thing is barely clinging to life support as it is, get in before it gives up the ghost."

I did as he said. Or was it ordered? It was hard to tell. Castillo was a friend, but he was also a cop. Sometimes I wasn't sure where to draw the line between the two sides of him.

"Seat belt," he said as he pushed a button and my window slid up with a faint whine. He hadn't been kidding about the air conditioner. It was, at best, a few degrees cooler in the car than out, and it was still early.

"What's with the blue and white?" I asked. Usually, he drove a rotating selection of generic, dark-colored, American-made sedans that came equipped with four extra antennas and dashboard lights. Frankly, I wasn't sure who they thought they were fooling. Unmarked cop cars might as well be more visible than an on-duty yellow cab.

"It's what was available," he replied. A grinding noise came from the dash and the tepid air coming out of the vents slowed to a trickle. "You seen Izzy this morning? She's not returning my calls."

"I thought she stayed with you last night," I said.

He shook his head.

"When I see her, I'll let her know you're looking for her," I promised, trying to not let it show that I was worried about her. If she wasn't at my aunt's place or Castillo's, where had she slept? I knew that Izzy was a big girl. She could take care of herself better than anyone else I'd ever met, but her idea of home and mine varied wildly. It wouldn't surprise me if she had a hotel room at Four Seasons or was setting up camp under a bridge somewhere. Either option was equally likely, and in Izzy's eyes, equally acceptable.

"You do that. I have some questions for her."

"About Vickie Marsh?" I asked.

He nodded curtly. "Inconsistencies have cropped up, and I need Izzy to clarify a few things."

"Inconsistencies? Like what?"

"Just give her the message." He pulled over behind a double-parked delivery van. "It's important."

"Got it," I said.

"Be careful, okay?"

"I'm ducky," I insisted. "I know how to take care of myself."

That much was an exaggeration, at best. But I was getting there, and that had to count for something.

"I just need to know you're staying out of trouble."

"You don't have to worry about me," I said, and let myself out of the car, careful not to slam the door. I was half tempted to ask for a ride for a few more blocks, but considering the state of the cruiser, I wasn't sure it would have made it.

As I trudged toward the river, I called Izzy. Her phone went to voicemail. Not a surprise. No one I knew used cell phones for phone calls anymore. I hung up and sent her a text message to check in instead of leaving a voicemail.

My phone vibrated and I glanced at my screen, expecting a response from Izzy. Instead, it was a text from an unknown number. Hey, beautiful. I blocked the creep and kept walking.

I ended up at one of my favorite hidden gems in Brooklyn. Nearby Domino Park drew tourists and families with its manicured grass, delicious taco bar, and well-maintained fountains. It had a great dog run and several picturesque Instagram spots. It was also crowded, even at this early hour, especially on weekends. But just a block away was a smaller park also along the river, tucked away behind a copse of trees.

Little more than a strip of land not much bigger than a suburban backyard, Grand Ferry Park consisted of a handful of benches overlooking enormous boulders that separated Brooklyn from the river. This morning, I was alone except for a man tossing a tennis ball to an off-leash Labrador retriever near the water's edge.

I chose a bench in the shade and sat cross-legged on it, sipping my coffee while I watched the river slap against the rocks.

There was a podcast on my phone calling my name, but I wasn't feeling it this morning. Instead, I listened to the sounds of the city, somewhat muffled by the park, and marveled at the view of the Manhattan skyline rising up from the brownstones of the Lower East Side. Or maybe it was Alphabet City. The lines between the neighborhoods were blurry from this side of the river.

I didn't want to think about all the nooks and crannies of New York I would never get a chance to explore now and instead wondered what Castillo wanted from Izzy. He said there were inconsistencies. Izzy might have left something out—by accident, of course—but she wouldn't have lied. Something new must have come to light since yesterday. I wondered what it was, not that Castillo would share such things with me.

Vickie and Izzy had gone to high school together, so that meant we were all about the same age. It was hard to wrap my head around the fact that Vickie had a successful career and I was still waiting tables. Then again, I was still able to enjoy a relaxing morning in my favorite park and Vickie would never again have that pleasure.

It wasn't fair.

Any time a life was cut short, it was tragic. But when she couldn't have been more than twenty-five, it was somehow worse. Even if she hadn't been a particularly nice person.

I barely knew Vickie. I'd met her, what, an hour? less? before she was murdered. To be completely honest, I didn't even know that I liked her that much. She was kinda rude to me. Bossy. Stuck-up.

Behind me, the now-familiar sound of a siren sped along the street. It was such a constant noise that it almost faded into the background. There were always emergency vehicles racing here or there. Fire trucks. Ambulances. Police cruisers.

Contrary to what I'd thought before arriving—I'd assumed that all of New York City was a hotbed of crime and murder—Williamsburg was relatively safe. It actually had a crime rate much *lower* than the national average. Even so, with so many people, that still equated to some danger, mostly from pickpockets and fender benders. Believe it or not, the murder rate in Williamsburg was close to null despite being a bustling neighborhood just a stone's throw from Manhattan.

Sure, there was the Williamsburg Slasher, but that had been the exception, not the rule. I'd followed his arrest, trial, and conviction closely on my favorite true crime blog. While the case gave me a serious case of the shivers, I knew the Williamsburg Slasher wouldn't be causing anyone trouble ever again.

Most deaths in this neighborhood were the more banal car-vs-pedestrian variety, or plain old age. But in the last two months, I'd met not just one but now two murder victims.

Talk about rotten luck.

I knew the full attention of the Brooklyn police force would be focused on solving Vickie's murder. Okay, maybe not the full force. But Detective Vincent Castillo, certainly. And he had a ton of resources at his disposal. A lot more than I did.

He certainly didn't need my help.

And yet, I couldn't seem to stop thinking about Vickie. She didn't deserve to die, and I couldn't shake the feeling that I had missed something.

None of us were in the library when she was killed, at least as far as I knew. Izzy and I were in the kitchen, along with Gen-

nifer. Or maybe it was Amanda? I'd been concentrating on finding clues, not who was where. Marlie had lagged behind the
whole time, so I assumed she was in the billiard room, but I
don't remember seeing her when Izzy and I backtracked to the
library. Then again, I wasn't looking for her. I hadn't even noticed that Vickie wasn't with us until we found her body.

I'd always considered myself an observant person, but since
coming to New York, I had to admit that I was a little over-
whelmed. There was just so much going on at any given moment
that it was nearly impossible to keep track of it all. The escape
room hadn't been as crowded as the neighborhood in general,
but the small rooms were crammed with clues and red herrings
and random distractions.

I took a sip of my coffee and was surprised to find my cup
empty. Sweat trickled down my back. I'd sat in the park longer
than I'd realized, lost in thought. I pulled out my phone and saw
multiple message notifications. I still had half an hour before my
shift started and Untapped wasn't even a five-minute walk away,
so I pulled up the notifications.

Ever since taking over the Untapped Books & Café's social
media accounts, my digital footprint had gone through the roof.
If I didn't check the accounts several times a day—whether or
not I was on the clock—it easily got away from me. The café had
a few dozen new followers. I scrolled through them, making sure
to follow back repeat customers while ignoring or blocking the
bots. All of the DMs were spam, so I deleted them without replying.

I opened Instagram, careful to avoid my page. I once lost a

few—and by a few, I mean ten—hours playing with Instagram filters. Hashtag never again. Instead, I searched for Vickie Marsh, and her account popped up. The last posting was a long-armed selfie shot of Vickie flashing a radiant smile at the camera, looking self-confident and happy. She'd tagged it "Winning!"

It was hard to believe that she was dead.

According to the comments below the picture, I wasn't the only person who was struggling to accept that the vibrant Vickie was gone with no warning. Dozens of people had expressed their shock and grief with everything from simple emojis to long-winded eulogies. She had a lot of friends, or at least a lot of on-line acquaintances.

Or maybe they were suspects.

Now that was a rabbit hole I wasn't going to go down. It wasn't my job to figure out who killed Vickie. It was Castillo's. My job was to serve cold craft brews and whatever delicious creations Parker was inventing in the kitchen. Sure, a few weeks ago when Bethany, one of my fellow servers, was murdered, I had managed to solve the case and bring the killer to justice before the police were even convinced that her death was more than an accident, but that was a fluke.

Right?

Besides, even if I did have a natural talent for solving murders—which was impossible; I think I just listened to too many true crime podcasts—I didn't want to get involved. The last time it hadn't ended well. I'd come awful close to becoming a second victim. Out of habit, I found myself rubbing the inside of my left wrist, where I'd gotten a colorful owl tattoo in memory of Bethany. I hadn't known her for long before she was murdered, but the tattoo was a constant reminder to live life at the fullest because no one ever knew when the end would come.

Just like it had come early for poor Vickie Marsh.

The police were looking into her death, I reminded myself.

Detective Castillo would never forgive me if I inserted myself into his murder investigation.

Again.

However, it wasn't actually investigating if all I was doing was looking at pictures on the internet, right? I recognized one of the commenters as Amanda, the woman who'd been in the escape room with us, and clicked on her username. By the looks of it, she posted multiple pictures an hour. She was the main subject in all the pictures. Other people occasionally popped up in the background, but Amanda was always front and center. I scrolled through the pictures until I reached a selfie of her in the NYPD waiting room. Not exactly something I would want on my public feed.

I could imagine it now. My mother would be so disappointed if she saw a picture of me inside a police station, surrounded by men and women in uniform as well as the flotsam of human society. Thinking of my mother, I knew I should update her on the Aunt Melanie situation. I wished I could text her, but she hardly ever had her cell phone charged, much less nearby.

As if my thinking of her ignited some kind of psychic mother-daughter connection, my phone rang and the caller ID displayed my home phone number. As in the landline number, the one I'd memorized back in kindergarten and would probably always remember. I accepted the call and could imagine my mother standing in our kitchen, the curtains decorated with sunbursts and a row of cookie jars shaped like chickens lined up along the buffet table.

"Hey, Ma," I said, answering the phone. "I was just about to call you."

"Odessa! Darling! I've missed your voice!"

I smiled. My mother had a way of making every person she met feel like the most special person in the universe, but I knew that position was really reserved for me. "Ma, we Skyped yesterday morning." I'd installed Skype on the computer in the den before I'd left so we could video-chat anytime she wanted.

"I know, but it's not the same. Did you get my package?"

"Yes, thank you!"

"I know you've been missing having your boots. I picked up a few patterns I thought you would like at the store yesterday. They were on sale. Wasn't sure if I should send them to you in another care package or wait until you got home. One of the dresses has those pretty panels you like so much, and it even has pockets!"

"Thanks, sounds great." My mother and I had vastly different ideas when it came to fashion, but it was the thought that counted. "Might as well keep them in Louisiana. Looks like I might be coming home sooner than expected."

"What? Really? What happened? You're not sick, are you? Have you seen a doctor yet?"

"Ma, don't worry, I'm right as rain. Promise." Maybe it was because I was an only child, but even after I turned eighteen and was legally an adult, she would immediately schedule an appointment with my old pediatrician if I so much as sneezed. "Aunt Melanie fractured her ankle."

"Honey, I know all about that. She posted it on Facebook."

"Then you know she had to cut her trip short, so I'll probably be headed home soon." At the thought of leaving New York, maybe to never come back, my heart sank. But it wasn't like I could afford an apartment here. Besides, I always knew this was temporary.

"Odessa Morgan Dean, I did *not* raise you to be like that!"

I blinked at the phone. It had been years since she'd pulled out my full name. The last time she'd done that, I'd gotten caught sneaking out after curfew to go meet up with my friends at the lake. I couldn't have been much more than sixteen at the time. "What'd I do?"

"You're not gonna leave my baby sister all alone in New York City with a broken foot, are you? You oughta be ashamed of yourself."

On one hand, I wanted to laugh. My mother knew Aunt Melanie better than that. She might not have seen her pin Izzy to the wall with her crutch, but she knew that my aunt was gonna do exactly what she was gonna do, and not nobody was gonna tell her different, cast or no cast. But on the other hand . . .

My mother might have inadvertently struck gold.

I had the perfect excuse to stay in New York for however long it took my aunt to heal. Weeks, at least. Months, maybe.

"You're so right, Ma."

I heard a soft snort on the other end of the line. A ladylike snort, of course, but a snort just the same. "I always am, darling dearest. Now, you get off the phone and go help your aunt this instant. Call me tomorrow?"

NO MEMES OF ESCAPE

"I will," I promised. "Love you."

"Love you, too, Odessa."

I ended the call and slipped my phone into my messenger bag, grinning from ear to ear. I had the perfect excuse to stay in New York!

9

Odessa Dean @OdessaWaiting · July 13
Raise ur hand if u 100% don't believe in ghosts, but also
kinda secretly 10/10 believe in ghosts? #whoyougonnacall
#cocacolaremovesbloodstains

WHEN I GOT to Untapped Books & Café—a full ninety seconds
before my shift started, thank you very much—I must have still
been smiling like a clown because Izzy looked up from her usual
position behind the checkout counter and said, "You look like
someone who just stumbled across a whole buncha free street
tacos. What's up with you?"

At the mention of tacos, my stomach grumbled. I hadn't
wanted to make breakfast at the apartment and risk waking up
my aunt, but now that I realized how long it was until my lunch
break, I was starting to regret that decision. "Hey, Izzy. I'm so
sorry about yesterday. You didn't have to leave like that."

She waved a dismissive hand. "No biggie. Besides, it was
time to move on."

"I tried calling you earlier but you didn't pick up."

"Oh yeah, I forgot to charge my phone."

"Uh-huh." I hoped that didn't mean that she had stayed someplace without electricity. I wouldn't put it past her. Izzy had a long, storied past of crashing wherever she could, for as long as she could. "I thought you were gonna stay with Vincent last night . . ."

"Changed my mind." She cocked her head, but her short, spiky hair barely moved. What she saved on rent she certainly invested in good hair product and revolving dye jobs. "How'd you know that, anyway?"

"Bumped into him on my way into work. He wanted me to pass along a message that you need to call him."

"I'm sure he did," she said. A customer approached the desk, several books in her arms and a young child glued to her leg. "Did you find everything you were looking for?" she asked the customer brightly.

That was my cue. Izzy would call Castillo back or she wouldn't. She'd tell me where she was staying or she wouldn't. Her life, her choice. I was worried about her, but I wasn't her keeper. It was none of my business. Besides, I needed to get to work.

I started to head back toward the café, but Izzy gestured at me to wait a sec. While I waited for her to finish up with the customer, I took a quick snapshot of one of our bookshelves. It was bulging with books ranging from newly released bestsellers to small-run, hard-to-find cult classics. I captioned it "Got books?" I doubted it would take off as a meme, but at least I could tell Todd I was trying.

As soon as Izzy finished her transaction, she told me, "I need five, ten minutes of your time before you clock in. Before you say anything, I already cleared it with Todd."

"And?" I asked suspiciously.

"He said it was fine. Come on." She stuck her head into the hallway and shouted for Todd to come relieve her, and then we hurried out the front door before he could object. "I've got a surprise for you."

"What is it?"

"If I tell you, it's not much of a surprise," Izzy said with a smile. "Trust me." We walked a few blocks before stopping in front of a building. I looked up at it. The first floor of the building was retail space. I could smell Thai food sizzling in one of the restaurants. The corner store was selling refurbished electronics, and the checkered awning next to it advertised exotic vacations.

The second floor was mostly windows, and judging from the tiny plants in the windows and cubicle walls, I assumed this was office space. I couldn't tell from here if it was one of those workplaces with standing desks and foosball tables in the break room or a button-down place, and I wondered what they did there. Never having worked in an office before, they were a bit of a mystery to me. Other than going to meetings and sending emails, I had no idea what sorts of things office workers did.

Above the office, I counted four flights of black iron balconies jutting out of the building, contrasting nicely with the light beige brick exterior. Judging from the size of the balconies, the units were spacious. There was no dirty laundry hanging off the rails or kids' bikes crammed onto the balconies. Instead, there were padded chairs and delicate tables, with lights strung along the railing.

But best of all was the location. The iconic four-story tall mural of a little girl staring off into space that had come to symbolize Williamsburg was right around the corner, and in the near distance, the Williamsburg Bridge rose out of the city streets and soared over the river.

"Whoa, nice digs," I said.

"Right?" Izzy led us around to an entrance between a lunch counter and the travel agency. She buzzed one of the buttons and the door popped open. We climbed the stairs to the third floor, and Izzy pushed a door open without knocking.

The apartment was enormous, with seemingly thousand-foot-tall ceilings and a single pane window where the far wall should be, letting the morning light stream in. It was also completely empty, bare of any furniture or knickknacks or any of the touches that made a house a home. However, the most noticeable feature by far, other than that enormous window, was that someone had splashed what looked like ten gallons of brownish paint over every surface.

The tightly woven industrial-grade carpet was splattered in paint. The walls, which featured floor-to-ceiling built-in bookshelves, were splattered in paint. Even the ceiling—a lovely checkerboard of white-textured drop tiles—was splattered in varying shades of brown paint.

And there was a smell that I couldn't place. Industrial cleaners, yes, but underneath it, something like the rotting vegetation in a Louisiana swamp, but sharper. More pungent.

"This place is so zhuzhy," Izzy said.

"Zhuzhy?" I asked. I hadn't heard that term before.

"You know, bougie, but zhuzhed up," she explained. "Can't you see me living here?"

I was fairly certain she'd made that word up on the spot, but it fit. "You could never afford this place."

"Never say never."

A woman entered from the kitchen, holding a disposable coffee cup in one hand and a tablet computer in the other. I recognized her. She'd been one of the escape room attendees, the older woman with the sour expression. "Lovely to see the two of you again," she said, beaming. Today she was wearing a white ruffled blouse paired with a tan pantsuit. She juggled her coffee, freeing up a hand to offer for us to shake. "Marlie Robbinson. I don't think we were properly introduced the other day. You're Izzy, right?"

"Yup. And I'm sure you remember Odessa," she replied. Izzy turned to me. "It's magnificent, isn't it?"

I blinked at her. "Well, yeah." The apartment was enormous, even larger than my aunt's. When I met Izzy, she'd been living in an abandoned public school with several other squatters. This wasn't just a step up, it was a whole year's worth of steps up. Maybe more.

"Let me show you around," Marlie offered.

Izzy started to follow her, but I grabbed her elbow and asked in a whisper, "What are we doing here?"

Izzy grinned. "I need an apartment, and a roommate. What do you say? Move in here with me?"

"I'd love to," I admitted. "But where would we get the money? I'm flat broke. We could never afford this place. It must cost like a gazillion bucks a month."

"That's the beauty of it. They're practically giving it away." Izzy followed Marlie into the kitchen. Like the spacious living room, brownish paint splattered all the surfaces, from the white grout between the light gray floor tiles to the shiny stainless steel appliances, the kind I'd always wanted.

"Ignore all the blood," Marlie said. "The landlord has cleaners coming out today, and it will be tip-top before you move in. It will be like nothing ever happened here."

There was a loud ringing in my ears like I'd been standing in front of the giant speakers at a rock concert, and my head felt too big for my body.

"Odessa, you okay?" Izzy asked.

I shook my head mutely, unable to think. I leaned against the counter to get my balance, but when I realized that my hand was clutching one of the brown stains on the white marble counter, I snatched it back. "Blood?" I finally choked out.

"Well, yes. There was a little, um, incident here a while back. But the police have cleared the scene and like I said, it will be good as new in a day or two. A fresh coat of paint and new carpet, and you'll never know that anyone was murdered here." She blinked at me, as if expecting me to speak.

When I didn't say anything, she continued, "I know it might seem a little gruesome, but it's old news now. The perpetrator has been convicted and sentenced to life. You're as safe as houses," she declared. But I noticed that she was careful not to touch any surfaces.

"The Williamsburg Slasher," I announced, putting two and two together.

"Why, yes, the papers did call him that. But the locks on the doors and windows have been replaced and there hasn't been a news crew or amateur ghost hunter try to break in for weeks."

"Wait a second, ghosts? You mean this place is haunted, too?"

"Of course not," Marlie said in a silken voice. "Ghosts aren't real. But the landlord knows he's not going to have an easy time finding renters, not even in this economy. So he hired me, and he's willing to let it go for a song. That's where you come in."

"Can we talk in the hall?" I asked. "I'm finding it hard to concentrate in here." Walking back through the living room was a little like walking through a minefield. With alligators. And snipers. When I'd thought the brownish stains on the carpet were paint, I'd stepped on them all willy-nilly, but now that I knew they were bloodstains I tiptoed from one patch of clean carpet to the next as well as I could.

"Why don't you two come back after the cleaners have done their thing?" Marlie suggested. "We can finish the tour then."

"No thanks."

"Come on, Odessa," Izzy urged. "Did you see those built-in bookshelves? South-facing windows? And there's two bedrooms, if you can believe it."

"I don't care if there's a sunken Jacuzzi tub in the en suite bathroom and a refrigerator that automatically orders groceries when you get low. I'm not living in the Williamsburg Slasher murder apartment."

"They have a generous pet policy," Marlie added. "All pet fees would be waived for the first year."

"A serial killer murdered an entire family here!"

Marlie continued as if I hadn't said anything. "As I told Izzy on the phone, the rent is simply unbeatable, and I'll even give you two the friends-and-family discount on my broker's fee."

"Nope," I said.

"But, Odessa," Izzy started.

"No stinking way," I repeated. I loved the idea of staying in Williamsburg, and I had to admit that the apartment was magnificent, but I'd never get the image of all that . . . brown paint, I reminded myself. It was easier to think of it that way . . . out of my head.

I wasn't naive. I knew the odds of someone dying in an apartment increased to 100 percent on a long enough timeline, and New York City was *old*. But now that I'd seen the raw, unfiltered evidence, I couldn't ever unsee it. A fresh coat of paint wouldn't change that.

It was bad enough that I'd seen a dead body yesterday. I couldn't live in a place where I would never be far away from the memory of all that blood and sadness. "Hard pass."

"Understood," Marlie said agreeably. The dour woman we'd met at the escape room disappeared, replaced by this cheery woman. This version of Marlie was pleasant and might even be fun to hang out with, unlike the one that had kept asking for unneeded hints, causing us to run out of time prematurely in the escape room. "I know you've got a tight budget, and that limits our options. There's one more building I'd like to show you ladies. It's not nearly as nice as this one, but as far as I know, it's never been featured on national news, either. Why don't you two follow me?"

"That's a good start," I said. I'd never figured that no recent mass murders would be my number one criterion when apartment hunting, but then again, before now I hadn't ever seriously shopped for a place to live. I still wasn't sure how I could possibly afford to live in Brooklyn, even with a roommate, but I could keep an open mind. "You're an apartment broker, right?"

"One of the top brokers in the city," she proclaimed with a proud note in her voice as she led us down the stairs and into the street.

"But not as good as Vickie was, right?" I asked before I could catch myself. I guess the shock of being inside the same apartment where the Williamsburg Slasher had, well, slashed, had rattled something loose inside of me. Like my filter. "That's what you were celebrating the other day, weren't you? Vickie had won an award for being top broker for like a whole year?"

"If she was the best, that makes you runner-up?" Izzy added.

Marlie's smile slipped. "Vickie was one of a kind, and we'll all miss her."

"Yeah, I'm sure," Izzy muttered under her breath.

I glanced at Izzy, and she gave me a little *Go on!* motion with her hand. I wasn't sure if we were really onto something or not, but Marlie was in the escape room with us, so she was one of the five possible suspects with opportunity. And she was obviously a professional rival of Vickie's. If the expression on her face was any indication, she was jealous of her coworker's success, which gave her a motive.

On top of that, she didn't seem even the slightest bit freaked out being inside the notorious Williamsburg Slasher's murder scene. Which either made her a cold, hard killer, a calloused soul, or an incredible actor. She was a much more viable suspect than Izzy was, in my humble opinion.

OLIVIA BLACKE

"What exactly does an apartment broker do?" I asked, study-ing Marlie's reactions closely.

"We match the right people with the right homes. I know how hard it is to find the perfect apartment in New York. With a million people apartment hunting at any given time, a good apartment goes off the market before an ad is ever posted online. The apartment I just showed you? It will be snatched up before end of day, and you have my word on that."

I had a hard time believing that, but Marlie knew more about New York real estate than I did.

She continued, "Landlords and supers don't have the time to show an apartment to a bunch of lookie-loos, much less wade through hundreds of applications. That's where I come in. When an apartment is coming up, they let me know and I arrange a viewing for my clients. Think of me like an Apartment Cupid."

"And how much does that all cost?" I asked. Renting an apartment in New York should be like anywhere else. I should be able to go online, submit an application, get approved, and move in. Everything was more complicated here.

"It's a minimal up-front fee. It depends on the property, of course, but it's usually a percentage, equal to a month or two's rent."

I came to a complete stop. "Wait one second."

"Yes?" Marlie said.

"You tell people about apartments that are already on the market for a living? You don't own the apartment or the building or anything? You don't even place an advertisement? And for this, people give you over a month's rent, in advance?"

"Sometimes more, sometimes less," she said with a guileless smile still plastered on her face. As if what she was doing wasn't

102

highway robbery, much less morally bankrupt. "Each apartment is different."

"How on earth do you justify exploiting people like that? And how can anyone afford those kinds of fees?" I did a little mental math. I wasn't sure exactly what my aunt's two-bedroom apartment rented for a month, but I had a rough idea of what a studio went for. Counting first and last months' rent, security deposit, and an apartment broker's fee, it would cost a small fortune to move in—and that wasn't even figuring in the moving truck!

"Not only do brokers have exclusive access to apartments that would never be advertised to the general public, we have already negotiated a more favorable price with the landlord. Say an apartment is going for three thousand a month. I could cut you a little slack and get you in there for twenty-seven fifty."

"Sure, you'd save someone two-fifty a month, but they still end up paying more up-front in fees. How is that fair?"

Marlie gave Izzy an exasperated look. "Can you please explain to your friend how life works in the city?"

Izzy nodded sweetly. "Of course." She turned to me. "You see, there are a lot of desperate, broke people that are trying to eke out a living, but public housing is practically nonexistent. Between slumlords and predatory apartment brokers, it's nearly impossible to find a decent apartment—affordable or otherwise— in New York. Once you do find a place, you never leave. Or you sublet it from one roommate to the next ad nauseam. Which is why people end up living with their parents or their exes or a stranger they met on the internet, subletting from a sublet of a subletter. Since no one can afford to move, new apartments never come up on the market, and when they do, vultures like

Marlie here charge people an arm and a leg for the privilege of not living in a cardboard box. Is that about right, Marlie?"

Marlie huffed. "I can see you young ladies aren't serious about finding housing. You have my number. Call me when you come to your senses." She turned and walked away briskly.

"I think I'm starting to understand your housing horror stories," I told Izzy as we headed back toward Untapped Books & Café.

She shrugged. "Finding a decent apartment is an art."

"How can you afford a broker, though?"

"I can't. Hardly anyone I know can. Which drives up competition and prices. And yet, she was telling the truth. That apartment will be rented within the day."

"How can anyone stand the thought of living there after what happened?"

"Odessa, you're not thinking like a New Yorker. For those windows? Built-in bookshelves? I wouldn't care if there was a pile of dead bodies in the living room and the kitchen was an active crime scene. But even if they slashed the rent in half to attract a renter, I would never pay up-front broker's fees."

"Then why did you make an appointment with Marlie?" I asked.

"Silly girl. We weren't there to find an apartment, although that place was gorgeous. We were there to interrogate her, to see if she was involved with Vickie's murder. Did you get any vibes off her, you know, before you noped all the way out of there?"

I stared at Izzy in surprise. I wished she would have told me her plan ahead of time. Then again, if I'd been in on it, I might have given us away. "Marlie doesn't come off as trustworthy, and not just because she makes a living ripping other people off. She doesn't feel genuine. Like she was smiling and cheery today, but the other day she was grumpy and disengaged."

Izzy nodded. "That could be her work face, though. Heaven knows we both do it. You think I smile at every customer because I like them? You're a cheery person in general, but when you're waiting tables, you're like a level twelve. *Howdy, folks, what can I get you today?*" she said in a falsetto.

"I do *not* sound like that," I protested.

"True. It's more like"—she slowed her voice down until it sounded like she was playing back a movie in slow motion, and added a drawl that even I could barely understand—"*Why, howdee, faulks, wyatt can eye gits y'all?*"

I pursed my lips. "Ha. Ha. You shoulda been a comedian."

"You know I love your accent." Izzy slung her arm around my shoulders. "It makes you sound like such a rube. Imagine what would have happened to you if I hadn't come along. This big, bad city would have chewed you up and spit you out."

"Yup," I agreed.

"What do you think? Is Marlie a suspect or not?"

I stopped on the front steps of Untapped to think about it. "She was clearly jealous of Vickie's success. Without the top salesperson in her way, she stands to make more in commissions, and maybe even win the top broker award for herself."

"Greed, the classic motive," Izzy said.

"Plus, she had an iron stomach. Marlie didn't even flinch in that kitchen, all covered in blood. She sat there like a serial killer, sipping her coffee. I betcha she could have killed Vickie and not even batted an eye."

Izzy nodded. "Definitely a suspect." She opened the door. We were greeted by the tinkle of bells and Huckleberry thudding his tail against the carpet. It was nice to know someone was always happy to see me.

"Where have you two been?" Todd barked at us. There was a line of several exasperated-looking customers queued up in front of the cash register.

"Told you, we had to step out for a second. Here, let me help you with that," Izzy said, maneuvering around him so she was directly in front of the first customer in line.

"Newsflash, Izzy, if you want to get paid, you're gonna actually have to do your job. Now get to work before I write you both up. Oh, and, Odessa, someone left those for you." He gestured at the counter, where half a dozen blue daisies with cellophane wrapped around the stems lay on their side.

I picked them up. There was a pink ribbon tied around the cellophane, but no note. "Who dropped these off?" I asked.

"Do I look like your secretary?" Todd replied, hurrying back to his office.

10

Untapped Books & Café @untappedwilliamsburg · July 13
Weekend sweets—what's better? Decadent coconut custard
pie or delicious vegan carrot cake? Both are *chef's kiss*
amazing. You decide! #vegan #cake #pie #Williamsburg

MY APRON WAS hanging from the same hook as always. We didn't have assigned hooks, but people were creatures of habit. I still had a temporary peel-and-stick name tag, which was starting to curl at the edges. I'd left the apartment this morning dreading telling Todd that I might be leaving soon, but now I was starting to think that I should—at the very least—ask for a new name tag sticker. This one was looking a lot worse for the wear.

"Morning!" I said as I squeezed into the kitchen. As usual, it was narrow and Parker was doing his best impression of a whirling dervish as he divided his attention between prepping plates, grilling hash browns on the hot plate, and whipping up something creamy in the mixer. In addition to the normal chaos, a new metal shelf blocked half the doorway. It was stacked with several pies, right out of the oven, if my nose wasn't deceiving me. "Smells amazing."

"Thanks," Parker said, glancing at the flowers. "Special day?"

I shrugged. "Not that I know of." I reached up and grabbed one of the Mason jars we serve tea or freshly squeezed lemonade in and filled it with water. I unwrapped the flowers, stuck them in the water, and threw away the cellophane. "Mind if I leave these here?" I asked. The kitchen was crowded and every inch of surface space was valuable, but I had no better idea where to put the flowers.

Parker moved the jar to the counter on the other side of the pass-thru that separated the kitchen from the dining tables. "Now you can see them without them being in the way. I'm trying a few new desserts today—coconut custard pie and vegan carrot cake. I'll need you to sample when you get a chance, and tell me what you think."

"Best part of my job." I tucked my phone into my apron pocket, along with a notepad and several pens, then shoved my messenger bag in its normal spot in the cabinet in the kitchen. "I'll take pictures of them later to post online."

"Sure thing." I turned to go, but then he asked, "Hey, Odessa, you and Izzy get into a tiff or something?" he asked.

"Nope. Why do you ask?"

"It's just I came in early today to get started on the pies, and she was already here, before you. I made a joke about her being on time for once, but she rolled her eyes and walked off."

That wasn't like her. Izzy was never, ever rude to her friends. Then again, she'd practically gotten evicted last night, she was going through a rough patch with her boyfriend, and one of her high school friends had gotten murdered yesterday, so if anyone had a right to be in a bad mood, it was Izzy. "She was acting fine this morning, but I'll ask her if something's up," I promised. "First, I need to check on my tables."

Untapped Books & Café patrons were as eclectic as Williamsburg itself, but it was unusual to find a woman dressed in full steampunk regalia nursing an ice water and nibbling on a flaky croissant. Despite the hot July day, she wore long, layered skirts with a corset over a long-sleeved blouse, accented with brass jewelry—all topped off by a tiny, jaunty hat and a pair of welder's goggles around her neck.

"Love your outfit," I said, heading to her table first since she didn't have an entrée in front of her. "Have you ordered yet?"

She looked at me over tiny round spectacles. "Aye." She had an accent. Irish, or possibly Scottish.

I noticed the water glass in front of her was nearly empty. "Can I get you a refill?"

She continued to stare at me, unblinking. "You're not from around here, are you?" she asked.

I blinked in surprise. Not exactly what I expected from someone with a foreign accent wearing a costume from an alternative history. "Not exactly. Refill?"

She finished off her water, ice clinking loudly, before setting it back down and pushing it toward me. "Aye," she repeated. "You don't by chance have a brunch drink menu? I'd kill for a cranberry mimosa."

"No mimosas," I told her. Even though we opened earlier than normal on the weekends, we didn't technically serve brunch, so no mimosas for us without a new liquor license. We could, however, serve beer. "We do have a selection of breakfast beers, including Maple Remover and my personal favorite, You Bacon Me Crazy."

"I'll give You Bacon Me Crazy a try."

"Coming right up." On my way back to the small drink station next to the kitchen, I caught the eye of the other server in the café. Emilie wore leopard-print tights and shiny black heels along with the standard neon green polo. Her hair was held back by a silver headband and her gold hoop earrings almost touched her shoulders. She waved at me, flashing fingernails that had to be at least two inches long.

I didn't know how she did it.

Between the constant handwashing and carrying hot, heavy plates, I was lucky if I could go a full shift without chipping a nail. I couldn't imagine wasting money on a manicure that wouldn't last a day. And those shoes! My cowboy boots weren't exactly practical, but heels? No thank you.

The tights, though, I could get behind those. I was happy wearing the long, flowy skirts I made in my free time, but her tights looked fun. At least, they seemed more comfortable than the corset Miss Steampunk was wearing.

I brought her water and beer and she gulped half of the bacon-infused stout in one swig. "Maybe you should pace yourself," I suggested.

She shifted ever so slightly so she could see past my shoulder. "Delish. Keep 'em comin'," she replied as she scanned the café.

"You waiting for someone?" I asked.

"Tinder match, if you really must know." She ran one hand over her curly hair, patting it into place.

"Good luck with that. Just so you know, if your date turns out to be a total bust, there's a back exit through there." I pointed at the open doorway under an "Employees Only" sign that led to the bathroom, alley, and Todd's office. Technically, customers weren't allowed back there, but that minor detail rarely stopped them.

"Thanks," she replied.

Making a mental note to keep an eye on her, I began circulating through the café. A dozen tables, each decorated with a different garish pattern under a Plexiglas topper, were scattered seemingly at random. Chairs with vinyl-covered padded seats ringed each table, with a few extra stools at a narrow bar in front of the kitchen. Several more tables, lower cast-iron ones, were in the garden courtyard out back. In the evenings, if the weather was nice, café patrons spilled into the garden for additional seating, but we hardly ever used the overflow space during the day and never when it was this hot outside.

Keeping with the theme that could best be described as garage-sale chic, the floral wallpaper on the back wall of the café clashed with the green vertical stripes on the side wall where a giant garage door could roll up to reveal the overgrown courtyard beyond. Pink flamingo party lights were strung along the ceiling. At night, it often got so crowded and noisy that it was hard to hear someone's order, but in the relative quiet of the late-morning crowd, all I could hear was the clanking of cheap silverware against thin plates and the music being piped in over crackly Bluetooth speakers. Today, it was nineties grunge rock.

Emilie motioned at me by putting two fingers to her lips and then slipped out to grab a quick smoke by the dumpsters out back as I circulated among the tables. Table Three was ready for their check, but for now they appeared to be content nursing their coffees and visiting with each other. A woman with three small children needed two more sets of silverware and a bottle of sriracha. A group that had pushed two tables together and were bent over a rousing game of D&D waved me off while arguing whether or not a level-twelve slingshot could pierce the armor of a mountain troll. Two men animatedly discussing the merits of a recent bestseller they'd just picked up in the bookstore ordered another round of beer.

I got their bottles out of the cooler and popped the tops with the bottle cap opener I kept on a string tied to my apron. When I first started waiting tables, I went through three of those before I learned to keep one tied to my person at all times, or they grew legs and walked away. As I headed back to the table, I felt the fine hairs on the back of my neck stand at attention.

I took a step backward and collided with someone.

"Oof!" I exclaimed. As I caught my balance without spilling the beers, I turned around and realized I'd just slammed into Todd. "Sorry, boss!"

Untapped Books & Café senior manager Todd Morris wore rimless glasses and his hair, short and receding, was shot through with gray. He'd changed clothes since my shift had started. Now his hair was slicked back, and he wore a gold braided bracelet. In place of his neon green Untapped polo shirt, he wore a short-sleeved button-down with a narrow blue tie. And instead of his usual blue jeans, he had on a blue and green plaid kilt.

He liked to think of himself as young, but he was only a year or two younger than my dad, and often waxed poetic about the days back before dial-up internet and MTV.

I didn't have the heart to tell him that no one watched TV anymore, not unless it's streaming.

Usually, Todd's appearance in a room was followed by a few barked orders or, if he'd been feeling friendly, an inappropriate joke. "Hey, Odessa, I've been meaning to talk to you," he said. I waited for the shoe to drop. The last time Todd wanted to talk to me, it was to ask me to regrout the tiles in the bathroom. "I liked your meme earlier. *Got books?* Funny stuff. It's already got a lot of likes on the Twitter."

"Um, thanks?" I was still uncertain, wondering when he would show his true form—the one with fangs and bat wings that was allergic to garlic and sunlight. But instead of coming back with some comment he thought was witty, he turned and continued on his way.

As soon as he was out of earshot, I took a few steps backward, until I could lean into the pass-thru to the kitchen. "Psst," I hissed at Parker.

"Sup?" he asked. "Don't let anyone order the tofu scramble. We've run out of turmeric and the chives are wilted."

"Does Todd have a twin brother by any chance?" I asked, unable to take my eyes off my boss. He crossed the room to stand in front of the steampunk woman. After shaking her hand, he pulled out a chair and sat down across from her.

"Not that I know of. Why?"

I angled my head so I could see Parker out of the corner of my eye while still watching Todd. "He's acting low-key weird."

"Weird how?"

"He was nice to me just now. I think he's on a date. And he's wearing a kilt."

Parker dismissed me with a wave of his hand. "He does that sometimes," he said, as if that was the most normal thing in the world. Then again, maybe it was. Brooklyn was filled with a wide range of people from all walks of life, spanning the entire rainbow of human possibilities. It was one of the many things I'd grown to love about New York.

Back home in Louisiana, it was nothing to see a man in denim overalls sans shirt, cowboy boots, and nothing else. In Brooklyn, a person could walk around in an Elmo costume and no one would blink an eye. Compared to some of the things I'd seen here, a man in a kilt didn't even register as a three on the weird meter, but this was different. This was Todd.

Todd shined his tennis shoes. He wore a calculator watch. His idea of a fashion shake-up was to wear dark indigo jeans instead of light indigo jeans, or if he really wanted to get bold, he would wear a black belt instead of his regular brown one. He got his hair cut on the cheap every other week at one of the nearby beauty colleges. He carried a briefcase instead of a backpack.

"You don't think . . ." My voice trailed off as I tried not to think about whether or not he wore the kilt in the traditional fashion or not.

"Don't ever ask," Parker said. He slid a plate piled high with chocolate chip pancakes onto the pass-thru. "For the lady with the kids. On the house."

I grabbed the plate and headed for the table, passing Emilie on her way back inside. She smelled faintly of cloves. "Table Three needs their check," I told her. I dropped off the pancakes and plastered a neutral smile on my face before stopping at Todd's table. "Can I get you something?" I asked.

"Beer," he said.

"Coming right up." I hurried back to the cooler and fished a can of Todd's favorite from the back. He might be the only person in Williamsburg who actually preferred the big-name stuff, not counting the people who only ordered it ironically. As I headed back to the table, I pulled my phone out and took a few surreptitious photos. Even if Parker was nonchalant about Todd's outfit and the fact that he was on a blind date, I couldn't be sure anyone else would believe me without photographic evidence.

Pics or it didn't happen, right?

"Excuse me, ma'am?" someone called, and I veered toward her table as soon as I'd dropped off Todd's PBR. I wasn't used to being called ma'am, not in New York. It was usually *Hey, you!* or *Yo!*

"Howdy, how can I help you?" She must have seated herself while I was rooting around for Todd's beer because I didn't see her come in. She was wearing large sunglasses despite the dim lighting in the café. Her short hair was cut in a cute bob, and I envied her cheekbones that let her pull off short hair and oversized glasses. I had a rounder face, so I wore my hair long to flatter the shape better.

Although, to be fair, I normally tossed it back into a ponytail.

"Do you have a braille menu?" she asked.

"Sorry, we don't do printed menus," I explained. "Our menu is different every day. I can tell you the specials, or if you have something particular in mind, I can ask the chef if he can accommodate." I rattled off the specials. "Anything catch your fancy?"

She ordered the orzo pasta salad, extra olives, and an iced tea, then asked, "What would you do for your hard-of-hearing customers if you don't have a menu?"

"There's a board on the wall we update daily." I fought the urge to gesture at the big, colorful board, knowing she couldn't see it. "Also, our day-shift chef signs and several of our waitstaff can sign enough to get by." I hoped to one day count myself in their number, as Parker had been teaching me a little ASL when we were slow. "I'll put your order in, and grab your drink."

Once the café was all taken care of for the moment, I took the couple of stairs leading up to the bookstore section. Izzy was behind the counter, alone for the moment. She was scrolling through her phone.

"Hey, glad to see you found a charger," I said.

She looked up guiltily and slid the phone under the counter. "Yep. Todd had a spare."

I found that hard to believe. Last I checked, Todd was still using a BlackBerry. Something about liking having a real keyboard. Which also explained why before I took over the store's social media accounts, the Instagram posts were either blurry or pixilated. In any event, Izzy wasn't telling the whole truth, and that hurt my feelings but I knew she must have a reason, so I let it slide.

"What's up?" she asked.

"Todd's on a date."

"Really? What's she like?"

I had to think about that one. I'd only had limited interaction

NO MEMES OF ESCAPE

with her and she seemed nice enough, but what kind of woman went out on a date with Todd? "Unique," I said.

"I for sure have to see this," Izzy insisted, hopping down from her chair.

"Don't make a scene," I warned her.

"I'm not a noob," she replied. She peeked into the café. "Is that her? The one with the steampunk hat?"

"That's her," I replied. "And you can't see it from here, but Todd's wearing a *kilt*."

"And?"

"And he's Todd. And he's wearing a skirt. Don't you think that's strange?"

"It's New York, Odessa. People can wear whatever they want and be whatever they choose. If Todd wanted to wear a skirt, or a full-on ball gown, that's his choice. But a kilt isn't a skirt. It's traditional Scottish clothing."

"But Todd's not Scottish," I insisted. I should know. I was a quarter Scottish, on my dad's side of the family. And an eighth Greek, Irish, German, French, Czechoslovakian, and a partridge in a pear tree.

"And you're not a boomer, but you were rocking those orthopedic loafers for a while, weren't you?" She had a point. "You come get me the second anything interesting happens."

I promised I would, and got back to work. For a Saturday, my shift was relatively uneventful. After Todd and his date departed, the most interesting thing that happened was Huckleberry, the shop dog, taking a nap in his favorite spot in the sun. Don't get me wrong, it was nice to have a low-drama morning at work but the slow trickle of customers meant few tips.

I did manage to get an amazing shot of Parker's carrot cake and posted it. Since my tables were all set for the moment, I took a few extra minutes to go back to Amanda's Instagram account.

Her selfie game put mine to shame. She was an absolute master at getting the most flattering angles, with perfectly framed backgrounds in her pictures. I caught a glimpse of myself in the background of a few of her shots from the escape room, as well as Izzy and the other attendees, but no shots at all of her with Vickie.

That was weird. Why go to an event and not take even a single picture of the guest of honor?

Then again, these were just the shots she posted. Despite the Game Master's warning that pictures weren't permitted inside, Amanda had snapped photos more or less constantly the whole time we were inside. She'd posted half a dozen, which seemed excessive to me but at the same time, I knew she'd taken more than that. Ten times more, at least.

Which meant that there were plenty of pictures she didn't deem post-worthy for one reason or another. Maybe the lighting was off. Maybe the angle was unflattering.

Maybe she'd caught a murder in the background.

11

..∘∘∘∘∘∘∘∘∘∘∘∘∘∘∘∘∘∘∘∘∘∘∘∘∘∘∘∘∘∘∘∘∘∘∘∘∘∘∘

Dizzy Izzy @IsabelleWilliamsburg · July 13
i hate 2 do this, but if you're in a giving mood, any1 wanna
contrib 2 my gofundme? who's with me? #payitforward

∘∘

MY UNEVENTFUL SHIFT dragged on for what felt like forever. I'd been on my feet a little over eight hours by the time the night crew started trickling in. Parker was replaced by Silvia Gómez, the second-shift cook. She wasn't as imaginative in the kitchen as Parker, but considering the later customers tended to order nachos or French fries more often than a fresh acai bowl—an intimidating dish I couldn't even pronounce a few months ago, but that turned out to be a deliciously simple fruit salad with granola—she wasn't as challenged, either.

I was surprised when Nan came in to take over my tables. I'd been at Untapped for almost six weeks, and I was usually stuck on the day shift where customers were quick to turn over and therefore left minuscule tips. Nan had been on staff for only a few days and she already had a Saturday-night shift? If I didn't know that my time in New York was limited, I might have been jealous.

Then again, Nan was a striking woman. She was tall and built like a professional athlete. She sported an intricate tattoo on her bald head and spoke in a Dominican accent. She had a great memory, stellar approach to customer service, and laser attention to detail, which undoubtedly led to amazing tips. I had to admit that she was a good choice to schedule for the busiest night of the week.

Kim Takahashi, a gorgeous waitress who typically wore all black except for her neon green uniform shirt, and Betty Davis—no relation to Bette—who was so quiet and unassuming I sometimes forgot when she was in the room, rounded out the rest of the waitstaff. Emilie had left after the lunch rush, leaving me alone until the dinner crowd started arriving, but now that it was getting late and business was picking up, there were three servers to handle the café.

I closed out my tabs and hung up my apron. When I ducked into the kitchen to retrieve my bag, Silvia gestured me over. "Don't tell the other waitresses, but when I told my mama how much you raved about her tamales, she insisted I bring you some more today."

My eyes grew wide. "You're kidding! Your mom makes the best tamales I've ever eaten in my life."

I grabbed the plain white bakery box that Silvia indicated and opened it. Six corn husk–wrapped tamales were lined up inside. I took a big sniff, and the delicious spices filled my senses. Silvia snapped the box closed. "Are you trying to start a riot? Put that away before everyone smells them."

"Tell your mom a million thanks for me," I exclaimed, shoving as much of the box as I could into my messenger bag and hoping no one noticed the edge of the box sticking out of the top. I waved and headed for the front door, feeling guilty that I wasn't sharing the tamales with the rest of the staff. Andre was working the front register, as he usually did at night. Izzy was tidying up a display of books on one of the endcaps. "You're still here?" I asked her. That was a change for her, to come in early and stay late on the same day.

"Waitin' on you," she explained. She waved at Andre and we went out together, the bell above the door chiming as we exited.

There was still at least an hour of daylight left, but after working inside through the heat of the day, it was starting to cool down. It was almost comfortable outside with the temperature hovering in the mid-eighties. "Whaddaya wanna do?" Izzy asked.

"I need to talk to Aunt Melanie," I replied. I wanted to run my mom's idea by her that I should stay with her until she was fully healed. I hoped she would say yes, because if not, I'd have to pack my bags and head back home sooner than I was ready. I patted my messenger bag. Bringing home half a dozen homemade tamales would go a long way toward buttering up my aunt. Since Izzy was vegan, I didn't have to feel bad about not offering her one.

"Been thinking about that," Izzy said, linking her arm through mine. "I don't think you should go back to Louisiana."

"You're right," I agreed.

"No, hear me out . . ." Izzy stopped so abruptly that a person walking behind us slammed into me. I apologized, but he glared at us anyway. "Wait a second, you're down?"

"Of course," I told her. "I've been thinking about what you

said this morning about us getting an apartment together, and I totally agree. I'm hoping to convince my aunt to let me crash with her for a few weeks in exchange for me helping her out while her foot's in the cast. During that time, we can look for something together."

"Brilliant. I'm so happy you still want to be roomies."

I smiled. "Of course I do! It would make things way easier. No way could I afford a place on my own, and I don't feel comfortable moving in with someone I'd only met online. Besides, you're my best friend." I hesitated, unsure how to phrase the next part. I didn't want to sound like a snob, but some of Izzy's past living arrangements were cringy, to say the least. "But, I wouldn't feel comfortable squatting in an abandoned building, either."

"No worries," Izzy said brightly. "Leave everything to me. But in the meantime, who do you want to interview next?"

"I don't know, Izzy. Shouldn't we leave the investigating to the cops?"

"You didn't think so after Bethany was killed. You were all eager to play detective then. Why is it different this time?"

"Solving Bethany's murder was a fluke. Not to mention it almost got me killed. I'd rather avoid murderers than chase after them," I said.

"But aren't you curious?"

"Well, sure," I admitted.

"And doesn't Vickie deserve justice?"

"Of course she does."

"What's the harm? I know you, Odessa. This is eating at you. I bet you've already considered your next move."

I sighed. She was right. As much as I didn't ever want to get tangled up in another murder investigation, I wasn't sure I could avoid it this time. Like it or not, Izzy and I were both already involved. "To tell you the truth, I wouldn't mind talking to Amanda. I want to see all the photos she took yesterday, the ones she didn't post. See if maybe she caught something we didn't notice at the time."

"I knew it," Izzy said, pumping her free fist in the air. "You're a brilliant detective. I bet we can solve this before Vince even gets his first real lead."

"Speaking of which . . ."

"Don't want to talk about him," she interrupted me.

"You know if you don't call him, he'll just come find you."

"I *said* I don't want to talk."

Alrighty then. I could take a hint. Really, I could. I didn't know what was going on between her and Castillo, but if she didn't want to discuss it, I couldn't exactly force her. "You know how to get ahold of Amanda?"

"I DM'd her earlier." The good thing about messaging was that as long as you knew someone's username online, you didn't need to know their phone number to send them a message. "She's got plans tonight, but she can meet us tomorrow morning."

"Can't. I'm working."

"Don't worry, Betty volunteered to swap with you, but she's gonna want a favor later."

"Thanks!" With most people, I'd be suspicious, but Betty was always reasonable when it came to swapping shifts. At worst, she'd ask me to cover the Sunday-night shift, when we were deader than Dracula. "In that case, I'm gonna go chat with my aunt. You've got someplace to stay tonight?"

"Of course," she said. "I'm good."

"Where did you end up?"

Izzy laughed. "Don't worry about me, *Mom*. I'll see you in the morning. Meet up at Untapped around ten?"

"Sure thing." Before coming to New York, I never would have considered ten to be early, but now that I was used to sleeping in and staying out late, ten in the morning might as well have been the break of dawn, especially on a day that I didn't have to work.

Izzy peeled off to do . . . whatever it was that she had planned. That could be anything from attending one of those wine-and-paint sessions to BASE jumping off the Verrazzano-Narrows Bridge. It was illegal—BASE jumping, not wine-and-paint—but Izzy loved anything that gave her a rush, and apparently parachuting off high places was on her bucket list.

My bucket list was a little tamer. I wanted to rescue a special-needs dog from a high-kill shelter. Learn how to crochet one of those adorable little amigurumi dolls. Visit the Eiffel Tower, but not to BASE jump. I wasn't that brave. Actually *complete* an escape room.

As I walked along the bustling sidewalk in my boots, I retrieved one of the tamales from my bag, removed the corn-husk wrapper, and savored every bite. Cars flew past, ranging from hybrid taxicabs to noisy charter buses belching fumes. The shadows lengthened, creeping up the sides of turn-of-the-century brick warehouses and glistening glass apartment buildings. In the distance, enormous cranes labored hundreds of feet over my head.

A woman led three young girls, each in pink tutus and sparkly tiaras with springy leashes connecting them together, past me. On the other side of the street, a man dressed in several layers of flannel despite the warm day pushed a squeaky three-wheeled shopping cart filled with Mylar balloons in the shape of SpongeBob. A rat the size of a well-fed Chihuahua eyed me from the steps leading into a high-end shoe store while next door, the owner of a pawn shop paced behind barred windows.

I could spend my whole life in the two-point-something square miles of just the neighborhood of Williamsburg and probably not experience everything it had to offer, mostly because things changed so rapidly. I walked past a storefront that had been advertised as the "Best Falafel in Brooklyn" when I'd come to town a mere six weeks ago. Now it was a florist shop. Next month it could be a gallery or a pop-up restaurant.

Which reminded me that I'd left my flowers at work. Shoot. Then again, they helped spruce up the café. I wondered who had left them for me, and why they hadn't included a note. Maybe they had come from a happy customer, which was nice, but I would have preferred a tip instead.

A bead of sweat rolled down my neck and tickled my spine. New York summers were brutal. The oppressive temperature got trapped in between the buildings with nowhere to go. In the middle of the day, the sidewalk shimmered with waves of heat. But multiple beaches were a short train ride away when I needed to escape.

Everyone said that fall was spectacular up here on the East Coast. As the air crisped up, the leaves turned miraculous colors before abandoning their trees en masse. Hot cider and pumpkin-flavored everything reigned supreme. I could finally take in a hockey game at Madison Square Garden and see what all the fuss was about.

And then as autumn merged into winter, frost would creep across the car windows and paint the tiny green spaces, whether they were planters on door stoops or narrow strips of grass between the sidewalk and the street behind tiny wrought iron fences. Eventually the snow would fall, turning even the shabbiest streets into a wonderland.

I wanted to buy a bulky peacoat at a secondhand store, crochet myself a pair of mittens, and wander down Fifth Avenue in December, marveling at the intricately decorated shop windows as the Christmas tree in Rockefeller Center sparkled over ice-skaters. Maybe I'd even give ice-skating a try myself. I wanted to catch a snowflake on my tongue. I wanted to smell the cloyingly sweet scent of spring as apple blossoms exploded on the trees and miniskirts began to replace down-filled puffy jackets.

Arriving at last at my aunt's building, I brushed my fingers against the kaleidoscope of broken pottery shards that someone had plastered around a lamppost, turning an ordinary pole into art. Sure, my hand came away filthy and there was something slimy dripping across my pinkie finger, but if that wasn't the perfect metaphor for my New York experience, I didn't know what was.

The front door was locked. Even though I could see the building's concierge sitting behind his desk at the far end of the lobby, he made no move to buzz me inside, so I dug my key out of my bag and let myself inside. "Hiya, Mr. Earl," I called out.

"Miss Odessa," he replied in his normal dry voice. Earl had

been born around the same time as poodle skirts, but didn't even have half of their flair. He always had a neatly pressed shirt and tie, a sharp eye, and a scowl on his face. Or maybe that was just for me. Izzy seemed to think he was a sweet old grandfatherly man who doted on her like she was a kitten, but then again Izzy brought out the best in people. Not that I was entirely convinced Earl had a good side. "I thought you'd be moved out by now. What with Miss Melanie being back and all."

I gave him a tight grin. Like I needed the reminder. "Soon enough, I'm sure. Any mail?"

"I already took it upstairs." That surprised me. He'd never gone out of his way to be helpful before. One time, I came down to check the mail and I'd forgotten the key to the box, and he'd made me go back upstairs and get it instead of using his master key. That wouldn't have been so bad, except it was one of the hundred-degree-plus days and the elevator was locked down except for emergency use to conserve energy, so I had to slog five flights of stairs up to the apartment and back only to find out the mailbox was empty save for a single flyer.

"That's awful kind of you," I said.

"Couldn't have Miss Melanie trudge all the way down here and back, not with her foot being in a cast like that, could I?"

"Of course not." The building had a fully functional elevator that let out mere steps from my aunt's apartment, but whatever. I tried to keep the begrudging note out of my voice, but if his smile—maybe the first genuine one I'd ever seen on his face— was any indication, I'd been unsuccessful.

"Well, you just let me know when you want me to call you a cab to the bus station. I'd be happy to do it."

"Gee, thanks." Gone were the days when New Yorkers needed doormen in their uniformed splendor to hail a cab, replaced with the Uber app. Most of Earl's position as concierge could be replaced with one app or another, but even with his surly attitude, even I had to admit it was nice to see a live human face when I came home.

"Sure am gonna miss you when you're gone, Miss Odessa," he said.

I ignored him and headed for the elevator, punching the call button a teensy bit harder than necessary. The doors slid open and I stepped inside, shoulders stiff. "If you say so," I muttered under my breath as the elevator doors sealed and the car rose.

The door to my aunt's apartment was, as expected, closed. Was I supposed to use my key and let myself in? Or was I supposed to knock? I compromised and knocked as I unlocked and opened the door. "Yoo-hoo, I'm home," I called out for extra emphasis.

"Odessa?" Aunt Melanie said, poking her head out of the bathroom.

"It's just me," I confirmed.

She stepped out of the bathroom. Her long hair was wrapped up in a towel. "Sorry, I'm just so used to living alone." She had wrapped a silk robe around herself. A white kitchen garbage bag covered the walking boot on her ankle.

"Aren't you supposed to take that off when you shower?" I asked.

My aunt looked down at the clumsy contraption. "Yes, but it's such a pain to get on and off. I'm not supposed to put any weight on my foot, and I was worrying about trying to balance in the shower. This is easier."

NO MEMES OF ESCAPE

"I've been thinking about that." I took my messenger bag off and looped the long strap over a hook near the door. I withdrew the box of tamales. "But first, tamale?" I opened the box and held it out.

"Don't mind if I do." She plucked one from the box. "These will go real nice with the chocolates."

"Chocolates?" I asked.

My aunt split open the corn husk and rolled the tamale onto a plate. She pointed her fork at a box of gourmet chocolates on the counter. "Those came for you earlier. I hope you don't mind, but I helped myself to one of the coconut creams."

I looked over at the box, and my mouth watered. I recognized the logo from a small local chocolatier, but I hadn't ordered anything from them. I'd bought a truffle from them as a splurge one day, but their big gift boxes cost more than I made in a good shift. "Of course I don't mind, but those aren't mine."

"Your name's on the box. Maybe your friend Izzy sent them as a thank-you?"

"Doubt it. Izzy couldn't afford those any more than I could, and even if she could, she's more the type to bring over a home-made treat than to have something delivered." I opened the box, selected the pink-coated chocolate, and popped it in my mouth. Divine. My name was in fact on the delivery slip, but there was no note to indicate who had sent them.

"I'm sure you'll figure it out." Aunt Melanie took a bite of the tamale. "Oh! This is spectacular," she said around bites. "Did you get this from that place on Grand?"

"Nope. A coworker's mom made them from scratch."

"Well, don't you forget to tell her this is hands-down the best

129

tamale I've ever tasted." She peeked into the box, which I'd set on the countertop, next to the mystery chocolates. "May I have another?"

"Help yourself." Rufus was winding himself around my feet, making it impossible to walk without tripping, so I picked him up and cuddled him. "I've been thinking. You shouldn't have to be alone, not when you're injured. When you're hobbling about, everything is more difficult. Maybe I should stick around and take care of you and Rufus for a few more weeks. Just until you feel better."

"Why, that's terribly sweet of you but totally unnecessary. I really appreciate you coming all the way up here to take care of Rufus for me while I was gone, but I don't need anyone making a fuss over me."

My shoulders sagged. Aunt Melanie didn't need me.

My brilliant plan to stay in Williamsburg a little longer crashed and burned.

I guess I wasn't going to be around long enough to see the autumn leaves change after all.

12

....

Odessa Dean @OdessaWaiting · July 13
Social media pro tip: post "how do I store leftover tacos?" & if
anyone responds with suggestions, block them
IMMEDIATELY. U don't need that kind of negativity in your life!
This is the hill I will die on. #eatmoretacos

I TOOK A BEAT to process the possibility of leaving Williamsburg.
I didn't like it. "Are you sure you don't want me to stick around
a little while?" I asked. "I can help."

My aunt gave me a cheery grin. "Sweetie, I've got everything
I need at my fingertips. If I get a craving for Ethiopian food or a
chocolate silk pie at three a.m., there's always someplace open
that delivers. I've got practically every book ever written and
every movie ever filmed at the push of a button. I'll be as right
as rain. Don't worry about me."

I hated to admit it, but I wasn't worried about her.

I was worried about me.

"I know, but who's gonna take care of your plants while you
recover?"

My aunt laughed. "You mean the plants you killed?"

She had me there. "What about Rufus's litter box? You can't hardly bend over."

Aunt Melanie leaned against the edge of the bar separating the kitchen from the living room. "It's all under control. When Earl came up earlier to drop off the mail and those chocolates, he volunteered to lend a hand if I need anything. Even mentioned the litter box specifically. He's got a cat himself, you know."

No, I hadn't known that. I didn't know much about him, except that he disliked me enough he would go so far as to volunteer to clean someone else's litter boxes just to get rid of me. I mean, that's some next-level passive-aggressiveness. I should know. I'm from the South. We *invented* passive-aggression.

"Oh." That's me. Odessa, undisputed queen of the witty replies.

"Really, you don't need to fuss over me. Your mom called earlier and said how you'd be sticking around awhile to lend me a hand and I told her that was just plain silly. Now, I know you'll need to quit your job and say bye to all your new friends, so take all the time you need. Mi casa es su casa."

My hopes rose. Not at the thought of leaving my friends. I wasn't sure how I would even begin to say goodbye to Izzy, Parker, or any of the staff at Untapped Books & Café. Even Todd. How could it even be possible that I could miss Todd? Huckleberry, the ancient shop dog, I knew I'd miss, but Todd? And yet the thought of never seeing him again stung.

Take all the time you need.

Mi casa es su casa.

It gave me hope. I couldn't mooch off my aunt forever, of

course. But maybe, just maybe, I could stay here long enough to find a place of my own. Not in Williamsburg, probably, but I could afford a place in Bed-Stuy with enough roomies. Or a little farther out if I had to.

Before I could open my mouth and thank her, my aunt continued, "What do you think? Would a few days be enough? I think Greyhound is running a deal, twenty percent off tickets for Wednesdays. My treat."

My heart plummeted. Wednesday. It was already Saturday evening. I had three days to either figure out a way to stay in New York or pack up and head home.

Three days wasn't long. It certainly wasn't long enough for Izzy to find us an apartment. Three days to say goodbye to everyone I'd met. Three days to cram in every experience I'd missed so far—like taking the Circle Line around Manhattan or exploring the Cloisters. I hadn't even visited the Bronx Zoo yet!

And there was the tiny little detail about having only three days to bring Vickie Marsh's killer to justice.

My phone beeped and I reached for it automatically. It's funny how even when the world was crashing down on me, I felt obligated to respond whenever my phone made even the slightest noise. Because maybe it was an emergency. Or maybe it was just a welcome distraction.

It was a text message. Whatcha doin?

I didn't recognize the number. If it had been a phone call, I wouldn't have answered. The only people who ever called me were telemarketers and politicians. Unexpected text messages didn't seem nearly as invasive. Who dis? I responded.

Contrary to what some people thought, text messaging wasn't

ruining the language. It was enhancing it. I could speak and write in perfect, grammatically correct English when the occasion called for such things. But when tweeting or texting with limited characters, I happily and easily truncated accordingly. Besides, why take forever to type out a complete sentence when a few characters would do the job just as well?

Rodney, he replied. Then he sent a picture. In it, he was surrounded by snowy mountains. I couldn't make out much of his face, since he was wearing ski goggles, a thick cap, and a colorful scarf. He had a scruffy, thick mustache that made him look like a walrus.

Even without fully seeing his face, I knew I'd never seen him before. That mustache made quite the impression. Sry, wrong #, I texted back. Then I blocked him. "Weirdo," I mumbled aloud. There was a 60 percent chance that Rodney was harmless, but if I was wrong and he was a creep, blocking him now was the simplest solution. I certainly didn't want him calling me, much less sending more pictures.

"Who's that?" my aunt asked.

I shook my head. "Nobody." She looked exhausted, like she might fall asleep standing up in the kitchen. "Can I get you something? If the tamales weren't enough, I can make dinner. If you'd prefer, I can run out and get anything you're in the mood for." I wasn't the best cook, but Izzy had taught me a few simple recipes that yielded surprisingly delicious meals. I'd never be as good as Parker, who was an absolute wizard in the kitchen, but I could make a mean mac 'n' cheese.

And I didn't mean the stuff that came out of a box with the sketchy orange powder.

"That's sweet, but I've got plans to meet up with some friends this evening." She'd been leaning against the counter, but when she started back toward her bedroom, she looked down with a sigh. Aunt Melanie had left a trail of water droplets from the bag around her walking boot. "Oh dear. I seem to have made a mess."

"Don't worry about it, Aunt Melanie. I'll get it." I grabbed one of Izzy's homemade dish towels and mopped up the water. I gestured at the garbage bag. "Want me to take this off, too?"

"Yes, please. It's just so annoying. I can hardly reach the silly thing, and oh, how it itches already." She held her leg out stiffly, the heavy boot weighing her down as she clutched at the edge of the counter for balance.

I took the garbage bag off. "Happy to help." I hung it up to dry in the bathroom shower so she could reuse it later if she needed to. It was obvious that she could use a helping hand, at least as long as she had to wear that clunky walking boot, but she was either too Southern to ask for help or too proud to accept assistance when offered. Or, I reminded myself, she was a grown adult used to taking care of herself and would have the hang of it soon.

My phone beeped again and I glanced at the screen. Huh. That was strange. Another unknown text message. Two back-to-back? Add in the creepy text from this morning, the blue daisies someone had sent me at work, and the mystery chocolates, and this was getting weird.

U busy?

Take a hint, Rodney, I replied.

Who's Rodney? This is Aiden.

I rolled my eyes. They said that persistence was a virtue, but

I preferred people who knew how to read a room. I didn't bother replying. My phone jingled, announcing an incoming video chat. I declined it, blocked the number, and set the phone to silent. That Rodney, or Aiden, or whatever his name was, needed to learn some manners.

My aunt came out of the bedroom wearing a long black skirt and a bright yellow sleeveless blouse. She was drying her hair with a towel. "I'm going to a gallery opening in Chelsea. Not sure when I'll be home, but if it's late, I'll try not to disturb you." She ducked into the bathroom, presumably to apply her makeup.

"Sounds like fun." I'd been on my feet all day. What I wanted most was to go up to the pool on the roof and soak my legs in the water while listening to a true crime podcast. But my time in Williamsburg was swiftly coming to an end, and I was determined to make the most of it. There was plenty of time to rest on the long—forty-two hours to be exact—bus ride home. "Mind if I tag along?"

"I don't know if it would be any fun for you. Just a bunch of us olds standing around complimenting each other while drinking cheap champagne."

"You're not old. And I like art," I told her. "And cheap champagne." That last part was mostly a fib. Champagne tickled my nose and made me want to sneeze. I was, however, starting to develop a taste for mimosas. My favorite were the cranberry mimosas they served at the 3rd Street Diner during brunch on the weekends. It paired perfectly with their homemade lemon tarts. But champagne by itself? I could take it or leave it.

"Well then, hurry up and get dressed. I've already ordered an Uber."

"Gimme just a minute," I replied. A few weeks ago, I'd repurposed a shapeless dress with pink roses on a field of silvery gray I'd found at a nearby secondhand store into a simple yet elegant sundress that fit me perfectly. It was a challenge, finding clothes I liked that flattered my shape. Luckily, I enjoyed sewing and had made most of my clothes ever since my grandma taught me how to use a sewing machine.

Plus, the dress paired nicely with my cowboy boots.

The new art gallery was in Chelsea, a small, artsy neighborhood on the west side of Manhattan. Like everything else, most of the art scene had been pushed to the outer boroughs due to soaring rents. It was why Williamsburg had become such a vibrant, thriving community back when it was more affordable. Still, some New Yorkers stubbornly clung to the belief that life didn't exist outside of Manhattan.

Vickie Marsh had been like that. It was a shame, really, that she had been murdered in Brooklyn. I wondered if in her last moments, she had been disappointed that she had to die somewhere other than her beloved Manhattan. Then again, she hadn't called out for help, so I doubt she knew what was happening until it was too late. At least, I hoped as much. There was something comforting about a quick, painless death.

I know, I know. My mind was wandering down a morbid path when I should have been enjoying an evening out with my aunt. However, the subject of the art show was a woman who dressed up like a ghost and posed in graveyards so she could get the perfect picture in the light of a full moon and then blow the print up beyond life-sized and hang it on the gallery walls. The artist turned out to be a tiny woman. She was a decade or so older than my aunt, and was the center of attention at the crowded gallery.

I hoped that one day I might get my life on a track like that.

Then again, I didn't see myself being famous anytime soon. I didn't have any special talents to speak of. I could sew, but I wasn't into designing haute couture. I was an excellent waitress. I had good coordination and balance—critical skills for anyone in food services—but I wasn't sure I wanted to spend the rest of my life standing on my feet for eight hours a day trying to survive on tips. It was a good job, but it wasn't what I wanted as a career.

I had zero idea what I wanted to be when I grew up.

Yeah, sure, I was only twenty-three. But I still lived at home. I never went to college. Other than the clothes I'd left in Louisiana, I didn't really own anything. The car I drove back and forth to work back home was in my dad's name. I wasn't even on my own insurance.

"More champagne?" a man asked, oblivious to the fact that I'd barely touched the glass I'd been carrying around all night.

I clutched the stem of the champagne flute, not caring that the drink was now warm and the bubbles had already bubbled themselves out. I wasn't planning on drinking it anyway. I just felt silly being the only person in the room without a drink in my hand, and after the six hundredth offer, I caved to peer pressure and accepted one. "Yeah, no. I'm good," I told him without turning around.

"You sure?"

"I told you, I'm just ducky," I said as I glanced over my shoulder to look the persistent waiter in the eye. I was prepared to give him some friendly advice, one server to another, about crossing the line from good service to pushy, but the man holding out the glass wasn't dressed in the black-pants-black-shirt-black-tie out-fit the other waiters wore.

Instead, his uniform was dark blue with gold piping down the pant legs with "Private Security" stitched in white lettering on the polyester blend button-down shirt. An oversized flash-light hung from his utility belt, the kind that doubled as a base-ball bat in a pinch. The flashlight, not the belt. A gun was clipped to the other side of his belt. The uniform was unfamiliar, but the face of the man wearing it was not.

"Detective Castillo? What are you doing here?"

13

•.•••••• • •••..•••••• • •••..•••••• •••

Odessa Dean @OdessaWaiting · July 13
I was today years old when I learned that champagne is
rarely ever (never?) "champagne color" #classy #culture
#cheapchampagne #bubbleseverywhere

•.•••••••••••••..•••••••••••••..•••••••••

SURPRISED TO SEE Castillo at the art gallery, I accepted the prof-
fered glass of champagne. I even took a sip out of habit, and the
bubbles tickled the back of my nose.

He flashed bright white teeth for a split second before the
stone-faced mask slipped back into place effortlessly. "You
should really call me Vincent when I'm not on duty." He looked
down at himself, and then shrugged. "Or near enough. Otherwise, it's weird."

Vincent Castillo was, above all, a snazzy dresser. As a plainclothes NYPD detective, he could wear pretty much anything he
wanted to. He typically straddled the line between professional
and business casual with dark, pressed blue jeans, a solid color
button-down, and a snappy tailored vest. When he was off work,

like when he came over for dinner with Izzy, he lost the vest. The stiff uniform looked out of place on him.

"Did you get a demotion since this morning?" I asked.

Expression not changing, he blinked at me.

"What are you doing working in Manhattan?" His precinct was across the river in Brooklyn. And why was he wearing not only a uniform but a private security uniform? It didn't make sense.

Unless he was working a case.

Maybe even Vickie Marsh's case.

I looked around the room, but other than my aunt and a few people she had introduced me to tonight, I didn't recognize anyone. Then again, why would I? I only knew three of Vickie's friends from the escape room. For all I knew, her family owned the gallery, or he had reason to believe a suspect would be here tonight. Maybe Castillo was here to gather evidence and eavesdrop on conversations. "Are you undercover?" I whispered.

Castillo laughed. Not to sound corny, but he had a really nice laugh. The kind that made everyone around him smile. He brushed his hands down the sides of his shirt. "Do I look inconspicuous in this getup?"

"Well, no," I admitted. "But let's be honest. You look like a cop. You look like a cop when you're picking up a pizza or doing a cannonball into the pool."

"So?" he asked.

"If you were in normal street clothes, everyone would know that you're a cop. But no one pays attention to a cop dressed like a security guard. If you're not undercover, what are you doing here dressed like that?"

"You didn't think I could afford an apartment in Williamsburg on a cop's salary, did you? When the minimum wage went up, the price of housing skyrocketed but my paycheck didn't budge."

To be honest, I hadn't thought about it. I'd never been over to his place before and had no idea if he had roommates or not, or if he lived in a bougie building like my aunt or rented a tiny room in a converted brownstone with a shared bathroom at the end of the hall. I guess I had assumed that Castillo had a real job, a grown-up job that covered his bills, and a grown-up apartment to go along with it.

Not that waiting tables wasn't a real, grown-up job. It just didn't pay a lot. If it weren't for tips, I wouldn't even make minimum wage. It wasn't easy, mentally or physically. I had to juggle a dozen things at once, all while making sure my customers were happy. It was a respectable job, one I was good at. One I enjoyed.

But being a cop was a whole different level. There were training programs and uniforms and ranks to move through. There were chains of command. There were guns and bulletproof vests. I guess I always figured that any job where people had to follow strict orders and got shot at on occasion came with a nice, fat paycheck.

Guess I was wrong.

If an NYPD detective with several years on the force had to take a second job to make ends meet, I would never make it on my own in NYC. Piney Island, Louisiana, wasn't exactly the most exciting place on the planet, but at least my parents didn't charge me rent.

Yet.

"So, you're a rent-a-cop on the side?"

"Freelance personal protection," he corrected me. "And yeah. I didn't realize this was your scene." He strained his neck to look around at the crowd. "Izzy with you?"

I shook my head. "Nah, I'm here with my aunt. She knows the artist."

"You seen Izzy today? You asked her to call me?"

"Yeah, she was at work today and I passed her your message. I think she mentioned something about her phone being out of data yesterday, and misplaced her charger today."

"Oh, really? Then I guess someone else was logged in as her on Twitter an hour ago," he said.

Gotta love the information age. It didn't take a cop to stalk someone on the internet. These days, any mildly curious, patient person with a Wi-Fi connection could learn a person's whole life story, including where they've been recently, if they weren't careful. "She was probably using the Wi-Fi at Untapped," I said.

"Funny, I stopped by there earlier, and she'd already gone home for the day."

"What do you want me to tell you? I have no idea where she is." I also didn't know what either Castillo or Izzy expected of me. I wasn't Izzy's keeper. I didn't have a clue where she was staying, and even if I did, it was her choice to reach out to Castillo or not. It was none of my business if they were going through a rocky patch.

"Lemme see your phone." He held out his hand, and I hesitated for a second. He cleared his throat and gave me The Look, the one I think he learned in the police academy, and I unlocked my phone and handed it to him. He tapped away at the screen.

I couldn't see what he was doing but then he held it up to his ear and waited. "Voicemail."

He handed my phone back to me and I saw a canceled outgoing call to Izzy on the screen. I didn't know if I should be relieved or annoyed that she hadn't picked up. I took a big gulp of champagne.

"Odessa, is something the matter?" My aunt clomped toward us, her walking boot practically dragging on the ground. She looked from me to Castillo with a concerned expression. The bags under her eyes had grown darker since we'd left Williamsburg, and even her hair was limp and dull.

"Aunt Melanie, I'd like you to meet my friend Vincent Castillo."

"Pleased," she said, offering her hand. It looked frailer than I remembered. Then again, I was used to seeing her hands covered in paint or plaster or chalk, depending on what project she was working on at the moment.

"You about ready to get out of here?" I asked her.

"Oh no, I couldn't possibly. Besides, you haven't even finished your champagne." She glanced down at my full hands. "Neither of them," she added with a hint of amusement in her voice. Or maybe it was just exhaustion. It was hard to tell when she was this lackluster.

Surprised to see that it was already half-empty, I finished the glass that Castillo had handed to me. My aunt raised one eyebrow. I drained the second glass.

For the record, flat, room-temperature champagne is decidedly *not* my favorite drink.

I put both empty flutes down on a nearby table.

"Odessa, the art!" my aunt chided me, picking them up.

That's when I realized that the metal-and-glass contraption I'd mistaken for a tray table was part of the installation. "Yikes." I took the glasses from her. "I'm gonna go drop these off, and then I'm ready to go. Why don't you order an Uber?"

Despite her protests, Aunt Melanie looked relieved at the idea of heading home. Between jet lag, the painkillers, and her awkward boot, she had to be drained. "Yes, dear. Nice meeting you, Mr. Castillo."

"Please, call me Vincent." He retreated to the corner of the room where he could observe the crowd while remaining relatively inconspicuous.

"Your friend is nice," my aunt pointed out as we waited on the curb for our car.

"He is," I agreed. I looked down and was spellbound by the way the sidewalk sparkled in the streetlights. I didn't know what it was about New York City sidewalks, but half the time, there's a chalk outline to walk around and the other half, they glittered like they were laced with diamonds.

Or maybe that was the champagne talking.

"And how do you two know each other?"

"He's dating Izzy."

"That handsome young man is your friend Izzy's beau? How is she, by the way? I am awful glad to get my apartment back to myself, but I hate the idea of kicking her out so suddenly."

I bit the inside of my cheek. I couldn't say anything about her apparent eagerness to get rid of me without sounding ungrateful. Besides, I had a place to go, and she had a point. It was her apartment. I was just the house sitter. Now that she was home,

I wasn't needed any longer. "Izzy will be just ducky, don't worry about her."

The car arrived, and I got in first so Aunt Melanie didn't have to scooch over the seat.

It was only a thirty-minute car ride to Williamsburg. In rush hour, it would have been quicker—not to mention cheaper—to take the subway, but it was late enough that there was little traffic. I wasn't sure if my aunt could navigate stairs in her walking cast anyway, and the elevators in the MTA were hit-or-miss. I couldn't even be positive that I could manage stairs right now, as I was feeling light-headed from downing so much champagne so quickly.

I leaned my head against the window and watched the lights of Manhattan fly past us, and the next thing I knew, Aunt Melanie was shaking me awake.

THE NEXT MORNING, I had a pounding headache and there was a cat asleep on my face. Now I remembered why I disliked champagne. It wasn't the taste. It was the aftereffects. Even if Rufus had decided to take a catnap somewhere other than curled up on top of me, my mouth would have still felt like it was sprouting fur.

Then again, in hindsight, maybe I shouldn't have drunk two full glasses of the cheap stuff in rapid succession.

I would have loved to pull the blinds, curl up under the blanket, and spend the day on the couch nursing my hangover, but that wasn't in the cards. For one thing, I'd made plans to meet Izzy and go talk with Amanda to see if she knew anything more about Vickie's death. For another, I could already hear my aunt clomping around her bedroom.

Aunt Melanie's apartment was gorgeous. The building was immaculately maintained with all the amenities, from a concierge at the front door to a pool on the roof and a small gym in the basement. It was pet-friendly. The elevator worked. The courtyard was clean and quiet. The units, at least my aunt's, were huge with enormous windows and eleventy-foot-tall ceilings.

The only problem was that my aunt had stuffed her apartment with everything she could get her hands on. The seven-foot-tall giraffe in the living room was just the tip of her collection iceberg. There was a life-sized chimpanzee statue, about a thousand books, and more tchotchkes than I could count. Even the bathroom was crammed full of unique pieces—all in a hippo theme.

The collection was fun. Whimsical. Unique. And took up a ton of space. When I wanted to get my sewing machine out, I had to shuffle a taxidermied raccoon and a Russian tea set off onto the counter to make room. I'd gotten into the habit of sleeping with a light on so I didn't crash into something in the dark. It was a good thing that my aunt had plenty of lamps to choose from—including one made of Barbie doll heads, a converted fishbowl complete with plastic goldfish, a tree fashioned from barbed wire and Christmas lights, and a lightsaber-wielding armadillo. The armadillo was fake.

I think.

Part of me wanted to sneak out of the apartment before my aunt could bumble her way to the bedroom door, but that wouldn't be polite. Instead, I went to her door and knocked. The door swung open.

Aunt Melanie stood in the narrow pathway between her enormous bed and her chest of drawers. Since the space between them was barely wide enough to open the drawers all the way even without the chunky boot on her foot, she was trying to squeeze her hand inside, but whatever she was reaching for appeared to be snagged on something.

As much as my friends liked to tease me for rotating the same four or five outfits all the time, one positive thing about not owning a lot of "stuff" was never running out of space. To be fair, I had more outfits back home, but considering I wore a uniform to work every day, it didn't make sense to own a closet stuffed with clothes I could never show off, especially since most of my wardrobe was made by hand, and that took a lot of time and effort. But it was worth it.

"Can I lend a hand?" I asked.

"Yes, dear. Please." She sank down onto the edge of her bed. I scooted around her and reached for a tie-dyed tank top she'd been trying to pull out of the drawer. "It's stuck."

"I can see that." I wiggled the drawer off its tracks and retrieved the tank top, which had been pinched against the back of the dresser. I shook out the top. It was made of thin cotton, perfect for a warm day like this promised to be, and appeared to be hand dyed. It was also ripped along the seam.

"Oh no!" Aunt Melanie reached for it. "That was one of my last clean shirts." I glanced in the drawer, which was packed with—of all things—more books.

"Don't worry about it. I'm sure I can fix it." I glanced over at her enormous suitcases. "Have you had a chance to unpack from your trip yet?"

She shook her head. "I've been exhausted. I should have stayed home and done laundry last night instead of dragging you to that gallery opening."

"I'm glad you did. It was fun." Maybe that was a fib. A tiny white lie. The art hadn't exactly spoken to me and the champagne had been a huge mistake. But at least I'd gotten to spend time with my aunt. And Castillo. "Why don't you leave this to me? I've got plans this morning, but I should have time to get a couple of loads done before I have to be at work this evening."

"Oh no, I couldn't," she insisted. "I'll just call down to Earl. He'll have it sent out for me."

"Don't be ridiculous." I closed the drawer and took the torn shirt back from my aunt. I shuffled toward the suitcases and maneuvered them around so I could take them with me. I wasn't about to be upstaged by the building's grumpy old concierge. Fortunately, the suitcases had those little wheels that could swivel and roll in any direction, and I was able to push the heavy hard-sided suitcases out of the bedroom in front of me. "I've got this."

After a quick repair of her tank top—a sewing machine really did make even the easiest job go so much quicker than it would have by hand—I lined the suitcases up against the door in the kitchen that led to her tiny washer and dryer. They were the micro-mini size that weren't good for much more than a few hand towels or maybe a small load of socks. They were convenient, but if I tried to wash six weeks' worth of clothes in them, I'd still be working on them come August. Instead, I'd drag the suitcases down to the coin-operated machines in the basement when I got home.

Speaking of which, if I didn't hurry, I would be late meeting Izzy. I rushed through my morning routine and started a pot of coffee. I didn't have time to drink it, but my aunt would appreciate it. I made sure that Rufus was fed and his litter box was cleaned, that there were no dishes in the sink, and that the curtains were open to let in the morning light before I headed out toward Untapped Books & Café.

The walk to work was always one of my favorite parts of the day. It was less than a mile and was a pleasant way to clear my head while getting some much-needed exercise. I'd thought about borrowing my aunt's bicycle and riding to work a few times, but to be perfectly honest, I was too intimidated by the constant flow of irritated traffic to be entirely comfortable riding a bike in the street.

Izzy wasn't outside when I arrived, not that I expected her to be. It wasn't hot yet, just bordering on warm, but Izzy wasn't the kind of person who waited around. She was probably inside, rearranging the shelves and chatting with repeat customers, even though she wasn't on the schedule this morning. I opened the door to the familiar chime of the bell hanging from the doorframe, and a completely unfamiliar whoosh of cold air.

I stopped in my tracks and let my head fall back so the cold air could wash over my face. Huckleberry gave me a happy doggy grin, and I could tell he was at least as happy about the fully functional air conditioner as he was to see me.

After all, he saw me pretty much every day. A working air conditioner was a novelty.

"You're not on the schedule this morning," an unexpected voice said, and I tore myself away from my unexpected enjoyment to look at the speaker. Nan, the new waitress, was behind the counter.

That was a surprise. Todd liked to have his staff do odd tasks around the shop just so he wouldn't have to do it, and wasn't above ordering one of the servers to man the desk for an hour or so despite making waitress wages. He just didn't trust easily. I'd been at Untapped several weeks before I was given the keys to the cash register. Nan had been on staff for days.

"Neither are you. I thought Betty switched with me?"

"And I switched with Betty," she said. "Wait a sec, if I'm covering for Betty and she's covering for you, what are you doing here?"

"I'm supposed to be meeting Izzy. Have you seen her?"

"You think if Izzy was around, I'd be at the front desk? Even on her day off?"

Nan had a point.

I liked my job. Really I did. The employees were great, with the probable exception of the boss. The customers were fantastic. The perks of a discount on food was a game changer. But I knew too well the perils of showing up at the bookstore on my day off. It was bad enough that I was expected to keep up with the store's social media accounts whether or not I was on the clock, but when I stepped foot inside, I was fair game.

Last time I'd made that mistake, I'd ended up running to the office supply store for toner for Todd's printer, to the grocery for a crate of lemons, and to the post office to drop off a package for Todd's mother.

"Well, if you see her, let her know I'm looking for her." I gave Huckleberry one last pat on the head and made a beeline for the café portion of the store. The only customers were seated at the bar, so Parker was able to take care of them.

Personally, I didn't think it was fair that Parker had to prep and cook all the food and then serve it as well. But the way Todd saw it was if there were fewer than half a dozen seats filled, the only server on shift could cover the bookstore and he could disappear into his shabby office in the back. Needless to say, despite being almost the exact same height, Todd and I were never going to see eye to eye.

"Heya," I said, waving at Parker. Instead of heading into the tiny, cramped kitchen, I took the barstool closest to the pass-thru window.

"Just the person I wanted to see," he said. "I was about to ask those two customers if they wanted to try my newest recipe, but I rather like it when you play guinea pig."

"Hit me," I agreed. While he was plating his new experiment, I pulled a bottle of Pour Williamsburg out of the cooler and popped the top. It was way early but I hoped a little hair of the dog could ease my throbbing hangover headache. Out of habit, I refreshed the other patrons' coffee. It seemed like a small price to pay to be the first to sample one of Parker's new culinary creations.

"I'm calling it breakfast chili," he said, sliding a soup bowl through the pass-thru. A quarter of a waffle poked up out of the center, separating a scoop of hearty chili on one side and scrambled cheesy eggs on the other. The eggs were garnished with paprika, and the chili with white onions and a dollop of sour cream. "Late last night, I was starving. I was in the mood for migas or huevos rancheros." I'd often had migas—scrambled eggs, tortilla chips, and chilis—in Louisiana, but I hadn't tried huevos rancheros—eggs, salsa, and beans—before coming to New York. It was delicious. "But I didn't have any cash, or chips in the house, so I threw this together instead."

I scooped a forkful of cheesy eggs onto the waffle, topped it with chili, and took a bite. "Yummy," I said, my mouth still full. I chewed and swallowed.

"Yeah?" Parker looked pleased.

"Although, it's more like migas meets Frito chili pie than huevos."

"Frito chili *what*?"

Now it was my turn to educate Parker on something culinary. I wasn't sure that had ever happened before, and certainly not to me. I might know a dozen ways to prepare a crawdad, but he knew at least twice that many. "You take a big double handful of corn chips," I told him, pantomiming the action as I talked, "and dump them in a big bowl. Cover them with hot chili right off the stove." I wasn't about to admit that nine times out of ten, I made Frito chili pie with chili that came out of a can that I popped in the microwave. He might faint. "Smother it with diced onions and shredded cheddar cheese, and add a dollop of sour cream on top."

"Sounds . . ." He seemed at a loss for words.

"Yummy," I supplied helpfully. "And warm, and hearty, and"—I rolled my eyes back into my head—"comfort food." I took another bite of his creation. "Delicious."

"I was thinking I could make an option with vegetarian chili, too, but I'm not sure if I can make it vegan. Do you think it would work with vegan scramble instead of eggs? Minus the cheese and sour cream, of course."

"Maybe? You're a genius." He blushed. "Most people couldn't even come up with a decent new idea in the kitchen to save their lives, and you're already thinking of ways to make a vegan version."

"It might be easier to stick with vegetarian for now. I've got a mean vegetarian chili recipe I was working on last winter."

"Speaking of which." I paused to take another bite. It was the perfect combination of sweet, savory, and spicy. I had to take a sip of my beer to balance out the chilis and spices. "Isn't this more of a, you know, cold-weather dish?"

"I was thinking that, too!" he exclaimed, gesturing wildly. "Except I got to work this morning, and the AC was running for once. Imagine having the comfort of a hot chili breakfast in a cold café. Brilliant, right?"

"Right," I agreed. "And you can always market it as a hang-over cure. I had the worst headache earlier but I feel much better now." I took another slug of beer, this time to build up my courage. If there was any chance I was going to be on that Greyhound bus on Wednesday, I ought to give Todd a heads-up so he'd have time to adjust the schedule. I'd known all along that I'd have to tender my resignation sooner or later, and I was a pull-the-Band-Aid-off-quickly kind of woman. "Is Todd around? He wasn't at the front desk."

"I think he's in his office. Why? What's up?"

I sighed. I liked Parker. He was fun and sweet and a great cook. He had an understated sense of humor and an irrepressible smile. He was always nice to me, and without his influence, I would have never tried half of the culinary delights that Williamsburg had to offer. I wouldn't have ever even tasted avocado toast.

He was my friend, and he certainly did not deserve to learn the news secondhand. "If Izzy and I don't find a place to stay soon, as in the next three days soon, I'm heading back to Piney Island on Wednesday."

"No way!" He reached through the window and grabbed my hand. "Hold off on talking to Todd. We'll come up with something, you'll see."

14

Untapped Books & Café @untappedwilliamsburg · July 14
Don't sweat it! We've got cold A/C and hot, hearty meals.
You know you want to see what Parker's got cooking in the
kitchen today! #Breakfastchili #yummy #Williamsburg

PARKER CROSSED HIS arms over his chest. "We'll figure something out. No way can you leave on Wednesday," he said. Like me, Parker had a slight build. He did *not* look intimidating, even when he scowled and brandished one of his enormous chef's knives at anyone who wandered into his kitchen if they didn't belong.

"I know, it sucks."

"It more than sucks," he replied. "Wednesday's my birthday. I'm planning a little get-together and I thought you'd join us. There's a new Italian café over on Montrose that I've been dying to try. I heard they have a terrific crab and goat cheese ravioli, and they make a divine Limoncello cake."

"Oh no, Parker. I didn't know your birthday was coming up. My aunt could not have worse timing."

"Can't you convince her to let you stick around for a few more days?"

"I already tried," I told him. "She's not used to having someone sharing her space. I think she wanted me out yesterday but is too Southern to say so. If I can't find something fast, I'm not gonna have much of a choice."

"Come crash with me until you can find your own place," he urged.

"Thanks for the offer, but you've told me horror stories about your apartment, remember? The cockroaches the size of dinner plates?" I held my hands out a foot apart. "What did you name them, again?"

"Randy and Jose," he said.

"And don't you have like a dozen roommates?"

"Two. Only two. But Suz is hardly ever home and Tony's real quiet. Sometimes I forget he's even there."

"You're awful sweet, but I'm pretty sure your roommates don't want another person in the apartment. Besides, what would Hazel think?" It broke my heart to have to leave Brooklyn, but I couldn't imagine putting up with the kind of living arrangements all my friends seemed to take for granted.

"Hazel wouldn't mind. But you're right, my roomies would," he assured me. "We're packed in like sardines as it is."

"Nothing is set in stone yet," I assured him. "I've still got a few days to come up with something, and Izzy said she could find us something. I don't know if she can do so on such short notice, but she's surprised me before."

"That's the spirit," he said with a wide grin. "Hey, how about we go try that Limoncello cake right now? We can pretend it's my birthday today."

"I'd love to, but you're working, and I've got plans with Izzy. Another time. Promise."

I had seventy-two hours to come up with an affordable place to live in Brooklyn, not to mention solving Vickie's murder. I had enough on my plate, but Parker's birthday celebration needed to be more than a dinner with a few friends. Who didn't love a surprise birthday party? I could arrange the whole thing, with Izzy's help. She was the absolute bomb at throwing parties. She once organized a wake that had gotten so packed, we had to turn people away. If she could do that well with a wake, imagine what she could do with a birthday.

I patted Parker's arm. "Chin up. It'll be all right." I pulled a few crumpled bills out of my wallet and laid them beside my plate to cover the beer and tip.

Izzy wasn't out front in the bookstore, in the tiny restroom, or out back by the dumpsters. I stuck my head into Todd's office on the offhand chance that she was in there. It was a dark, dank room with no windows, filled with an old army surplus desk and the overflow of stock or inventory that didn't fit in the storage room next door. On the desk was a computer that hailed from the era of beige cases and big, clunky monitors. From the doorway I could hear its fan running.

Todd's desk ran along the wall. Since the computer no longer had a working Wi-Fi card, it had to be physically plugged into the router mounted above his head. I'd once asked Todd why he never locked his office door, but he'd just laughed at me and said anyone so hard up that they would steal his sweet setup was welcome to it. That might have been the most magnanimous and humanitarian thing I'd ever heard him say.

"Knock, knock," I said, even though the door was open.

He glanced over his shoulder at me before returning to his keyboard. "Odessa, you're not on the schedule."

"Nope. Have you seen Izzy?"

"I'm sure she's around. She always is. Hey, since you're here, something came for you." He rifled through his desk and came up with a padded mailer. He tossed it to me. "Shut the door on your way out."

Once I was back in the hall, I ripped open the envelope and upended it. An Untapped Books & Café name tag fell out into my hand. I'd been wearing temporary stickers ever since I started—had it been less than six weeks? It felt like a lot longer—but now I had a legit plastic name tag with my name on it and everything. If I believed in signs, I'd think this was the universe's way of telling me everything was gonna work out.

A man I didn't know was waiting for me as I emerged from the hallway into the bookstore. "Odessa?" he asked. He was tall, close to six foot, maybe a hair over. He had a neatly trimmed goatee and whiter-than-white teeth. Toothpaste commercial white. His dark, almost black, hair was slicked back so it was hard to tell how long it was. He wore a soft-looking ringer T-shirt with the silhouette of a bigfoot under the logo for a summer camp. Both arms were covered in black-and-white tattoos down to the wrist.

I'd never seen him before in my life.

To the best of my knowledge, I didn't owe anyone any money, so he wasn't a bill collector. He didn't live in my aunt's building and he wasn't one of the dozens of friends Izzy had introduced me to. I hadn't waited on him before—I would have remembered him—but he could have been at one of the other tables and escaped my attention if it had been busy, and he could have seen my hand-lettered stick-on name tag. Part of my brain screamed, *Stranger, danger!* but my curiosity was piqued.

"Do I know you?" I asked.

He pointed to himself. "Raleigh."

"Nice to meetcha, Raleigh, but my friend's waiting for me." I was half tempted to stick around and get to know this Raleigh fellow a little better, but I had things to do. "I'm off this morning, but you should go ask the cook for an order of breakfast chili. Trust me." I caught a glimpse of Izzy's silhouette outside the door, and continued, "Sorry, but I gotta go." I hurried out the front door onto the sunny sidewalk.

"Morning," Izzy said as soon as I stepped outside. "We need to dash or we'll be late." Her hair was still aquamarine, but now there was a bold white streak that ran from the middle of one eyebrow to the back of her head.

Izzy started walking. I let her lead the way because, as usual, I had no idea where we were going. I could find my way around, and I'd gotten pretty good at navigating subway lines and city streets, but I didn't even know what neighborhood we were heading into, much less Amanda's address.

"I texted you to let you know I was on my way."

"My phone's out of minutes."

"That explains why you didn't pick up the phone last night when Castillo tried calling you from my phone, but you should still get texts."

She shrugged. "I'm out of data, too."

I pulled my phone out and checked my account balance. I had exactly $21.32. I used PayPal to send her $20. "I've got a little extra this week, so I contributed to recharge-Izzy's-phone fund."

"You didn't have to do that," she insisted. "Save your money. We'll need it for our new apartment."

"About that, I talked to Aunt Melanie last night and she doesn't want me sticking around."

"Did she say that?" Izzy asked.

"Not in so many words, but she offered to buy me a bus ticket back home as long as I leave by Wednesday."

Izzy frowned. "That's not very long from now."

"I know," I agreed.

She flapped her hand in a dismissive gesture. "Don't worry, I'll come up with something."

"In three days?" I asked skeptically.

"Have I ever let you down? I've got this. And seriously, keep your money."

"Too late," I told her. "And I know you won't transfer it back, because you don't want it getting eaten up in fees. Use it to buy more minutes for your phone and then you can call Vincent."

"Maybe I don't want to call Vince," she said.

"He's worried about you. What's going on with you two?"

"I don't want to talk about it. But what was he doing calling me from your phone?"

I shouldn't push. It was none of my business. Well, it was sorta my business, in a roundabout fashion. They were my friends. Plus, Castillo was a good guy. I didn't want to let the subject drop, and was glad that she'd finally opened the door a crack by asking about him. "I bumped into him last night."

"Oh, you did?" Her tone of voice sounded bored, but I could tell by the way her shoulders stiffened and her pace slowed by a hair that I had her attention.

"He was moonlighting as a security guard at an art gallery that my aunt took me to."

"Yeah, he does that sometimes." She slowed down enough that I could almost keep up with her.

With the difference in our heights, Izzy had a longer stride than I did. I usually had to jog to stick close to her heels whenever we walked anywhere. It was good exercise, I grudgingly admitted, but I was enjoying the brief respite. "He asked about you."

"Uh-huh. And what did you tell him?"

"Nothing. I hadn't seen you since work, and I have no idea where you're staying." I paused, but she didn't take the bait and offer any new information. "I told him maybe your phone was dead, and that's why you weren't picking up."

"Good thinking."

"Except he's a *cop*, Izzy. He's nosy. You'd liked something on Twitter a few minutes earlier, so he knew you were online."

"Oh." She chewed her bottom lip.

"Just call him."

"I can't," she said.

"Why not? What's going on? Was he brusque to you when he was questioning us after the escape room? Because that's his *job*.

He did it to me, too. He can't give you special treatment. He probably has to show the powers that be that he's impartial or they'll pull him off the case and whoever they replace him with would undoubtably be worse."

"I know that," Izzy said. "Being impartial isn't the problem. He's not calling to ask me out. He wants to talk with me. Like *talk*, talk. At the station." She turned to me. The soft tissue around her bloodshot eyes was puffy and pink. A tear sparkled in the corner of her eye. "He wants to bring me in for further questioning, Odessa. And he told me to get a lawyer."

"What?"

She nodded. "He thinks I had something to do with Vickie's murder."

I stood there flabbergasted in the middle of the crosswalk until a car honked at me. I sidled out of the way, but continued to stare at Izzy. "That's just silly. Vincent knows you're innocent."

"Sure, Vince does. But *Detective Castillo* isn't convinced." She grabbed my elbow and propelled me back onto the sidewalk. "Doesn't help that the last thing I said to Vickie was 'Knock yourself out' and then someone bashed her over the head with our trophy. It looks bad."

"I can talk to him."

"And say what? Remind him that it's impolite to accuse your girlfriend of murder, even if her fingerprints are all over the murder weapon?"

To be completely honest, I wished we'd never won that silly trophy. So much had happened in the last few days, it felt like the cornhole tournament was a lifetime ago. "Well, I know I didn't kill Vickie and I know that you didn't kill her . . ."

Izzy interrupted me. "Oh yeah? How do you know?"

"First and foremost, you might be capable of killing someone, in like a life-or-death situation, but you wouldn't murder anyone. Besides, even if you hated Vicki Marsh with every fiber of your being—and you're not a hateful person—you had no idea we were going to bump into her on Friday. It was my idea that we invite ourselves along to the escape room, not yours. And practically the whole time we were inside, we were together."

Although, to be completely honest, I couldn't be 1,000 percent sure about that last bit. I'd been paying attention to the room, not the people around me. Could Izzy have slipped back into the library when no one was looking to kill Vickie? Maybe. Would she have? No way.

"And you told Vince that?"

"When he questioned me, I had no idea he considered you a suspect. I'll talk to him. And you should, too. Dodging his phone calls and refusing to come in doesn't exactly scream 'innocent.'"

She glowered at me. "It's hard to have faith in the system when even my own boyfriend treats me like a criminal. The only way I'm voluntarily stepping foot in that station is with hard evidence that I'm innocent."

I nodded. No wonder Izzy was pushing so hard to get me to look into Vickie's murder. She wasn't just a concerned friend or a bored busybody. She was a suspect, a prime one if Castillo thought she needed a lawyer. "So how do we get proof?" I asked.

"You tell me. You solved Bethany's murder, even before anyone else believed that she *was* murdered. The way I see it, that makes you more qualified to solve Vickie's death than anyone at the NYPD. And that includes Vince."

I had a bad feeling about this.

"My money's on Marlie, but I think we should talk to Amanda to cover all our bases," she continued.

"You just want Marlie to be guilty because you hate apartment brokers," I said.

"True, but to be fair, *everybody* hates apartment brokers."

15

Odessa Dean @OdessaWaiting · July 14
do kindness
hydrate
practice self-care
hydrate
wash your hands
hydrate
don't EVER feed the trolls
hydrate (craft beer counts as water, right?)
#cleanliving

TWENTY MINUTES AND two trains later, we arrived at our destination. To pass the time, I popped in my earbuds and listened to a podcast and people-watched while Izzy played a game on her phone. For the record, people-watching on the New York City subway was better than scripted television most days, almost as good as my favorite YouTube channel.

Amanda's apartment was in an older building. None of that alternating colors of brick with steel and glass with staggered pop-out balconies and freshly painted trim here, just a solid multifamily-style building with bars on the windows and a broken buzzer on the front door. The front door was propped open with a rock. Inside, all but one of the lights was busted out, leaving the dingy lobby in deep shadow. Cubbies lined one wall. Once upon a time, they'd probably had locking doors but now the residents picked up their mail on the honor system.

Someone had left their bicycle, the kind with a huge rack on the back for deliveries, propped up against the wall. The front wheel and seat were both missing.

There was an elevator straight ahead, which surprised me. Elevator buildings in New York were few and far between, outside of giant high-rises. Having one in the relatively short five-story building my aunt lived in was a luxury.

This elevator looked like it had been installed around the time that Calvin Coolidge was president. It was an ornate metal cage with a smaller cage tucked inside. There was a chain holding the door closed, and the top U-shaped bar of a padlock looped through the chain. The padlock itself was nowhere to be seen. The message was clear. Out of order, and for some time, if the dust on the chain was any indication.

"Take the stairs?" I suggested.

"Hundred percent," Izzy said.

By the time we reached the seventh floor, I was dripping with sweat. Between all the stairs and the complete lack of air-conditioning, I'd felt like I'd just run a marathon. Izzy looked better but she was also out of breath. "And to think some people waste good money on a gym membership," I quipped between gulps of air.

"Suckers," Izzy agreed.

She knocked, and Amanda opened the door. After studying her Instagram feed, I would have been hard pressed *not* to recognize her again. Although, in her own home with barely any makeup on and poor lighting, she wasn't the best, most picturesque version of Amanda. That much was certain. It gave me hope that with the right eyeshadow, I, too, could be a ten.

Yeah, right.

I wasn't perfect, but I was perfectly content with the person I saw in the mirror every day, even if I didn't have enormous eyes, glossy hair, and a flawless complexion like Amanda. She had one of those completely symmetrical faces that no amount of makeup could replicate. It was no wonder that she was an Instagram sensation.

"Come in," she said, inviting us inside. "Make yourself at home."

"Thanks," I said, glancing around. Amanda's studio apartment was small but neat. My room back home was decorated with secondhand furniture and old photos from high school. Amanda's was decorated like a catalog with coordinating throw pillows on the daybed—which was made up like a sofa—and a vase of fresh flowers on the window ledge. Even the books on her shelves were organized by the color on their spines.

"Can I get you anything? Coffee? Water?"

"No thanks," Izzy said for both of us.

"You guys had a question about the escape room we did on Friday?" Amanda moved a fuzzy pink blanket so she could sit on the narrow armchair by the bookshelf, leaving the daybed for us. "Is it okay to call you two 'guys' or is there something else you would prefer?"

"'Guys' is fine," Izzy said. While everyone up north liked to make fun of my accent, I had one major advantage over them. I'd been using the gender-neutral "y'all" as long as I could remember, and didn't have to worry about offending anyone by using the wrong plural pronoun. As a bonus, "y'all" could be used in a pinch as a singular pronoun if I wasn't certain what pronouns someone preferred but didn't feel comfortable asking.

Who would have guessed that the South—backward as it could be on delicate social issues—would hold the answer to gender-fluid language?

"You have a killer Instagram feed," I said as I sat.

"Aww, thank you," Amanda said, raising her chin slightly, as if a camera was pointed in her direction.

"I noticed that you were taking a ton of pictures in the escape room, but you only posted a few."

"Sure. I mean, you only post the best, right?"

"Yeah, but I was wondering if I could peek at the other pictures? The ones you didn't post?"

"Why would you want to do that?" Amanda asked.

"Because you might have captured something we missed," I said.

"Don't you mean something that the cops missed? I mean, why are *you* so interested? You didn't even know Vickie."

"No, but I think it's horrible what happened to her." It wasn't a straight answer, but it was a lot better than *My best friend is on the suspect short list and I want to clear her name.*

"Further evidence that you didn't know her very well. Am I right?" she asked Izzy.

"Big mood," Izzy agreed. "To be fair, I hadn't seen Vickie in ages. Not since high school, and even back then, we weren't exactly besties."

"I gotta ask, what was she like in high school?" Amanda asked.

"That was a different time. We were young. She was the entitled, stuck-up cheerleader, and I was the drama nerd."

I could picture Izzy onstage. I bet she'd been great at it.

"So, nothing much has changed. Look, when I saw the invite on Facebook I clicked Maybe as a lark. I'm not really into escape rooms and Vickie and I haven't been in touch since NYU except for an occasional like on each other's posts. Then the day came and I thought why not? Now I'm wishing I'd stayed home."

"I get it," I said. "I really do. I wish Izzy and I hadn't come along, too. But since we did, we're all suspects. Maybe if I could have a look at the pictures on your phone, I might be able to figure out what really happened."

"You're too late," she replied.

"Oh. Did you give your phone to the police already?" I gave Izzy a sideways glance. If Castillo had the pictures, then surely he was able to build an accurate timeline and prove whether or not Izzy was anywhere near Vickie at the time of her death.

"Nope. They didn't ask. But I deleted the pictures already. My phone is always running out of space. Sorry, I'd love to be of more help."

"Do you mind if I took a look?" I asked, holding out my hand.

Her hand tightened around her phone. "Like I said, I deleted them."

"Yeah, but it's real easy to undelete photos, especially if it's only been a few days."

OLIVIA BLACKE

"Whatevs." She unlocked the phone, rose so she could reach the daybed, and handed her phone to me.

I went into her photo gallery and navigated to the deleted photos option. Hundreds of pictures popped up, many of them from yesterday. Amanda really did put a lot of effort into her Instagram. At best, I would take two or three pictures and post the one that was the least blurry. I put a little more effort into what I posted on the Untapped Books & Café accounts, but not by much. Amanda took dozens of pictures of everything, each from a slightly different angle and sifted through them all, removing every possible imperfection.

It took a minute to scroll back to Friday afternoon. When I started seeing pictures inside the now-familiar Brooklyn police station, I slowed down. There were way too many pictures for me to email or text to myself. "Do you have a cloud account?" I asked. There were lots of free services that made it easy to back up, store, and share files on the cloud.

"Yeah, but it's full," she said.

"That's all right, I've got space on mine." I opened her file-sharing app, logged in as myself, and started transferring pictures. This was gonna take forever. I handed the phone back to her. "The pics are still uploading."

I wasn't entirely comfortable leaving while Amanda was still logged in to my account. I didn't have anything of value saved there, no embarrassing pictures or anything like that, but still, it was *mine*. I'd rather stick around until the transfer was complete, so I needed to keep her talking. "You and Vickie went to college together?" I asked.

"Yeah, she was a business major and I was into art, but we

were in a few clubs together. Save the Planet and something else I don't remember."

"Save the Planet?" I hadn't pictured Vickie as an environmental crusader, but then again, I didn't know her very well.

"I think she only joined clubs to meet boys. That's how she met my boyfriend freshman year."

"Sounds like Vickie," Izzy muttered.

"Yeah, she could be a real piece of work," Amanda agreed. "Although, college, you know? He ended up dropping out and that's the last I heard from him."

"I don't get it. If you and Vickie had bad blood between you, why spend the day celebrating her big award with her?"

"Like I said, a lark. And the boyfriend stuff was water under the bridge. Besides . . ." Amanda paused. She seemed to be considering her next words carefully. "Have you ever been friends with a bully?"

"Not exactly friends. There was this girl, Carin Butcher, who bullied me when we were kids, but my parents still forced me to invite her to birthday parties anyway. I try to be nice when I see her now, and we used to end up at the same events a lot because Piney Island is so small, but I don't think we're ever gonna be friends. She's still mean to me to this day."

"Bullies are the worst."

"Hashtag fact," Izzy agreed.

"Then you guys understand. Part of me was hoping that Vickie had grown up and become a nicer person. The other part of me was hoping she had split ends or a botched nose job. I was wrong on all counts. But by the time I figured that out, I'd already paid my share of the escape room, so I tried to make the best of it. And we all know how well *that* turned out."

Izzy grunted in affirmation. "For reals."

Amanda's phone chimed, and she glanced down at it. "Looks like the pics have transferred." She pushed a few buttons. "I'm logged out of your account. Anything else?"

"Nope," I said. "Thanks for everything."

"Sure, anytime," Amanda said, walking us to the door.

"You really think those pictures will help?" Izzy asked as we trudged down the stairs. They were a lot easier going down than they had been coming up, but there were still a whole lot of steps.

"Who can say? They certainly can't hurt your case."

Izzy looked over her shoulder, back toward Amanda's apartment. "You think she did it?"

I shrugged. "Hard to tell. She tried to play it off as no big deal, but I think she was still salty that her freshman boyfriend left her for Vickie. She wouldn't have given me those pictures if she thought there was any evidence on them, but she sure wasn't eager to let me see them in the first place."

"Oh, please, she was worried that you might see a less-than-flattering angle. It's Sunday morning, and even though she was at home alone, she had on makeup and she's redone her nails since we saw her on Friday."

Izzy was more observant than I'd previously realized. "So?"

"If her Instagram obsession and her neatly designed apartment are any indication, she really cares about appearances. A lot. You know how when you take a selfie, you're always supposed to take it from above you, and off to your 'good' side?"

I nodded. "Yeah." I knew how to work the angles to look my best in selfies. It was one of the perks of practically growing up with a smartphone in my hand. It was hard to work all the tricks while getting touristy landmarks in the background, but I'd gotten better at it since coming to New York, where practically every street corner was photo op–worthy.

"Whaddaya wanna bet there's a picture in there where she's got a booger or something?" We both giggled at the thought. For someone who seemed to care about appearances as much as Amanda did, that would be *devastating*. I made a mental promise to myself that if we did find a picture like that, unless there was vital evidence in that shot, I would delete it.

Once we got out onto the street, I looked around, uncertain which neighborhood we were in. The street was lined with everything from tattoo parlors to holistic massages to one place with blacked-out windows and a hand-lettered sign that read, "Appointments only." We'd passed a small park on our way over. In typical New York fashion, half of its occupants pushed strollers and the other half pushed grocery carts piled high with all their earthly belongings. "Where exactly are we?"

"Alphabet City." She pointed to a street sign. "We're on Avenue C. Where the avenues run out of numbers on the edge of the East Village, Alphabet City begins, and continues to the river. This neighborhood had the best twenty-four-hour café back in the day. We'd sneak out and come all the way from Staten Island to sit in the garden until the wee hours of the morning. And the food! I mean, Parker can cook, don't get me wrong, but their menu was divine."

"What happened to them?" I asked.

"Like everything else, they eventually folded. I think there's a dry cleaner in that spot now."

"Want to walk by and see?" I suggested.

"No way. Too depressing." Izzy led the way back to the subway, and I hurried to keep up with her. I glanced down at my phone to check the time. "Got someplace to be?"

"Between the long subway ride and transferring all those pictures, that took longer than I'd expected. It will take a while to get home, and I promised Betty I would cover for her tonight. If I wanted to get all of Aunt Melanie's clothes washed, dried, and folded before work, I should have started an hour ago."

"Leave it to me," Izzy volunteered. "I'm off tonight."

"I can't ask you to wash my aunt's laundry."

"You're not asking. I'm volunteering. Besides, I like doing laundry. It's soothing. Gives me a chance to think."

"You sure?" I asked.

"Positive."

"Well, if you insist . . ." I handed her my keys, knowing she couldn't access the building, much less my aunt's apartment or the laundry room in the basement without them, and she'd given her keys back when she moved out abruptly. "Thanks."

"No worries," Izzy said.

On the train ride back to Williamsburg, I brought up the idea of throwing Parker a surprise birthday party. Izzy was all over it and was eager to get started. "You know, I don't want to hijack Parker's special day, but I'm sure he won't mind if this doubles as my going-away party," I suggested.

"Don't even say that. Trust me. I know the murder apartment wasn't your speed, but we'll find something."

"Even if we could find an apartment, and could manage to swing the exorbitant broker's fee . . ."

"Extortion is more like it," Izzy grumbled.

"Agreed. Even if we scraped together enough money to rent a place, the clock's ticking. My aunt wants me out in three days."

"So, we get creative. Leave it to me."

Izzy had regaled me with stories of some of her previous creative housing solutions, and frankly, they horrified me. "I'm not squatting in a schoolhouse or pitching a tent in a graveyard or any of your other wacky ideas."

"Never even crossed my mind," she said. "Don't you worry. Like I told you, I'll find us something. I've got this."

16

Cosmic Raleigh @RealRaleighRousedale · July 14
.@CosmicPossumBrooklyn is playing Clubsburg Thursday,
9PM—come out for the best Bluegrass, Banjos, & Beer this
side of the bridge! #livemusic #bluegrass #banjonation
#CosmicPossum

THE SUNDAY-NIGHT SHIFT at Untapped Books & Café was usually quiet, but tonight it was deserted. I glanced at the time. It was nine o'clock. We hadn't had a single customer in almost an hour, and didn't close until eleven.

Normally, if it wasn't busy, I would hang out near the kitchen and chat with Parker. He was teaching me a little sign language, and in exchange, I was trying to teach him how to juggle. But Silvia was covering the night shift as usual, and while I enjoyed her company—she had a wicked sense of humor—she got annoyed if the waitstaff spent too much time hanging out in the cramped kitchen. Andre was running the register, and he'd sent the other server home at seven when it became clear that we could handle the evening on a skeleton crew.

When a customer did finally walk in, I was able to give him my full attention. Which was fortunate, because it was the same guy who'd come in earlier, the one who had called me by my name. Now it was my turn. "Raleigh, right?" I'd been waiting tables on and off since I was seventeen, and nothing brought in the tips quite like a big smile and remembering the names of the regulars. It was harder in Williamsburg than it had been in Piney Island, Louisiana, where I'd practically grown up with most of the patrons of the Crawdad Shack, but it didn't hurt to try.

I glanced over at the sea of available tables. "Sit anywhere."

His face blossomed into a grin, and he ran one hand through his slicked-back hair in an unconscious gesture. "Don't mind if I do. Which one's in your section?"

I liked the way he spoke. His voice had an almost rhythmic cadence to it, and while there wasn't even the slightest hint of an accent I could detect, he spoke slower than most New Yorkers, so I didn't have to concentrate to keep up with what he was saying. I waved my arm at the dozen empty tables. I grinned at him. I enjoyed feeling like we shared a joke, even if it was a silly one. "The one with the spaceship."

Out of all of the unique tables, my favorite looked like someone had upcycled a kid's curtains into a tablecloth. On it, green space invaders with bulbous heads shot ray guns at astronauts in bulky white spacesuits while behind them, UFOs and other spacecraft battled among the stars. It was fun, and the more I looked at it, the more details I found, such as a startled black-and-white dairy cow caught in the tractor beam of a flying saucer.

Raleigh settled at the table I suggested. "Do you have a menu or something?"

"We have rotating options," I told him. "In other words, a limited selection that changes at the whim of the chef." Parker handled the creative side of the kitchen and Silvia served similar dishes in the evening, until the ingredients ran out or the kitchen closed. "Vegan? Vegetarian? Dietary restrictions or food allergies?"

"None of the above," he replied.

"Then I would recommend the turkey club on locally baked wheat bread, grilled flatbread pizza with chorizo and olives, or an all-American grilled cheese sandwich with a cup of gazpacho." In the winter, the grilled cheese would come with tomato soup, but in the hot summer months it was served with a cup of cold gazpacho.

Once Todd realized that the air conditioner was working properly for the first time since I'd been here, he promptly turned it up until it was a balmy seventy-three degrees inside. To save money. Despite that, Parker's breakfast chili had been an immense success and had sold out before the lunch rush started.

"Can I get pickles on that grilled cheese?"

I raised my eyebrows in surprise. I liked pickles as much as the next person. With a burger. I'd never tried them with grilled cheese. "Yeah, sure, if that's what you want. And to drink?"

The residents of Williamsburg liked their beer. No, scratch that. The residents of Williamsburg liked their *craft* beer—beers brewed in small batches, with a wide range of flavors. At Untapped Books & Café, we specialized in local craft beers and had an impressive selection. However, by Sunday night, we're usually down to just a few remaining choices until the delivery arrived on Monday morning.

In order to prevent me from having to run back and forth between the cooler and my tables to let them know that their selection was unavailable, would they like to make another choice? I tried to memorize what we had at the beginning of each shift and check back often when we're running low. I've learned to appreciate the subtle differences between different brews, but it never hurt to memorize the beer's info sheet as well.

"Tonight, we have Landlord's Lunch, a hearty seven percent stout, Butcher's Hyperbole where, ironically, the flavor is under-stated, and Pursuit of Hoppiness, a rich nine and a half percent IPA. Of course, we always stock Pour Williamsburg, the local favorite. Now, if you're in the mood for a nonalcoholic beer, we might have a bottle or two of Crafty Like A Faux left."

"PBR?" he asked.

I nodded, "Of course." Everyone had different tastes and opinions. That's what made the world go round, and why we had so many choices. Some people liked taking chances on craft beers. Since batches were small, and they're always experiment-ing with different flavors, there's no real way to guarantee any-one ever got the same beer twice. Mass-market beer, like Pabst Blue Ribbon, was consistent, which held a certain appeal, too. "Coming right up."

I swung by the kitchen and gave his order to Silvia before pulling a can of PBR out of the beer refrigerator and grabbing a glass off the shelf. When I delivered it, Raleigh pulled out a chair for me. "Sit a spell."

I sat. If Todd ever saw me sitting on the job, I'd be out of work before I could say *bedazzler*. But since Andre was supervising, I didn't see how it could hurt. Even so, I sat on the edge of the chair so I could jump up if we got any more diners, as unlikely as that seemed on such a slow night. "Where are you from?" I asked. I could tell he wasn't a native New Yorker, but beyond that I was stumped.

"Upstate," he replied. "But you probably already knew that."

I guess if I'd been a local, I might have recognized his speech patterns. The state of New York, especially upstate, was as different from New York City itself and the surrounding suburbs as Piney Island, Louisiana, was from New Orleans. For one thing, Manhattan, Staten Island, Queens, and Brooklyn were all on islands. Queens and Brooklyn shared an island—Long Island to be precise, which continued far out beyond the city proper to form its own community. The only borough of the city that was on mainland New York state was the Bronx, which I hadn't visited yet despite having heard amazing things about their world-famous zoo.

Upstate New York was its own separate world. Stretching up to Canada and the Great Lakes, upstate was marked with the Catskill Mountains, rolling farmland, and frigid winters. It was remote, rural, and rustic—in other words, everything that New York City was not. From what I'd heard, upstate might as well be a foreign country compared to New York's most populous metroplex.

"I hear it's lovely up there."

"It is," Raleigh agreed. "Gorgeous. Especially if you like looking at the back end of bears."

"That sounds so interesting. I've never seen real mountains before, much less bears in the wild."

"Seriously?"

"Where I'm from is mostly at or below sea level, and the closest mountains are about seven hundred miles away. We've got bears, supposedly, but I've never seen one. Seen plenty of gators, though."

"Louisiana, right?" he asked.

I looked at him with newfound respect. Most people, if they could recognize a Louisiana accent at all, could at best recognize a Creole or Cajun from New Orleans, not the northern part of the state. "You have an incredible ear."

"I better. I'm a musician. Surely you've heard my band? Cosmic Possum?" He looked at me as though I should know that, and I felt a teensy bit foolish.

Izzy had been slowly introducing me to the local music scene, which, like Williamsburg, was vast and eclectic. So far, we'd seen an all-woman band called Deep Fried Cigarettes; Shamble and Roarke, a jazz band with a flamboyant lead singer; and a free-form choral group named Cauliflower Explosion. They had all been very . . . Williamsburg.

"I'm still exploring the local music scene," I said.

A bell rang behind me, and I turned to see Silvia wave at me from behind the kitchen pass-thru. "Order up."

I jumped up and grabbed Raleigh's sandwich and dropped it off at his table. "Well, I'll leave you to it. Let me know if you need anything."

"You should come see us play sometime. We've got a gig Thursday." He pulled a folded piece of paper out of his pocket, smoothed it out on the table, and passed it to me. "We go on at nine."

Despite Izzy's reassurances, there was still a slim chance that I'd be in Louisiana by then, and I didn't want to make a promise I couldn't keep. "Not sure I'll be in town Thursday, but thanks for the invite," I told him. It was a shame. I was curious to see if his band was any good. I ambled away. I felt silly standing by the counter and staring at the only diner in the café, so I stepped into the kitchen.

"Who's the dude?" Silvia asked. "You were looking pretty cozy out there. Friend of yours?"

"Name's Raleigh." I traced my finger along the list of band names on the flyer, until I got to the nine o'clock slot. "Said he's in some band called Cosmic Possum. Heard of them?"

"Have I heard of Cosmic Possum? Are you kidding?" She stuck her head out of the pass-thru. "No fricking way. That's Raleigh Rousedale! You're telling me I just made a grilled cheese sandwich for Raleigh Rousedale? If I'd known it was him, I would have buttered the inside of the bread before I slapped it on the hot plate!"

"I take it the band's a pretty big deal?" I asked. I'd never seen Silvia so excited before.

"You could say that," she replied. "They're easily one of the top five best bluegrass bands in Williamsburg."

Which raised the question—exactly how many bluegrass bands were there in Williamsburg? At least five, I assumed.

"Why don't you go out and say hi?" I suggested.

"Oh no. I couldn't. I get so weird around musicians." She picked up a nearby pot and studied her hazy reflection in it.

Silvia's dark hair was twisted up underneath a hairnet. Her forehead glistened with sweat and there was a smear of something on her cheek. "Besides, he's not my type but he seems really into you."

"He does?" I asked with surprise. I hadn't gotten any kind of vibe from him. "He's just being friendly. Even if he was interested, there's a chance I might be leaving town soon."

"I've heard the rumors. Have a little faith," Silvia said.

I nodded. "I'm trying. Izzy's never let me down before. If I'm still here on Thursday, we can go to the show together."

"I'd love to, but I've got to work," Silvia said.

"That's a bunch of malarkey. Cosmic Possum doesn't go on until nine. Thursday nights are so slow that Andre could cover the kitchen, and he probably wouldn't even need to put on a hairnet since he wouldn't get any orders."

"What's this I hear about hairnets?" I hadn't heard Andre come up behind me. "It's nights like this I wonder why we're even open past six, amiright?"

Sunday evenings were usually quiet, but tonight was painfully so. "Would you cover the kitchen Thursday night if Silvia wanted to leave early to see a band?"

"Sure thing. No one orders much of anything other than beer after eight." He leaned against the countertop. "This have anything to do with that adorable, lonely-looking patron out there with an empty beer glass?"

"Oh, right," I said. "I'll go check on him."

"You do that, Odessa," Andre said with a chuckle.

Raleigh had finished his sandwich and gazpacho and didn't need another beer. He told me he needed to get to practice, and settled his bill. "Are you sure I can't talk you into coming to the show on Thursday?" he asked.

I shrugged. "Maybe," I told him.

"Hope to see you at the show." He winked at me and left.

"What do you say we close up early?" Andre asked. Silvia and I both agreed, so we hurried through the cleaning and closing chores. By the time we finished, it was almost normal closing time anyway, so I didn't feel too bad about leaving a little early.

"Huckleberry going home with you tonight?" I asked Andre. The shop dog didn't actually belong to anyone as far as I could tell. Legend had it that he just showed up one day and never left. Since he'd been around longer than anyone else, I figured he had as much right to be here as anyone. Sometimes he followed employees or customers home at night, and then showed up again the next morning. Other times he slept in the shop.

There might have been a few health code violations in there somewhere, but considering the health inspector only dropped by to flirt with Andre, barely giving the kitchen a passing glance, no one made a fuss about it.

"He's been staying here at night lately," Andre said. "Plus, my sister's friend moved in with us, and things have gotten even more crowded than normal." Last I heard, Andre lived with his boyfriend at his mom's house, along with a few grown siblings and a cousin or two. I got the impression that his mother's house wasn't nearly big enough to accommodate everyone, but she wasn't the kind to turn anyone away, not even a big, floofy dog.

"Alrighty then. Night." I pushed open the front door and almost walked smack into Izzy. "Hey," I said, once I got over my initial surprise. "What are you doing here so late?"

"Just swung by to return your keys. Your aunt's laundry is all washed and folded and put away. She was still in a lot of pain, so she took a pill and turned in early. Thought I'd let you know so you don't go home and make a ton of noise."

"Shoot, I was gonna practice my Riverdancing tonight," I said.

"Maybe you should try it barefoot?" she offered with a grin. Izzy always got my sense of humor, even when no one else did.

"You'll never guess who came in tonight. Raleigh, um, somebody. He's in that band Cosmic Possum."

Her eyes got wide. "Really? What's he like?"

"Nice guy."

"So, you like him?" Izzy asked.

That was a weird question. "He's funny and a good tipper."

She nodded, looking pleased with herself. "That's a start."

Something wasn't adding up. Izzy mostly worked in the bookstore half of Untapped. While she was friendly and helpful to her customers, she had little interaction with the café regulars and had never shown much interest in them before. "What's going on?"

"Going on? Nothing. Nada. Why do you ask?"

Before she could answer, Silvia appeared behind me. "Walk me to my car, and I'll give you a lift. You, too, Izzy."

Izzy gave her a dismissive gesture with her hand. "Thanks, but I'm good. Besides, I think I left something earlier and I'm gonna grab it before Andre locks up. You working tomorrow?"

"Morning shift," I confirmed.

"Call in sick," she told me.

"I can't do that. I need the money," I said.

"Sure, don't we all? But I got to thinking, how come Vickie booked an escape room for six but only four people showed up? I doubt the police have questioned the two that flaked out. We should talk to them."

"Why?" I asked. "They weren't in the room with us, so they couldn't have possibly killed Vickie. Besides, how would we even find them?"

"Easy. Amanda said there was a Facebook invite, right? I'll ask Gennifer who else was on the invite. Then we'll know who RSVP'd but didn't show."

Silvia lifted a finger. "I hate to interrupt, but do you guys want that ride home or not?"

"Go ahead," Izzy said. "I'll call you in the morning."

I nodded. I hated the idea of calling in sick and leaving the café shorthanded, but if there was any chance I was leaving Williamsburg in a few days, time was running out to figure out who killed Vickie and clear Izzy's name. "Alrighty."

As much as I'd grown to love walking, it was nice to have a free ride home. After a long shift, my feet hurt whether I wore cowboy boots or orthopedic shoes, so it felt good to sit down and be chauffeured. As Silvia cut up Metropolitan Avenue, I asked, "You're not gonna dime me out to Todd, are you?"

"Are you kidding? I wouldn't pass Todd a cold." I took that to mean no.

She pulled up in front of my building. "Thanks for the ride. Oh, and before I forget, I shared those tamales with my aunt yesterday and she wanted to tell your mom those were the best tamales she's ever had in her life."

Silvia grinned. "She'll be happy to hear that."

I got out of the car, and she took off, heading toward the highway. After a recent breakup, Silvia had moved back in with her parents in Queens and commuted to Untapped Books & Café while she figured out her next step. Maybe I should ask her if she was looking for a roomie, in case Izzy and I needed a third.

Not wanting to wake my aunt, I was as quiet as possible coming home. Rufus meowed persistently as soon as I put my key in the lock, and I tried to shush him before realizing he was closed up in the bedroom with my aunt. I opened the door a crack, and the cat slipped outside, weaving between my legs and purring loudly. "Happy to see you, too, Rufie," I said, bending down to offer my hand for him to rub against.

When he was satisfied, he retreated to one of his favorite spots, an empty shelf near the top of the bookshelf. Apparently there used to be books and knickknacks there like every other surface in my aunt's apartment, but he kept knocking them over until she relented and gave him the whole shelf all to himself. Once he was settled, I went out on the balcony.

Aunt Melanie's apartment was on the top floor of the building, but because hers was an interior unit, there was no view to speak of except for the other balconies in the courtyard. I could see a twinkle of lights over the roof of the building, but Manhattan was too far away to be more than just a glow on the horizon from this angle. It was quiet tonight, or at least as quiet as it ever got in Brooklyn. I tuned out the distant buzz of traffic and ever-present wail of sirens, opened my phone, and navigated to the pictures that Amanda had uploaded earlier.

Most of the pictures were exactly what I'd expected to see—well-composed selfies of Amanda with glimpses of the escape room in the background. I reached the end of the set and found nothing useful, so I went back through them, slower the second time. That's when I noticed it.

There were pictures missing.

A lot of them.

The file names were numbered, and there were huge gaps. One picture was 712_357, and the next started at 712_374. I identified several jumps like that, where at least a dozen pictures were missing in between.

Not knowing that someone would come by and ask for her deleted pictures, Amanda had deliberately, permanently erased a whole bunch of photos that might have contained evidence.

Now, why would anyone go and do a thing like that?

17

Odessa Dean @OdessaWaiting · July 15
Am I laughing because I'm happy? Yes. Am I laughing
because I have ZERO CLUE what I'm doing and don't really
have a fallback plan? Also yes! #zerochill

THERE ARE FEW things more glorious than waking naturally instead of being yanked out of dreamland by a blaring alarm, even if it was barely nine in the morning. I might have felt a tiny smidgeon of guilt about skipping out on work, but I'd already sent a text to Todd—on a delay so he wouldn't receive it until seven a.m.—and it was too late to back out now. Besides, it wasn't like I was up for a promotion.

Plus, I had a murder to solve.

I sat up and stretched. My aunt's couch wasn't exactly a room at the Ritz, but if I was being completely honest, it was at least as comfortable as the well-worn mattress back at my parents' house that I'd had ever since I'd graduated from a toddler's bed.

Huh. That was new. When had I started thinking of it as my parents' house and not "home"? Probably around the time that

I'd stopped seeing Williamsburg as an alien planet and started feeling like I belonged here. Like this wasn't just a summer visit.

I picked up my phone and texted Izzy. My first instinct was to ask her if she'd found us a permanent place to stay, but if she had, she would have called, texted, or kicked down my aunt's front door to tell me the good news. So instead, I simply asked, Where we meeting? When?

Her answer was instantaneous, which was a surprise. Unless she was working, Izzy rarely rose and shone before noon. Meet me @ 53 & Lex 1 hour.

I hurried through my morning routine, pulling my hair back into a ponytail in lieu of washing it. It was lazy, but considering that my weather app predicted soaring temperatures I was being practical. Equally practical was my long cotton skirt which barely brushed the tops of my cowboy boots, and a blousy top I'd scored at a local secondhand resale store.

Before leaving, I downloaded a few podcasts to listen to on the long subway ride into Manhattan. Feeling like a legit New Yorker, I walked to the nearest subway station and jumped on a train without even consulting my app. However, I sat across from one of the electronic screens in the car and stole surreptitious glances at the map display to make sure I was heading in the right direction.

I might be more comfortable getting around the city, but I wasn't sure anyone had the full map memorized. Anyone who said they did had to be lying.

The New York City subway system was a confusing tangle of numbered and lettered colored lines that spiderwebbed between boroughs. Lines merged and split with transfer spots whenever they crossed other tracks. I took the subway into Manhattan and then made a rookie mistake at the transfer station. Rather than waiting for the right train, I got on the first train that pulled up, which took me several blocks out of my way. Instead of trying to backtrack and get on the correct train, I walked the extra blocks aboveground, where it was only slightly less confusing.

I was in the business district, commonly known as Midtown, surrounded by medium- and high-rise geometric steel-and-glass office buildings. Traffic—delivery vans, yellow taxis, and sedans ranging from beat-up 1990s-era Hondas to sleek, silent electric cars—crept past. I was glad that I'd opted for the subway instead of taking an Uber, not that I could afford morning-rush-hour prices. I heard a sharp whistle, the kind I had been trying with no success to learn, and looked up to see Izzy waving with both hands over her head from the corner diagonal to me.

I waved back to let her know I saw her and hurried across the crosswalk at the tail end of the flashing walk signal, quickly sidestepping out of the way of a bicyclist who couldn't care less that I was in his path. I had to wait a few seconds for the next light, and then gave it a few more seconds as an impatient driver blew through the red. When I finally made it to Izzy's corner, my heart was racing. I might have fallen in love with New York, but I doubt I'd ever be comfortable playing Frogger through the intersections.

"You made it," Izzy said, beaming at me. She checked her phone. "And with minutes to spare." She handed me an insulated thermos I knew would be filled with hot coffee. Izzy was always prepared, but the most impressive thing wasn't that she'd brought not only her own reusable coffee container but she'd brought one for me, too. Talk about thoughtful *and* eco-conscious!

"Thanks! Was there any doubt?" I craned my neck to study the high-rises surrounding the intersection. In the distance, I caught a glimpse of the familiar spire of the Chrysler Building. I knew it was several blocks away still, and was impressed with the sheer size of any building that could stand out in this teeming steel metropolis.

"You know, it's gonna be high nineties today. You might want to consider making yourself a pair of shorts," she said, checking out my long skirt.

"Believe it or not, with the right pattern and material, this is as cool if not cooler than your shorts. Besides, subway seats, right?" I was no germaphobe, but New York City mass transit was every bit as dirty as the worst bayou back home. It was bad enough knowing that the folds of my skirt were the only thing between my skin and the seats, but it would be worse if my legs were bare. "So, who are we here to see?"

I had to admit that after watching a gazillion TV shows and movies set in swanky New York office buildings, I was curious to see one up close in person. Would there be some geeky kid pushing a squeaky mail cart among a sea of cubicles? Would everyone be dressed in pin-striped suits, with women in their Louboutin shoes and ruffled blouses? I bet someone was screaming at their poor assistants from a corner office right now, ordering them to bring them that memo, stat!

"Nadia works here," she said, gesturing at the drugstore on the corner.

My face fell. My hopes of finally touring a real Manhattan

office were dashed. I'd been in a hundred drugstores, and they looked exactly the same in New York City as they looked in Piney Island, except bigger.

"Whatya waiting for?" Izzy asked, already in motion. The automatic doors whooshed open and she disappeared inside.

I followed her. An air-conditioned chill washed over me. The store smelled like industrial cleaners with a hint of flowers, which grew stronger as we wove between aisles of hair products to arrive at the pharmacy desk in the back. The white-coated pharmacist behind the counter was serving a customer. Her name tag read "Nadia." The dark-skinned woman was tall and built like a runner—long and lean. Her curls brushed the top of her shoulders and she wore pink-framed glasses.

"Can I help you?" she asked in a pleasant, if slightly bored voice when it was our turn to approach the desk.

Izzy flashed a smile at her and stepped forward. "Izzy Wilson," she announced. "And this is Odessa Dean."

"Do you have a prescription?" Nadia asked in the tone of someone who repeated the same questions ad nauseam all day long. I know exactly how she felt. *Can I get you some water to start? Do you need a minute to decide? Would you like some ketchup with that?*

"Actually, we need to speak to you on a personal matter. Do you have a minute?"

She pushed her glasses up higher on the bridge of her nose with one finger and studied Izzy. "Do I know you?"

"Not yet. We're friends of Vickie Marsh."

Personally, I thought *friends* was stretching the truth.

Nadia rolled her eyes. "This is about that stupid escape room, isn't it? I already PayPal'd her my share. I'm sorry I couldn't go, but my fiancée wasn't feeling well." She shook her head. "I can't believe Vickie's still sore about that."

Izzy elbowed me, hard. "Tell her," she whispered.

"Why do I have to be the one to break the news?" I whispered back.

"News? What news?" Nadia asked.

I was impressed. Between my accent and lowering my voice, she would have had to have some kind of superpower to catch that. "Um, I hate to break it to you, but Vickie, um, passed."

"Passed?" Nadia stared at me incredulously, her dark eyes boring into me. "Passed what?"

"She was murdered," Izzy clarified. She was just trying to help, but seeing the shock on Nadia's face, I think she was making things worse.

"I'm gonna need a second," Nadia said, leaning her weight on her palms, which were braced against the counter.

"Maybe you should sit down?" I suggested.

"You think?" she snapped. Then she took a deep breath. "Sorry." I don't think I'd heard a New Yorker apologize before now. That, more than any physical reaction Nadia had shown, was evidence of her shock.

Izzy vaulted over the counter and took Nadia's elbow. "Let's get you a seat."

Unlike my athletic and adventurous friend, I wasn't a vaulter. Or even a jumper, really. I was more of an ambler. Besides, I didn't relish the idea of trying to clear a counter in a skirt. Practicality being the better part of valor and all that, I hurried around to a hinged section of counter and tugged on it. It didn't move. I had to hop up a little, resting my stomach against the edge, and reached over to unlatch the door before swinging it open.

A buzzer sounded and one of the technicians in the back noticed me for the first time. He looked up, put down the enormous pill bottle he'd been holding, and approached menacingly. "Customers aren't allowed back here," he said in a stern voice.

"Oh, I'm not a customer," I explained, then realized that probably sounded worse. "I'm here with Nadia." I waved at the back of her white lab coat as she retreated with Izzy toward an unmarked door.

"Employees only," he said, blocking my way.

A man in a security guard uniform appeared at my side. He towered over me, arms straining the sleeves of his polo shirt. When he clapped a hand on my shoulder, it felt like a sandbag. "You ain't goin' nowhere," he told me, his voice a rumbling bass.

"Odessa?" Izzy called out. She appeared around the corner. "You coming?"

"Apparently not," I told her, trying not to move, lest the giant guard crush me by mistake.

Izzy tilted her head, taking in the scene. "Myke?"

He nodded at her. "Izzy."

I let out a sigh of relief. It came in handy, having a friend that knew pretty much everyone. Considering over eight million people lived in New York City, that was impressive. More than impressive. Supernatural.

"What's going on?" he asked.

"We need a sec to talk to Nadia," she said, as if that explanation was enough.

Apparently it was, because Myke the giant released his grip on my shoulder. "Make it quick."

"Sure thing." Izzy reached past the angry tech, grabbed my hand, and propelled me through the open hatch toward the back of the pharmacy.

We took a sharp turn and ended up in a bland employee break room. Two plain round tables took up most of the room, each with four simple stackable chairs ringing it. A small microwave balanced on top of a dorm-style refrigerator, squeezed between a soda machine and a snack dispenser. Considering the better selection of food and drinks available for purchase in the drugstore, I doubted either machine saw much action.

The room was completed by a sagging couch that looked like it had survived through more presidential administrations than I had. Nadia sat in the center of the couch, clutching a coffee mug. Izzy sat down next to her. I pulled up a chair and sat in front of her.

"I'm so sorry," Izzy said, patting Nadia's knee. "I thought you would have heard by now."

"I should have guessed something was wrong when Vickie didn't call and light into me for standing her up."

"But y'all were Facebook friends, weren't you?" I asked. I wasn't directly connected to Vickie, but even I was seeing posts about her death on all my social media feeds. Salacious news spread faster than wildfire over the internet.

"I'm taking a break from social media," she said. Her phone chimed once, inside her lab jacket pocket. She didn't even flinch, much less reach for it. She had a whole lot more self-control than I ever dreamed of having. "What happened?"

"We were at the escape room," I explained. "There were a couple of connecting rooms, and when the time ran out, they found her, still in the first room. Looks like someone hit her over the head with a trophy, and she was dead." I didn't mention that it was *our* trophy, or that Izzy and I had been among the first to discover her body. Frankly, I didn't want to think about it.

"Wait a second, she died in the escape room? How is that even possible?"

"No clue," Izzy said. "We were hoping you would know something about that."

"How could I? I wasn't there. Like I said, Becks wasn't feeling well. A migraine. I didn't feel right going out with her friends without her, so I stayed home to keep her company."

"Becks was Vickie's friend, not you?" I asked.

Nadia nodded. "I wouldn't exactly call them friends. Coworkers, more like it. Becks manages a bunch of buildings in Hell's Kitchen. Vickie was one of her brokers."

"I thought Vickie only managed apartments?" Izzy asked. Hell's Kitchen, despite the ominous name, was a popular neighborhood just west of Midtown. Historically, it had been filled with low-income housing but like almost every square inch of Manhattan, it had been gentrified into submission. The rent-controlled apartments disappeared, replaced by expensive condos and Airbnb units. "How many apartment buildings remain in Hell's Kitchen?"

"More than you might think," Nadia said. "But most of Becks's buildings are condos. Vickie manages those openings, too. She is . . . was a full-service agent." Nadia bit her lip.

"I'm sorry for your loss," I said, leaning forward.

Nadia shook her head. "I'm fine. Truth be told, I didn't get along with Vickie all that well. But Becks is going to be devastated."

"Were they close?" I asked.

"Not to speak of. But do you know how hard it is to find a good broker?"

Izzy gave me a knowing look. I wasn't sure she believed there was such a thing as a *good* broker. But I guess being on the property end of things, Becks had a different point of view. "You seem pretty upset for someone who wasn't close to the victim," I said.

"Wouldn't you be?" she asked. "I might not have been her biggest fan, but we saw Vickie all the time, and my fiancée works closely with her. So, yeah, I'm shook. Oh, I should call Becks." She pulled her cell phone out from her pocket, then stared at it for a second as if she'd forgotten how to use it. "Will you two excuse me?"

"Of course!" Izzy jumped up and pulled me with her. "See ya, Myke," she said, waving at the enormous security guard as we made our way out of the store.

"How do you know that dude?" I asked as the door closed behind us and I adjusted to the heat and brightness of the crowded sidewalk.

"Myke? He works with Vince." She glanced back behind us. "You know, he's single. A bit of a gym rat, obviously, but a real softie. I could set the two of you up if you want. Hold on, I'll be right back."

"No way," I said, grabbing her wrist before she could go back into the drugstore. "He's so totally not my type."

"Oh yeah?" She looked back again, and I noticed that Myke was still watching us. "He's cute, isn't he?"

"Cute? Sure," I agreed. "But I keep telling you, I'm not interested in starting a relationship right now."

"Check," she said. "What about that guy from the café last night? You liked him, right?"

"Raleigh? He was nice. We get a lot of nice customers at Untapped."

"He asked you to his show, didn't he?" she pressed. "And he came into the café just to see you."

"I'm sure he was just trying to drum up more people for the audience. Besides . . ." I thought about it for a minute. "What do you mean he was at the café last night to see me? How could you possibly have known that? And how did he know my name in the first place?"

"Life's a mystery," Izzy said, shrugging.

"Oh no, you don't get off that easily. You know something. Spill."

"Okay, I might have set up a Tinder profile for you. And Raleigh might have been one of the guys who wanted to meet you. I know what you're going to say, but he's hot, right? And sweet. And tall. And in a band. You could do a lot worse."

18

•.•••

Dizzy Izzy @IsabelleWilliamsburg · 15 July
u can never go home again. wait, no, i meant you *should*
never go home again. fight me. #homesweethome
#statenisland #ferrylife

•••••••••••••••••••••••••••••••••••••••

I STARED AT MY best friend in disbelief. "I can't believe you did
that!" I told Izzy. "All those weird text messages? The blue daisies? The expensive chocolates? The seemingly random encoun-
ters I've been having with Raleigh, those were all you? It's bad
enough you're trying to trick me into going on a date, but pretending to be me online on a dating app? That's crossing a line."

"It's not like I'm catfishing them or anything," Izzy protested.
"I mean, sure, I told them I was you, but I'm not trying to scam
anyone. I'm trying to nudge you in the right direction. I mean, if
Todd can find someone online, why not you?"

"I told you I'm not interested in dating right now. Even if I
met Prince Charming, what's the point, when I might be leaving
in two days?"

"I already said I'd take care of that. Don't you trust me?"

Five minutes ago, I would have said yes without any hesitation. But that was before I found out that she was pretending to be me online. "I know you have the best of intentions, you always do, but I'm not as adventurous as you are. You'd be perfectly comfortable living out of a tent in the middle of Times Square, but I need something more conventional. Even if you found us something, how can we afford it?"

Izzy clapped her hand on my shoulder. "Don't worry. I've got this."

I paused to think about it. Izzy knew New York like the back of her hand, and more importantly, she knew people. If anyone could pull this off, it was her. I couldn't keep hedging my bets—hoping for a miracle while planning on being at the bus station on Wednesday morning. "All right, I'm all in. The apartment, not the online dating. Promise me this place is going to have electricity and running water."

"Nothing janky. I swear."

"And one more thing. Let me see your phone." I held out my hand. She gave me her phone. I scrolled through the apps and pulled up Tinder. "What were you thinking?" I muttered. I know that internet dating no longer had the stigma it had held decades ago, long before I was even *thinking* of dating. More people met through the internet than in real life these days, and I thought that was great.

For other people.

People who were actually looking to date.

Not me.

"Seriously?" I mumbled to myself when I opened the app and

saw that I had 257 new matches. "What did you put on here to get so many responses? Let me guess, you said I was a Vickie's Secret model?"

"Nope," Izzy said, grabbing her phone out of my hand. "Your profile is accurate. Hundred percent."

"Except that *I* didn't write it," I pointed out.

She ignored me. "Look at this guy. He's a transplant, too. From Tennessee. He works on Wall Street, in IT. So he's smart."

"Says here he's 'family oriented.' He's probably got a wife and kids back home," I said.

Izzy swiped his profile away and another popped up on the screen. "What about this one? He's cute and likes dogs."

"And he's fifty," I said.

"Nothing wrong with an older man."

"He's more than twice my age. Swipe left."

Izzy rolled her eyes skyward. On either side of us, pedestrians streamed past us, hurrying from one destination to the next without so much as noticing us other than as a minor obstruction. "And this guy? Employed, twenty-four, even lives in Williamsburg. Oh, never mind."

She started to swipe, but I stopped her. "What?" I peered over her hand at the screen and recognized Parker's face staring back at me. "Oh, great. Now Parker thinks I'm on Tinder, too."

"Yeah, well, he matched with you."

"That's even worse!" I felt a blush creep up my cheeks. "Now I'm gonna have to explain to him that this was all your doing and it's gonna embarrass both of us."

"How is it embarrassing? He's totally your type, right? I see how you guys act together. You should go out with him."

"We're friends," I protested.

"So what?"

"And he's dating that Hazel girl," I said. I wasn't about to ruin a perfectly good friendship by going out on a date with Parker.

"It can't be that serious, if he matched with you on Tinder," Izzy pointed out.

Changing the subject, I asked, "What about the other person who RSVP'd to Vickie's party but didn't show up? Nadia's fiancée, Becks. Think we should talk to her?"

Izzy closed Tinder. "Even if I thought she had any information, it's too soon. She just found out that Vickie's dead. I don't see much point in talking to her and making things worse. Do you?"

I shook my head. "Don't see how it would help. Obviously, they weren't there, so it was a stretch even talking to Nadia, not that she had anything helpful to add. What about Gennifer? Shouldn't we talk to her?" Granted, I don't think that Izzy had ever met a stranger, but it was a little weird that we were running all over Manhattan talking to Amanda and Nadia, who wasn't even in the escape room, and we hadn't interviewed Izzy's friend Gennifer yet.

"If she knew anything, she would have already told me," Izzy said.

"It wouldn't hurt to sit down with her. Maybe she knows something she doesn't realize that she knows."

"You've got a point." She scrolled through her contacts and sent a text message. Less than a minute later, her phone beeped. "She's home right now and says it's okay if we drop by. Come on, if we time this just right, we might not even have to wait on the ferry."

"The ferry?" I asked, eyes widening.

Izzy gave me a toothy grin. "Hey, it was your idea to talk to her. Hope you don't get seasick."

I didn't. At least, I didn't think I did.

Staten Island was an island that sat in the harbor south of Manhattan Island. There were bridges connecting it to Brooklyn on one side and New Jersey on the other, but the only direct route from Manhattan was the famous orange Staten Island Ferry.

According to the Wikipedia article I read on the bus ride downtown, something like seventy thousand passengers used the ferry every day to travel between the Whitehall Ferry Terminal in Manhattan and the St. George Ferry Terminal in Staten Island. During rush hour, the ferry was packed shoulder to shoulder as people pushed and shoved their way onto the boat, but now that it was creeping toward noon, the only people on the ferry with us were folks that rode the free ferry as long as they could for lack of anything better to do, a school trip group that clustered around the open-air balconies to catch a glimpse of the Statue of Liberty, and a handful of off-hours commuters hiding behind oversized headphones and e-book readers.

I followed Izzy as she picked out a bench she liked and plopped down on it. She didn't seem to notice the gentle rocking of the boat or the gorgeous view of the Manhattan skyline out the back windows. Over the roar of the engines, I could hear a smattering of giggles from the assembled schoolkids as salty spray blew into their faces.

I stared out the windows, taking in the scenic views. When that got old, I turned to Izzy. "So, Staten Island," I said.

"Yup," Izzy replied.

"What was it like growing up there?"

She shrugged. "Same as anywhere, I guess." She gestured out the window at the unassuming view as we neared the island. "There's a pretty good mall, or at least it used to be. A couple of movie theaters. Some of the best diners on the East Coast. A real scenic landfill. And of course, the whole Sleepy Hollow thing."

"Wait, what?"

"Sleepy Hollow?" she repeated. "You know, the headless horseman? Ichabod Crane?"

"Yeah, of course I know the headless horseman. I just didn't know that was Staten Island."

"Not exactly. The town of Sleepy Hollow is up north a ways, but the original Ichabod Crane is buried right here on Staten Island, and there's a Sleepy Hollow Road, too. Not sure if it's really haunted. We used to go down there every Halloween, but I never saw any ghosts."

A chill ran down my back. I was pretty sure I didn't believe in ghosts, but the legend of Sleepy Hollow always gave me chills. "Ichabod Crane was a real person?"

"Sure enough."

The ferry lurched and the engines whined. We bumped against something, and I grabbed the back of the seat in front of us to brace myself. There was a loud scraping sound as the boat swayed hard to one side. "What was that?" I asked. "What's wrong? Did we hit something? Are we sinking? Please tell me we're not gonna sink."

"Nothing's wrong, silly," Izzy said, standing and stretching. "We just docked. Welcome to Staten Island."

The inside of the Staten Island side of the ferry terminal could have been any generic bus station in any city in America. There was a large holding area ringed with seating and newsstands that probably did a brisk business in the morning. The terminal could have used a coat of paint to brighten things up, but I was too busy trying to keep up with Izzy to see much. We passed signs for buses, taxis, and parking before heading down a long hallway. I could imagine during rush hour that this place would be packed with people, but now we were practically the only ones in sight.

We swiped our MTA cards at the turnstile, and Izzy muttered something about getting ripped off as we walked down a short platform and boarded a waiting train. Similar to many of the subway lines in Brooklyn, the Staten Island Railway was an elevated train. But unlike the tangled lines that serviced the rest of the city, the SIR was a single track stretching in a straight-ish line from the ferry terminal to the far side of the island.

We rode for several stops, with me plastered against the window the whole time. I didn't know what I was expecting to see— a headless ghost riding an enormous black horse perhaps—but instead, the train rocked along a track through a pleasant suburban neighborhood of modest, well-kept homes. Yards were mowed and kids played basketball in driveways. In many ways, Staten Island looked more like Louisiana than it did New York.

"Come on, Odessa," Izzy said, yanking me out of my reverie. "It's our stop."

I followed her off the train to a narrow platform overlooking a sea of roofs of two- and three-story homes. We took the stairs down and wound around a steeply sloped street. Izzy pointed to the right. "The beach is a few blocks that way. I spent pretty much every summer there as a kid until I was old enough to just go to flirt with the lifeguards, at which time my dad decided I needed to get a summer job to keep me out of trouble. Didn't work, of course." She winked at me. "But it did keep me away from the lifeguards. More or less."

We came to a stop sign, and Izzy walked across the street without hardly glancing around for traffic. Not that there was any. She gestured to a house with pale green siding. "My best friend lived there. She married a wise guy and moved to Trenton."

Izzy slowed down in front of a cream-colored house that had been converted to a duplex with two entry doors side by side. The grass was neatly trimmed. Oblong topiaries flanked a cast-iron mailbox in the shape of a horse-drawn carriage. "This is where I grew up. We had the left side. There used to be a shed out back that I transformed into a clubhouse. I used to charge neighborhood kids a dollar to hide out there if they wanted to run away from home. When it got dark, they'd get scared and ask my dad to walk them home, but one guy, Brad Maplecourt, stayed three whole days before his aunt came and dragged him back home." She grinned at the memory.

"Where are your parents now?" Izzy rarely talked about her childhood, and up until now, I'd never heard her mention her family at all. It was strange, in a city where so many grown adults still lived at home, for Izzy to seem to come out of nowhere.

"Florida." She rolled her eyes. "Palm Beach, I think. It's been a while since we talked."

I didn't push it any further. If she wanted to talk about it, she would. "Do you think the shed's still there?"

"Nah. Collapsed after a particularly bad snowstorm." She walked briskly away from the house, without looking back. Three houses later, she turned and walked up the path to a glass-front door obscured behind a barred security door. She knocked and a second later, the door opened. Gennifer stepped onto the front porch.

Gennifer swept Izzy up in a huge bear hug. "Oh my goodness, I didn't think I'd ever live to see you step foot in Staten Island after graduation."

"I'm as surprised as anyone," Izzy said. "I'm dying out here. Can we come in?"

"Of course! But we've got to try to keep it down, please, the baby just went down for a nap." I was impressed. I didn't even know where I was going to be living in a few days, but Gennifer seemed to have it all figured out—a husband, a baby, even a cute little house in the suburbs. It was hard to wrap my head around the fact that people my age were already having babies of their own, while I was still sitting at the kids' table.

I wasn't ready for adulting.

Gennifer ushered us inside and disappeared into the kitchen. "Water? Soda? Coffee? Beer?"

"Water's fine," Izzy said, and I agreed. This morning's coffee was long gone, and I didn't realize how parched I was until she offered. Traipsing around three of the five boroughs in this heat would do that to a person.

We settled onto couches with a bright floral pattern preserved underneath a thick plastic cover and waited for Gennifer to return from the kitchen. She handed us our drinks and then placed coasters on the coffee table in front of us. "So, Vickie," Izzy prompted.

"Yup. Her service is next Tuesday. You coming?"

"I'll have to think about it. Maybe. To be honest, I'm kinda surprised you two hung out. She was a real jerk to you back in high school."

Gennifer shrugged. "She's not so bad. We got to talking at the five-year class reunion. Missed you, by the way." Izzy made a noncommittal sound in the back of her throat, and Gennifer continued, "She's trying to get me to sell Mom's house and buy something bigger in New Jersey, but we like it here, you know? Plus, Pete's job is on the island and this is a good school district for when Penny gets older."

"So you guys were, what? Friends?" Izzy asked.

"I mean, we weren't close, not really. You know how she is." Gennifer flinched, and then corrected herself. "Was. She wasn't mean to me like she was back in the day, but she could be intense."

"Amanda called her a bully," I said, because Gennifer seemed to be dancing around the fact. "Is that what you meant when you said she used to be mean to you?"

"We were just kids," Gennifer replied.

"She picked on everyone, but you were a favorite target," Izzy added.

"I wouldn't say that. Sure, she was opinionated and used to stick gum in my hair when we were little. But it wasn't like we spent a lot of time together."

"Then why were you at her celebration?" I asked.

"Do you know how hard it is to make friends as an adult?" Gennifer asked. When I nodded, vigorously, Gennifer grinned. "The struggle is real."

I turned to Izzy. "That's why I'm so lucky to have you. And Parker. And why I wouldn't risk blowing that for a date."

"Yeah, sure. Heard you the first time," Izzy said, but she still didn't sound convinced.

I turned to Gennifer. "Did Vickie have any close friends? It was supposed to be her special day, but as far as I can tell, the only people that she got to come out with her were a coworker, some clients, and women she went to school with who didn't even like her that much."

Gennifer laughed. "Far be it from me to throw shade, but Vickie's not exactly the friendly type. She wasn't what I'd call easy to get along with."

"But who would want to kill her?" I asked.

"A couple of years ago? I would have said Izzy."

"What?" I looked back and forth between her and Izzy.

Izzy stared daggers at Gennifer. "Go ahead. Spill the tea."

"Not to put anyone on blast, but Vickie has . . . had . . . a reputation. She liked to steal anything anyone else had, especially boys. But *especially* boys that Izzy wanted. There used to be a saying back in high school that the easiest way for a guy to get Vickie's attention was for them to ask Izzy out on a date. Wasn't that true?"

Izzy's jaw moved as if she was grinding her teeth together. Instead of answering, she gave a terse nod. Then she relaxed her jaw. "That was ages ago."

"Sure, but back in the day, I wouldn't have been surprised if you took a crowbar to her. Who was that one guy you had such a huge crush on, but then he dumped you on prom night? Brad something?"

"Brad Maplecourt," she supplied.

"Wait, is that the same Brad that hid out in your shed?" I asked.

"Aw, yes, I'd forgotten about that!" Gennifer exclaimed. "We used to smuggle soda pops out of your house and hide in the shed for hours cutting pictures out of magazines. Good times." She leaned forward and lowered her voice conspiratorially. "You know that girl Amanda that was in the escape room with us? Vickie stole her boyfriend just last week. I mean, honestly, some people just never grow up. Vickie was even bragging about it Friday right before Amanda got there, like it was some kind of contest and she was winning."

"Amanda's current boyfriend was cheating on her with Vickie? Are you sure they weren't talking about old news?" I asked. I gave Izzy a knowing look. Unless Gennifer was mistaken, it sounded like history was repeating itself. Funny how Amanda hadn't mentioned that to us when we interviewed her yesterday.

"That's what Vickie said. And I overheard the two of them arguing while we were walking. They tried to keep their voices down so we couldn't eavesdrop, but Amanda sure was mad about something."

My phone rang and I glanced at the screen. I expected it to be Todd, calling to yell at me for ditching work, since he was pretty much the only person I knew who called instead of texting like everyone else. Then I saw the caller ID. Vincent Castillo. I showed the screen to Izzy, and she waved me away. "I'm not here," she said.

I jumped up and moved to the hall before answering, "Hey."

"Izzy with you?" he asked, no greeting, no anything. Then again, that would have been a waste of time since I already knew it was him.

"Nope," I said, crossing my fingers to ward off the white lie. I mean, Izzy wasn't *with* me. She was in the other room.

"Odessa," he growled, his voice low and warning.

"I don't know what to tell you. I'm not Izzy's keeper. Besides . . ."

"If you try to tell me her phone's dead or out of minutes or some such nonsense, I'll, well, I'll arrest you for obstruction of justice."

"Look, I'll tell her you're looking for her next time I see her, alrighty?"

"Promise?"

"Pinkie swear," I said, keeping my fingers crossed.

The doorbell rang. Upstairs, a baby began to cry.

"Rats," Gennifer said, sprinting up the stairs. "Get that for me, will ya?"

I opened the front door.

Detective Vincent Castillo stood on the front step. And he did not look happy.

19

Odessa Dean @OdessaWaiting · July 15
Does anyone even pinkie swear anymore, or is it just me? It's just me, isn't it? #pinkieswear #sorrynotsorry

AS USUAL, VINCENT Castillo's dark hair was buzzed short. He wore tight, dark indigo jeans with a pale green shirt and a coal gray vest. He held his phone up to one ear and the other hand was poised to ring the doorbell again. He glared at me as he hung up the phone.

Before I could say anything, Izzy appeared from the living room. "Who is it?" She froze, then let out an exaggerated sigh. "Might as well come on in and join the party."

Castillo brushed past me. "Pinkie swear?" he asked, shaking his head. "I expected better from you." I shrugged and followed him. When he sat down on the sofa, the plastic cover let out a squeak. "You've been dodging my calls," he said to Izzy. "And worse, you got Odessa to cover for you."

"I wasn't covering . . ."

He silenced me with another glare.

"Vince, I was about to call you," Izzy said. Overhead, I could hear creaks coming from old, loose floorboards as Gennifer presumably paced with the baby, trying to quiet her. "How did you find me?"

"I'm good at my job." He glanced around the living room, taking in the floral furniture, the baby playpen in the center of the carpet, and the framed photographs on the walls before focusing on the stairs leading to the second floor. "Is Ms. Buckley available?"

"She's upstairs. I'll go get her for you," Izzy volunteered.

"Nice try," Castillo said, rising from the sofa. "Then you can shimmy out an upstairs window to what, the drainpipe? A trellis?"

"I feel seen," Izzy said.

"Which one is it? A drainpipe or a trellis?" Castillo asked.

"The garage roof," Izzy admitted. "The yard slopes up to meet it. There's only a three-foot drop from there."

"What'd you do, scope the place out before you came over?" he asked.

"Gennifer grew up here and I was over a lot. We might have snuck out once or twice when we were in high school. Odessa, do you mind asking Gennifer to come downstairs?"

As I mounted the stairs, I heard Castillo chuckle. "I have to admire your spirit, Iz." If he was laughing, maybe he wasn't arresting Izzy. Or me, for that matter. Was I harboring a fugitive? Aiding and abetting? I sure hoped not.

"Hey, Gennifer, Detective Castillo is here to see you," I said, sticking my head into a room that looked like the pink factory had exploded. The walls were pink. The carpet was pink. The curtains were pink. The five-foot-tall bear shoved into a pink rocking chair was pink. On seeing me, the baby's cries escalated to wails.

Little Penny had chubby little cheeks and chubby little fists that she waved about in frustration. She had a full head of dark hair and if her screams were any indication, very healthy lungs. Poor thing. I often felt like crying when people woke me up from naps, too.

Gennifer nodded at me over the baby's head. "Coming."

I followed them back down the stairs, wondering if Vincent would notice if we slipped out while he was interrogating Gennifer. Izzy must have been on the same wavelength, because as soon as she saw me, she announced, "We'll just give you two some privacy," and headed for the front door.

"Sit," he told her. Izzy sat.

Gennifer stood in the center of her living room, bouncing the fussy baby on her hip. "Can I offer you something? Coffee? Water?"

"I'm fine," Castillo said. "I'm here to follow up on Ms. Marsh's death. Have you thought of anything new?"

Gennifer shook her head. "Sorry, no."

"Okay, then, I think we're finished here."

"That's it?" Izzy asked, popping up off the couch. "You've been hounding me for days and all you have for Gennifer is one lousy question?"

"Ms. Buckley has been very forthcoming and cooperative. And her fingerprints weren't found on the murder weapon."

"Yeah, well, did she tell you that there was a Facebook invite that went out for Vickie's little celebration party? Instead of focusing on the people who *did* show up, maybe you should be interrogating the ones that didn't."

"I'm sure there were plenty of people that weren't locked in the escape room when Ms. Marsh died. That's over eight million solid alibis in New York City alone. I'm more interested in the people that were in the room at the time." He shifted his focus to Gennifer. "But as long as I'm here, mind sharing that Facebook invite?"

Gennifer nodded. "Screenshots okay?" She handed Penny off to Izzy, retrieved her phone, and started scrolling through the app.

Castillo handed her his business card. "If you could email that to me, I'd appreciate it."

"Send me a copy, too," Izzy mouthed, pantomiming with her free hand.

Castillo's phone chimed. He scrolled through his email before standing. "Thank you very much, Ms. Buckley. Izzy, Odessa, let's go. I'm giving both of you a ride back to Williamsburg."

"I'd love to, but Penny just fell back asleep," Izzy said, rocking the baby. She really did look like a tiny angel, when she wasn't screaming at the top of her lungs.

"Give the baby back and get in the car," Castillo ordered.

We complied, following him back to his car. Izzy got in the front seat, and I climbed into the back. It wasn't the same marked cruiser Castillo had been driving the day before—or was that two days ago? The days were starting to blur together—but it was obviously police issue, from the nondescript paint job to the smell of one too many stakeouts. I sat in the back, in the middle so I wouldn't miss a word from the front seat. I mean, it's not eavesdropping if everyone's in the same car, right?

Right?

Which might have been true if anyone was talking.

"Are we under arrest?" Izzy asked.

"For what? Hanging out in Staten Island? They might revoke your hipster card if anyone finds out, but last I checked, it wasn't an arrestable offense. Technically, you haven't even left New York City."

"We're not hipsters," Izzy protested.

"You live in Williamsburg. You work in a bookstore that sells craft beer. You won a cornhole tournament. You might as well both have man buns and ironic mustache tattoos on your fingers."

"That doesn't make us . . ."

"You've been dodging my calls," he interrupted her.

"It's been a hectic few days."

"Yup, imagine it has been. Good thing I can save you, what, an hour or so on transit." He merged into a line of traffic heading for the Verrazzano-Narrows Bridge. At almost a mile long, the Verrazzano was one of the longest suspension bridges in the U.S. It was certainly the longest and highest bridge I had ever seen, and crossing it made my stomach coil up in knots. I wasn't scared of heights, not really, but flying across a double-decker bridge at what felt like a gazillion miles per hour with multiple lanes of traffic was where I drew the line.

"Thanks," Izzy said, looking out the passenger window. I didn't understand how she could do that so casually, when what I really wanted to do was close my eyes and hold my breath until we were safely on the other side. Of course, that wouldn't block out the sound of the wind buffeting the car or the heart-stopping thud of the tires going over supports. "Sorry. I know you're mad."

"I'm not mad. I'm disappointed." He let the silence stretch out again, before asking, "Where are you staying?"

"Around," Izzy responded.

"I'm not familiar with that neighborhood. Sorta hard to drop you off at 'around.'"

I breathed a sigh of relief. Not only was the end of the bridge in sight, but *dropping us off* seemed a whole lot more encouraging than *locking us up and throwing away the key.*

"You can drop us at Untapped," Izzy said, shifting in her seat. I could tell by the weariness in her voice that she was waiting for the other shoe to drop. The silence stretched out between us. I was half tempted to ask Castillo to turn on the radio, just to break the tension. But Izzy broke first. "I haven't been avoiding you, you know. I've been busy. Plus, after our last conversation, I wasn't sure you wanted to talk to me."

"Sure. I've left you twenty messages a day because I didn't want to talk."

"I told you . . ."

"Yeah, yeah. Your phone is dead. It's out of minutes. You can't find your charger. The dog ate it." He took one hand off the steering wheel and dropped it on her knee. "Here's the problem, Iz. I know you're not the murdering type, but as lead detective on this case, I need to convince my captain that I'm completely objective or she's gonna replace me with someone who isn't dating you. Someone who is gonna take one look at your finger-

NO MEMES OF ESCAPE

prints on the murder weapon, review the witness statements that all say the same thing—you didn't get along with the vic—and bring you in for a forty-eight-hour hold while they interrogate you and wait for you to slip up."

"I didn't *do* anything," Izzy protested.

"To some cops, that might not matter." He paused and let that sink in. "Here's the deal. You had beef with the vic. You provided the murder weapon—your cornhole trophy. I've only got five possible suspects, and none of you can give a full accounting as to where the other suspects were at any given time. It's impossible to narrow down the vic's death to less than an hour-long window when you all were in a locked room together, so all I have to go on is fingerprints. *Your* fingerprints. And you were one of the people who discovered the body. You see why this might be a problem?"

"I didn't do it," she repeated.

Castillo sighed. "I know." He squeezed her knee. The he let go so he could reach up and adjust the rearview mirror so he was looking at me. "Your fingerprints were on the trophy, too, Odessa."

I swallowed down the lump in my throat. "Well, yeah. It was our trophy."

"Every bit of evidence that points to Izzy could apply to you, too, except for one thing. You didn't know the vic, so you've got exactly zero motive."

"And what's my motive?" Izzy asked. "I got into a couple of hair-pulling matches with her in high school? I haven't even seen her in five years. I was as surprised as anyone to bump into her."

"Except that's not exactly true." Castillo turned his attention back to her. "You were on the Facebook invite."

"I was?"

"You hadn't replied one way or the other, but you were on the invite, according to the screenshots that Ms. Buckley provided," he said. "Something I wouldn't have even known existed if you hadn't brought it up."

"I haven't checked Facebook since, I don't know, since forever. I don't even remember my password anymore."

"And that is easy enough to check, if you grant me access to your phone and laptop. Or do I need a warrant?" He held out his hand. "Your phone. Please."

To her credit, Izzy handed it over without argument. With any other person, police or otherwise, she would have been better off holding on to it but if she truly had nothing to hide, this might be exactly what she needed to dig herself out of this hole.

"And your laptop?"

"It's at the bookstore," she said.

"Good." Castillo expertly navigated the streets of Williamsburg. Instead of circling the block to look for a parking space, he pulled up in front and double-parked, blocking in another car and taking up a whole lane of traffic. He put his flashers on, waited for a break, and got out of the car. He walked around and opened both of our doors at the same time. "Ladies."

"I'd rather wait here if you don't mind," I said. "You see, I called in sick earlier and . . ."

"The problem is, I can't trust you right now, Odessa. You lied to me. You pinkie swore you didn't know where Izzy was, when she was five feet away from you. Izzy's a bad influence. Which puts me in an awkward position and makes me less sympathetic."

Well, since he put it that way, I guess he did have a point. I got out of the car and looked up at Untapped Books & Café, at the familiar display in the window that was long overdue for a rotation and the faded awning that sagged a little in the middle. A few people browsed the shelves inside. A man walking by on the sidewalk paused to check out a poster advertising a local band, which someone had taped to the glass.

A wave of emotion hit me and I realized that sometime in the past two months, this unassuming bookstore-slash-café had become more than a job. It was my home away from home. My safe haven.

"You coming?"

I realized that Castillo was holding the door open for me, and I hurried up the steps.

Todd wasn't behind the front desk—thank goodness. In his place was Nan, again. "Thought you called out sick," she said, seeing me.

"I'm feeling better," I told her.

"Beer delivery didn't show up," she said. "Todd had to rent a van and drive to Queens to pick it up. Won't be back for"—she checked her watch—"another fifteen minutes or so. He's already in a mood. If I were you, I wouldn't be here when he gets back."

"Thanks for the heads-up."

"Where's your laptop?" Castillo asked Izzy.

"In the back," she replied, and led the way to the narrow hallway that separated the public spaces from the employees-only area. I assumed she was going to Todd's office. We had a cabinet in the kitchen where we stored our purses and bags when we're on shift, but when it got crowded, sometimes Todd would let us lock valuables in his bottom desk drawer. A laptop would be safer there than in the kitchen, where despite my co-workers' best intentions, it might grow legs and hop off.

But Izzy didn't stop at Todd's office. Instead, she continued to the stockroom.

Like the rest of Untapped, the stockroom was crammed to the brim with merchandise waiting to be sold. Only today, it felt even more cramped than normal. The boxes that held excess inventory were piled to the ceiling, and the extra uniform shirts and other supplies were pushed off to one side. "Whoever did inventory last did a lousy job of putting everything back where it belongs," I mused aloud.

Izzy wove her way through the boxes and disappeared behind a stack. I followed her and Castillo, and noticed that the store-room felt more claustrophobic because the boxes had been pushed forward away from the wall to create a narrow walkway. Only it wasn't a walkway. An unrolled sleeping bag was spread out in the narrow space, alongside an assorted collection of gar-bage bags and thirdhand luggage I recognized as Izzy's.

"Oh my actual goodness, you've been staying *here*?" I asked incredulously.

"NBD. It's just temporary, until I find something for us," she said, waving a hand at me.

But I knew it *was* a big deal. "Todd would lose his entire mind if he found out. You'd be out of a job on top of being homeless."

Izzy shrugged. "Nah. I fixed the air conditioner, scrubbed the walk-in, and kept Huckleberry company. If anything, he ought to be paying me overtime."

No wonder Huckleberry had been content to sleep in the shop instead of following random employees and customers home lately. I should have guessed that something was up. Izzy had been staying here under everyone's noses and no one had noticed, not even me.

Castillo pursed his lips. He grabbed the nearest bulging garbage sack and shoved it at me. Then he knelt and rolled up the sleeping bag. Once he looped the elastic around the bundle, he handed that to me as well.

"What do you think you're doing?" Izzy asked, positioning herself between him and the rest of her belongings.

"You're staying with me tonight," he said, brushing past her to pick up a battered suitcase that had seen better decades. "Bring the laptop."

"Won't you get in trouble if your captain finds out that Suspect Numero Uno is sleeping at your place?" she asked.

"Not nearly as much as if you get arrested for trespassing here after hours and I knew about it." He grabbed another bag. "Let's go."

I had no choice other than to retreat, as there was nowhere else to go. I lugged the heavy bag through the storeroom and into the hall. "It was just for a few nights," Izzy protested, bringing up the rear. "It's not like I was hurting anyone."

I bit my lip to keep from saying anything. This was my fault. She'd given up her previous living arrangement—as odd as it had been, staying in an abandoned schoolhouse with other squatters—because I'd convinced my aunt to let her stay with me. Then when my aunt showed up a month and a half early, Izzy hadn't had a backup plan.

The worst part was I should have figured it out sooner. Izzy showing up at the bookstore first thing in the morning and right before closing, even when she wasn't scheduled to work. The AC miraculously starting to work. Izzy popping up in the store when I never saw her come or go.

It was all totes obvious, in hindsight. And to be completely honest, it wasn't even the worst idea. There was a working bathroom—sans shower—and a fully functioning, well-stocked kitchen. She knew everyone's schedule, and like most of the employees, knew the alarm code if she accidentally set it off. The only thing she didn't have was a key to the door, and that wouldn't be a problem as long as she slipped in and out during operating hours.

To be completely honest, it was brilliant.

And sad.

"I'm sorry," I said as she drew even with me.

"For what?" she asked brightly. All traces of the embarrassment and annoyance she had shown in the stockroom were gone, replaced by her usual cheeriness.

"I've been a bad bestie," I admitted.

"Odessa, you've been a better friend to me the last coupla weeks than people I've known for years. You let me stay in that big, bougie apartment with a washer and dryer and a big kitchen and that gorgeous pool on the roof. You taught me how to use a sewing machine and split the grocery bills without complaint."

"You were the best roomie I've ever had," I told her, propping the front door open with my foot so she could follow me outside.

"I'm the only roomie you've ever had," she pointed out.

"True, but you made me coffee in the morning, then made

dinner *and* did the dishes. You even cleaned the cat's litter box and somehow got the old grump at the concierge's desk to like you."

"I've got a way with folks," she said.

"You do," I agreed.

Castillo unlocked the trunk of the sedan. Then he yanked at it. Nothing happened. He smacked it a few times, and the creaky trunk finally relented. He pushed the trunk open and stared inside it in dismay. It was filled to the brim with crumpled fast-food bags and what smelled like sweaty gym clothes. "Back seat it is," he said, slamming the trunk and walking around to open the passenger door.

As we filled the back seat, I asked, "Where am I supposed to sit?"

Castillo gave me a sideways glance. "Izzy will call you later."

I looked at her, not wanting to ask aloud if she was all right. She nodded and gave me a hug. "I'll be fine. Don't worry about me. Text me later." She got in the front seat and buckled her seat belt before Castillo pulled away from the curb.

I had the rest of the afternoon to kill, so I started down the sidewalk toward my aunt's apartment. A windowless white panel van pulled up next to me, then jerked over at such a sharp angle that the front-right tire jumped the curb. The van screeched to a stop and the driver's side door popped open.

20

Untapped Books & Café @untappedwilliamsburg · July 15
We might not sell coffee-scented beard oil, but a case of It's
Nine A.M. Somewhere coffee-flavored stout just arrived if
you're thirsty! And come on, who isn't? #coffee #craftbeer
#youknowyouwannatryit

I JUMPED BACK AND peered around the windshield to see an annoyed Todd Morris glaring back at me. Todd hollered at me from
the front seat of the delivery van, "Looks like someone's feeling
better."

"Um, yeah, I guess," I said, my heart still racing. I wasn't sure
what was worse, thinking that I was about to be run over, or bumping into my boss after lying and telling him I was too sick to work.

"Good. You can help me unload these."

"Shouldn't you, I don't know, go around back?" Most of the
deliveries came up the alley, where they were not blocking traffic and could unload directly into the kitchen instead of having
to lug their wares all the way through the bookstore, navigating
several steps inside and outside.

"Some son of a gun's been futzing with the dumpsters again, and there's no way I'm squeezing this beast back there. Go ahead, there's a trolley in the back."

It served me right for showing up to work after calling out sick, but I knew if I wasn't careful, Todd would make sure I didn't get paid a dime for helping him. "Sure thing, let me go clock in first."

"You're not in uniform," he pointed out. "Which means you're not on the clock."

I rolled my eyes. I was never gonna win this argument. I swung open the back doors of the van to reveal several crates of beer and a handcart. I pulled the trolley out and set it upright on the sidewalk. I carried the first crate to the trolley, noting that Todd was back in the driver's seat, enjoying the air-conditioned van. "Can I get a hand?" I asked.

"Not my job," Todd replied.

"Not my job, either." I was a waitress, pulling down less than minimum wage, plus tips—when I was lucky. That didn't stop Todd from demanding that I manage the store's social media accounts, help with the bookstore's inventory, and even walk the shop dog whenever Huckleberry needed to go outside. Now he wanted me to finish the beer delivery, off the clock.

Typical.

I dragged the first load back into the stockroom, forgetting that Izzy had rearranged things and there wasn't enough room. I had to stack the crates in the hallway instead. I went out with the trolley, and Todd helpfully pointed out, "You know, this would go a lot quicker if you took bigger loads."

"It would go even faster if you helped," I said. Maybe Castillo was right, and Izzy was a bad influence on me. Or living in New York City for six weeks was enough to override my ingrained Southern manners. In any event, I wasn't the quiet, overly polite person I'd been before arriving in Williamsburg.

"Like I said . . ."

"Except," I interrupted him to my surprise. I hardly ever interrupted anyone. I once caught myself apologizing to an automatic door. Another time I'd thanked a canned announcement played over the crackling subway speakers. ". . . this really *is* your job, a lot more than it is mine. You're the manager, but that doesn't just mean you sit on your keister all day and tell everyone else what to do. Sometimes you gotta get your hands dirty, too."

Instead of bursting into flames or whatever I might have expected, Todd turned off the engine, got out of the van, and came around to the back. "You know, I liked you a whole lot better when you first started working here," he said, grabbing a case of beer and moving it to the trolley.

I lugged the heavy load up the stairs into Untapped, navigated through the narrow pathway between bookshelves—honestly, how come the fire marshal hadn't shut us down yet was anyone's guess—and down the steps into the café. The beer refrigerator was almost empty, so I pulled out the cold ones, shoved as many of the newly delivered ones as I could fit inside, leaving just enough room to put the cold ones back in front before I closed the door. Beer fridge stocked and ready for business, I rolled the trolley toward the stockroom and offloaded the remainder in the hallway.

That done, I headed toward the kitchen. Parker had his back to me. He reached into the walk-in refrigerator and came out with a flat of eggs. "Oh! I thought you weren't coming in today," he said as he put the eggs on the counter. "Todd said you called out sick."

"I was playing hooky," I admitted. "I've been wanting to talk to you."

"Oh?" Parker wiped his arm across his forehead. "I guess I've been wanting to talk to you, too."

Great. Way to make this even more awkward. "I found out this morning that Izzy opened a Tinder account for me. And apparently has been talking to a bunch of guys, as me, on my behalf."

"Oh," he said, for the third time in as many minutes.

"I was trying to explain to her what a bad idea that was because I'm really not looking for a relationship right now when I noticed that you were one of my matches."

"And?" He was staring at me with a deliberately blank expression.

"And you know how important our friendship is to me," I started.

"Of course. I matched with you as a lark. I thought it was funny. I'm not even really active on Tinder anymore, not since I started going out with Hazel."

"So, it's serious with you two?" I asked.

"Not sure. Maybe it could be. She's nice."

"That's good to hear," I told him. "I hope this doesn't change anything between us."

Parker reached out and punched me on the shoulder, lightly, like we were old buddies instead of two coworkers having an awkward conversation about dating profiles on an app that I never even intended to use. "No worries. Hey, Odessa, why don't eggs tell each other jokes?" Without waiting for me to respond, he said, "Because they'd crack each other up."

I groaned. Parker had the worst sense of humor.

He began cracking eggs into a large bowl. "I'm playing around with tomorrow's menu. What do you think, chicken and apple salad for the carnivores, and toasted walnut and avocado sandwiches for the vegans? And I've got a recipe for gluten-free, dairy-free fudge brownies I've been wanting to take for a test-drive."

"Yum," I said. My horizons, and palate, had been vastly expanded, thanks in no small part to Parker's culinary creativity and the wealth of food trucks parked on every street. "Thanks, Parker."

"For?" He looked genuinely confused.

"For encouraging me to try new things."

Nan stuck her head into the pass-thru window. "Are you working or what?" she asked me. "I've been covering the cash register in the bookstore and waiting tables at the same time since we opened this morning. Good thing we're slow today, but I could really use a smoke break."

"Yeah, I'm working. Give me a second."

I headed back into the hall and finally punched in. Then I grabbed an extra neon green polo shirt from the box in the stockroom. It seemed like a waste, knowing this might be my second-to-last shift, but I hadn't expected to go into work, so I hadn't brought a shirt with me. I could wash it and return it, but I doubted even Todd would notice a single missing shirt. I fastened my apron around my waist, pinned my shiny new name tag to my shirt above the Untapped Books & Café logo, and reported for duty.

Nan was right about it being slow. In between serving tables, I had time to rearrange the beer cooler so that the servers could easily see what was in stock. Along with the usual labels, we had some new flavors, including It's Nine A.M. Somewhere coffee-flavored stout, Beam Me Up Berry lager, and Orange Is the New Beer IPA. The last one sounded intriguing, and I promised myself I'd sample it after it had a chance to chill.

The lunch rush was long over when a woman entered the café alone. That in itself wasn't unusual, but when she settled into her chair and waved me over, I bit back a sigh. Marlie Robinson, the Realtor. Today's ensemble was a suit dress in various colors of purple and green that was almost vintage enough to be cool again. A ginormous necklace of interlaced peacock feathers graced her long neck.

If the death of her coworker was bothering her, I certainly couldn't see any outward sign.

"Marlie," I said, as genuinely welcoming as I could manage, "what can I get for you? Water? Tea? Or would you like something stronger?"

"Odessa, dear, I feel like we might have gotten off on the wrong foot."

Whatever could have given her that idea? That she'd tried to convince me to rent a murder apartment? Or maybe it was that Izzy had called her—and by extension, all apartment brokers—a vulture.

"Nothing to worry about. We've got a delicious cold-cut sub

on locally baked honey-wheat bread as the special of the day, or if you'd prefer, we have several meatless options as well. If you're lucky, we might still have a serving or two remaining of the cook's infamous five-cheese macaroni. If you're looking for something sweet there are homemade lemon bars."

"Why don't you have a seat?" she asked, instead of ordering.

"I'd love to, but I've got several tables to attend to." I swept my arm out, indicating the other tables in the café. Not exactly rush hour, but a plausible excuse to remain standing.

"Suit yourself. I understand your friend has a chip on her shoulder about apartment brokers."

"That's an understatement," I agreed.

"It can be hard, paying a little extra for a service that seems unnecessary. I just want to help you find an apartment you love that's in your budget. But more than that, I can help you navigate the murky waters of real estate. I can tell you what neighborhoods are safe and which landlords are responsive to problems. More importantly, I act as your go-between even after you move in and am available to resolve disputes or address concerns in a way that property owners rarely are. And I'll have you know that my interests are always with the renter."

"Are they?" I blurted out. "Are they really? It seems to me that apartment brokers make money whether or not the renters are happy. Since people can't afford to move, you don't get a lot of repeat customers from renters. Which means the real money is keeping the building owners happy, right?"

"That's how a lot of brokers see it," Marlie admitted. "Goodness knows that Vickie was one of them. Vickie had a killer instinct. That's why she was always going to outperform me. She focused on commission, not customer satisfaction."

"And that's why she was number one in your office."

Marlie nodded amicably. "Exactly. Although I suppose I'm number one now. For the time being, anyway. Another Vickie will come along, eventually. Can I give you some free advice?"

"Sure," I said. What could it hurt?

"No matter how good you are at what you do, there is always someone hungrier than you are nipping at your heels."

"Waiting tables isn't quite as competitive as real estate," I pointed out. Then again, Nan had only been working at Untapped a few days and already got the best shifts and extra responsibility. At the rate she was going, she'd be assistant manager within the month.

"Don't fool yourself. Everything's a competition. Speaking of which, if you want to beat someone to an apartment, you need someone like me in your corner. How about I set up some viewing appointments for you tomorrow. How does eleven o'clock sound?"

"I'm sorry we got our wires crossed, but I'm set." To be strictly honest, as much as I wanted an apartment in Williamsburg, I didn't have the up-front money for a broker. I had to trust that Izzy would come through for us. "Can I get you something from the kitchen?"

"Coffee will be fine," she said.

"Comin' right up." I poured her a mug and set it down on the table in front of her. "Holler if you change your mind about ordering food." I hurried away before she could try any of her hard-sale tactics again, and hid just inside of the kitchen, where I could keep an eye on the occupied tables without having to talk to Marlie.

"Friend of yours?" Parker asked.

"Some apartment broker that is trying to get me to open a vein for her."

"Vampires," he said, knitting his brows together. "When I first moved to Brooklyn, I fell for the broker racket. Ended up closing on the apartment, then finding out I couldn't move in for three whole months because it was suddenly 'under construction.' When I finally got the keys, the electricity and water only worked intermittently. The range was broken. The toilet didn't flush, and don't even get me started about the water pressure in the shower. There was only one tiny window in the entire place, and it was busted."

"That sounds horrible! What did you do?"

"I lodged a complaint. A lot of complaints. I tried to get my money back, but the broker never returned my calls and was always out of the office when I went by. Landlord wasn't much better. I even filed a grievance with the city but nothing ever came of it. I'd already sunk so much money into the place that I didn't have a lot of options left."

"Where did you end up living?" I asked.

"There. I fixed up the window best I could with duct tape and cardboard. Bought a new toilet from the hardware store and installed it myself. It's annoying not having a working stove on the regular, but we bought a multiuse air-fryer-slash-toaster-slash-oven and use the range for storage. With a few creative curtains and a lot of respecting each other's privacy, I converted a studio into a one bedroom that I split with my roomies."

"Wait a sec, you *still* live there?"

"Why not?" Parker asked. "It's on a great block, and the rent is reasonable, split three ways. I've already invested a fortune in broker's fees. What else can I do? Get suckered into someplace even worse and have to start all over again?"

"Izzy was right. Apartment brokers are the worst," I said.

"The absolute worst," Parker agreed. He ducked his head so he had a clear view through the order window, and one side of his lip curled up mischievously. "How about you send over a little something? On the house."

I shook my head. I didn't particularly like Marlie, but I didn't want to be party to Parker doing something untoward to her food. "She's not worth it."

"Speak for yourself," he grumbled, then went back to stirring something in a large bowl.

Marlie finished up her coffee and left a few dollars on the table to cover the cost of the drink with a few cents left over for a tip. Coming from a woman who survived on commission, I thought that was rude. If I could afford to eat, I could afford to tip. Generously.

She also left her business card, which I promptly tossed in the recycle bin. For the past few days, I'd been obsessed over the murder of Vickie Marsh, but the more I learned about her, the harder it was to empathize with her. She bullied her "friends." She reveled in stealing other people's boyfriends right out from under them. And to top it all off, she was a ruthless apartment broker.

Not that she deserved to die. No one did. But if I absolutely had to choose between, say, a sweet nun who fostered rescue kittens and an apartment broker, I know who I'd save first. And it wouldn't have been Vickie.

I still had no idea who had killed her, but now that it was obvious that Castillo wasn't planning on charging Izzy with a crime anytime soon, I wasn't sure if it mattered to me personally. I hadn't known Vickie for more than an hour. I didn't like the idea of a killer getting away with literal murder, but was it really any of my business? Castillo was a competent cop, and he was on the case.

For now.

What would happen if his boss found out that Castillo was currently living with the prime suspect? Would he get removed from the investigation? If so, would the detective that replaced him be so reasonable? I doubted it.

Which meant I needed to figure out who the real killer was, and I was running out of time.

21

Untapped Books & Café @untappedwilliamsburg · July 15
Looking for a good mystery? Romance? Comedy? Thriller?
Have we got some great suggestions for you! Swing by the
bookstore to check out the latest arrivals in traditional and
indie novels. #bookstore #newarrivals #Williamsburg

THE GOOD THING about working in food service—or any service
job, really—was that except when it's slammed, there's plenty of
time to think.

The *bad* thing about working in food service was pretty much
the exact same thing.

I mean, there were drawbacks, don't get me wrong. It's hard
work for little pay, but I did enjoy meeting new people and serving them stellar food along with an amazing selection of beers.
Speaking of which, Orange Is the New Beer turned out to be a
delicious addition to our menu, and I hoped that Todd would
keep ordering it. It was light and hoppy like most IPAs, but without a bitter aftertaste.

I wondered how many beers Izzy sampled while she was living in the stockroom, and how many meals she made out of the contents of the walk-in fridge. If she had stayed much longer, Todd would have eventually noticed. He might not take strict notice of how many heads of lettuce were in the walk-in at any given moment, but he knew exactly how many bottles of beer we had at any given time. He was kind of a genius when it came to inventory, at least for the valuable stock.

But I wasn't worried about Izzy drinking a beer or two from the cooler, especially knowing that she likely put money in the till the next morning to cover it. I was relieved she was staying with Castillo for the time being. I was mostly anxious about what would happen to her in the long run. On the plus side, if she was tried and (wrongly) convicted of Vickie's murder, she'd have guaranteed food and lodging at the hands of the Bureau of Prisons. The irony that the prison system was likely better than the apartment brokerage racket in New York City did not escape me.

Izzy wasn't going to jail. Not if I had any say about it. She was innocent. I was fully convinced of that. Which narrowed the possible suspects considerably to the people locked in the escape room.

Except, the escape room wasn't *precisely* locked.

I thought back to what the Game Master had said when he closed the first door behind us. I hadn't been paying close attention, with everything else going on, but I distinctly remembered hearing him say that due to fire regulations or something, the door wouldn't be locked behind us, but if we opened it and walked out, the game was over.

Anyone could have come into the room after us, and we might not have ever noticed.

I wondered if Castillo knew that. If he had never been in an escape room—and I didn't have any reason to believe he had—he might believe that we were physically locked in the room. I thought back to him interrogating me to try to remember if the subject had ever come up, but I'd still been shook over Vickie's death and a lot of things had happened in the last few days. I couldn't be expected to recall every single detail.

Even if we weren't exactly locked in together, we might as well have been. It wasn't like anyone could have walked in off the street and joined the room without the Game Master noticing them. Sure, there were other games going, but they were all busy in their own rooms. I'd only seen one proctor—Brandon in the ill-fitting tuxedo. I had to assume his attention was split between multiple games. I guess if someone was really motivated, they could book one of the other rooms at the same time as we were in the Clueless room, wait until everyone was distracted, and sneak in to kill Vickie.

Who knew we were there, in that particular escape room, at that exact time?

Potentially, anyone on the Facebook invite.

Nadia and her fiancée, Becks, certainly knew. They'd paid their share with every intention of joining the outing, so they would have had precise details. I needed to get my hands on the Facebook invite to see how much information Vickie had shared, and how many people she had shared it with. Castillo would never show me, but Izzy had been invited and she certainly would.

I loved growing up in the information age. Even when I was a kid, practically everyone had internet in their homes. Computers became relatively inexpensive and existed almost everywhere from the classroom to the living room. I got my first smartphone when I was in middle school, about the same time I opened a Myspace account. I literally could not recall a time that I wasn't on the internet—surfing, searching, and sharing.

It never seemed like a big deal before. It was second nature to check in on the current social media platform of the moment anytime I went somewhere even slightly interesting. It wasn't until I moved to Williamsburg that I started to be more conscious of how much information I was actually sharing online, and even then, I didn't know if I actually grew that much more careful. I still broadcast my location without giving it a second thought half the time.

What if Vickie's Facebook invitation had given her killer everything they had needed to find her and murder her?

But that was silly, wasn't it?

Even if someone really, really wanted her dead—and for all of her flaws I couldn't imagine anyone hating her enough to murder her—it was a little *too* complicated. Book an adjoining escape room, somehow manage to get Vickie alone, kill her, and slip out without anyone else in the group seeing them or getting caught on camera? That seemed a little far-fetched even for my admittedly overactive imagination.

I wasn't completely ready to rule out Nadia, Becks, and the other invitees as suspects, but even if any of them wanted to hurt Vickie, they weren't in the room with us. Not like I could prove that Becks had a headache that day, or even that they were both together, but they had if not an iron-clad alibi, at least a plastic-clad one. As for the other invitees? Maybe they *could* sneak into the game in progress but there were easier ways to kill someone.

That limited the field to the six of us in the escape room. Vickie didn't bludgeon herself over the head. I trusted Izzy implicitly and I certainly hadn't hurt anyone. That narrowed the list down to the three original suspects.

Marlie was my first choice. But if I was being honest with myself, I was biased because she was an apartment broker. I forced myself to be objective. Marlie worked with Vickie in a competitive industry. What was it that Vickie was celebrating? She had won an award for being the best in the office for twelve months in a row. Marlie played it off as nonchalant that she was always second fiddle to Vickie, but she had to be jealous. She was at least fifteen years older than Vickie. How must it feel to know that someone practically half her age was crushing it?

I paused in my musings to bring refills to the table with the subway map table topper surrounded by men who looked—and smelled—like they had spent the last hour or two in the gym. They'd spent ten minutes grilling me on the caloric content of every item on the menu, especially the beers, before deciding on plain grilled chicken and room-temperature water, which seemed like a waste of Parker's culinary genius, if you asked me.

As soon as there was a lull, my thoughts wandered back to the escape room murder. Unlike Marlie, Gennifer seemed nice. I'd caught a glimpse of a competitive streak at the escape room, but Izzy liked her. They went way back, but they hadn't been in contact for years, and people changed over time. Gennifer was a mother, so her focus was probably more on raising a little one instead of competing with someone she'd gone to high school with half a decade ago. They weren't even in the same industry, as far as I knew, so if there was any jealousy, it wasn't professional. Gennifer seemed happily married and didn't need Vickie's Realtor services, so I was at a loss for a possibly motive.

From all accounts, Vickie hadn't been the nicest person. She'd bullied Gennifer when they were kids, but high school was long enough ago to cool even the hottest tempers. Gennifer didn't seem to hold a grudge. Which, come to think of it, was weird. I put on a friendly face when Carin Butcher, my childhood bully, came into the Crawdad Shack back home, but I was never going to like her, much less hang out with her. I had to chalk it up to Gennifer being a *very* forgiving person.

That is, unless she was lying and still held a grudge, but she didn't seem the type.

Then there was Amanda. I'd love to talk to her again. She admitted that Vickie stole her boyfriend back in college, but conveniently forgot to mention it had happened again recently. Gennifer told us that Vickie was even bragging about stealing Amanda's current boyfriend and that they were arguing about something on the way to the escape room. What were they arguing about, if not boyfriends?

Plus, there was the matter of Amanda's missing photos. Amanda seemed completely obsessed with Instagram and kept a ton of pictures on her phone that didn't make the cut or she wouldn't always be running out of space like she claimed. Why had she deleted a chunk of them around the time that we were in the escape room? What was she trying to hide?

The table with faded birthday wrapping paper under the Plexiglas protector had finished their meals fifteen minutes ago and I'd brought their check already, but no one seemed in a hurry to leave. Which was just ducky with me. Most of the tables were empty anyway, and the longer they lingered, the greater the chances were that they would order something else that would add a few more dollars to their tip.

My only other customer was an older gentleman who wore a bulky hand-knit sweater despite the heat wave outside. He'd sat himself at the counter and ordered coffee, black. I checked on occasion to see if he needed a refill yet, but as far as I could tell, he hadn't even touched it. "Can I freshen that up for you?" I offered.

"No thanks, doll," he replied, winking at me.

I knew I should have been offended, but as a waitress, I'd gotten used to more than my share of overly familiar customers. "Let me know if you change your mind," I told the older gentleman.

I retreated to the corner of the café where I could survey the tables without hovering and wondered what I was going to do about Vickie. As far as I could tell, none of the top three suspects popped out at me. None of them were exactly Vickie's biggest fan, but that didn't mean they had murderous intent. Had I been asking the wrong questions? Or maybe they were all just really good actors.

In any event, I wasn't going to solve this case by thinking about it in between serving tables. I needed to *do* something. I loved listening to true crime podcasts. One of my favorites featured a big dramatic scene at the end when the police detective corralled all the suspects in one room and asked a few vague questions to confirm their suspicions before making the big reveal.

If only I could do something like that.

Then it hit me—I could.

I pulled out my phone and called Izzy. She answered on the second ring, to my surprise. "Hey, glad to see you're picking up for once," I teased.

On the other end of the line, I could practically hear her roll her eyes at me. "Doofus. What's up?"

"I've got an idea."

"Uh-oh," she replied.

"Bear with me. We round up everyone who was in the escape room and convince them to go back with us and try the game again."

"To what end?" Izzy asked.

"We get them to return to the scene of the crime and trick one of them into confessing. Easy, peasy. Vickie's killer is exposed, and you're off the hook with all the loose ends tied up in a neat little bow."

"I'm totally here for it. Gimme a minute to see what I can do, and I'll get back to you soon about Escape Room Two: Escape Harder."

"Thanks," I told her, ending the call. If anyone could arrange to get everyone back together to the scene of the crime, it was Izzy.

Sure enough, fifteen minutes later, she texted me to say we were on. She was even able to use the coupons we got last time to lower the cost. I didn't know how she'd managed to reserve the escape room on short notice or get everyone to agree to it, but we were set for this evening. If Izzy ever got tired of working at Untapped, she'd make a killing as an event planner.

I would have just enough time to go home, check in with my aunt, and change before meeting up with Izzy, assuming that my relief was on time. She wasn't. A mere five minutes before I had to leave to get to the escape room, Emilie breezed in. Her hair was rolled into big poufy curls held back by a black handkerchief decorated with pink skulls. She wore a coordinating black-and-pink-checkered skirt fluffed out by layers of petticoats that whooshed when she walked. The garish Untapped Books & Café neon green polo shirt was such an incongruous addition to her outfit that she *almost* made it work.

Almost.

I untied my apron and tossed it over my shoulder. "Table Seven is ready to order, Table Eleven is debating dessert, the dude at the counter has been sitting there for ages but swears he's good, and Table Six should be ready for their check." I handed her the notepad where I kept track of orders.

"Hello to you, too," Emilie said, grinning widely. Her lips were fire-engine red. I was more of a lip gloss girl, but I was impressed with her ability to have perfectly applied makeup at all times.

"Hey. Sorry, didn't mean to be short, I'm in a hurry."

"No need to apologize," she replied with another toothy grin.

"Push the potato salad, Parker made a ton, but it's not moving. We're out of pita bread and just got in a shipment of beer so we have a great selection. I recommend the Orange Is the New Beer IPA. And by the way, cute scarf."

"Thanks! And sorry for being late, I forgot I was scheduled to work tonight, until Andre called and asked me where I was."

"No worries." That was odd. Normally, it was Todd who ended up hassling anyone who was late for their shift. Then again, the downside for this new, more relaxed Todd might be that now that he was distracted by his internet dates, he was dropping the ball at work. I wondered if today's beer shipment had been the shipper's fault after all, or if Todd had forgotten to place the order last week.

I turned to wave at Parker but he was busy. I headed back toward the hall, where I hung my apron on its hook with a pang of sadness. This might be my last time using this hook. If I didn't find an apartment in the next twenty-four hours, tomorrow at the end of my shift, I would have to turn my apron in. It would be washed and reissued to my replacement, or more likely, a string of replacements. Turnover at a café like Untapped was high and the average server lasted six months or less.

I stopped to check on Huckleberry. He'd managed to knock over a stack of books in his never-ending quest to find the best spots to nap, and was on his back, sound asleep in a bright shaft of sunshine, surrounded by this month's employee picks. One ear was flipped inside out, his tongue lolled out of his mouth, and there was a thin line of drool coming from his muzzle. I snapped a picture and posted it with the caption "Untapped Books & Café—books *and* craft beer? What could possibly go wrong?" I reshelved the scattered books and scratched his belly without ever waking him up.

The bell over the door jingled and Raleigh stepped inside. Like last night, his hair was neatly buzzed, but tonight he had on red plastic-rimmed glasses and his T-shirt advertised the 1988 Calgary Olympics. "Fancy bumping into you here," he said, resting his hand on my shoulder.

"Hey, Raleigh. I've got to run, but Emilie can seat you."

He shook his head, a look of confusion on his face. "I thought you wanted to meet here."

"What are you talking about?"

"You said something about an escape room?"

I groaned. Izzy. "Sorry for the mix-up. Let me guess, you got a message on Tinder?"

He chuckled. "Of course. That's how we've been communicating."

"Not exactly." The door chimed and I stepped into a cross aisle to make room for the new customer to enter. Raleigh followed my lead, standing a little closer to me than I would have liked. He was tall enough to reach the top shelf with ease, which meant I had to crane my neck to look up to him when he was this close. "I'm not the person you've been talking with online."

22

Chef Parker @2_Bee_Or_Not_2_Bee · July 15
What did the Millennial do for their 25th birthday? They
worked a double. Because they're poor, have overwhelming
student loan debt, and have no medical insurance. #dadjokes
#happyalmostbirthdaytome

RALEIGH SHRUGGED. "COME on, no one is exactly who they say they
are online. Although, I have to admit I was pleasantly surprised
by you. You're the real deal."

"But that's just it. You weren't talking to me. You were talking
to my friend, who was pretending to be me."

"Are you telling me I've been catfished?" Raleigh asked, his
brow wrinkling.

Unlike some men who let their facial hair explode in whatever direction it liked, including their ears and neck, Raleigh
probably spent more time on personal grooming than I did. His
eyebrows were as neat and ordered as his goatee, with nary a
sign of the dreaded unibrow. Despite his dark hair, I didn't see
any telltale black chest hair peeking out of the collar of his ringer

tee. His skin looked moisturized and if he had any pores, they would only be visible under an electron microscope. Add in long, full eyelashes and I was almost jealous of him.

None of which made this conversation any easier.

"Not exactly. I told her I wasn't interested in dating, but she went ahead and opened a Tinder account for me anyway. I just found out she's been talking to my matches without my knowledge so she can set me up on dates." I thought back to the all of the odd text messages, gifts, and the attempted video chat. Izzy had been busy.

"What a horrible friend!" he exclaimed.

"She meant well," I said, defending her. I could get mad at Izzy for doing all this behind my back, but I wasn't gonna let Raleigh talk smack about my bestie. "She thought she was helping."

He took a deep breath, unconsciously scratching at his elbow. "Sorry. That was uncalled for. It's cringy, you know. I really liked you, or at least the you that I had such great conversations with."

Great. Apparently, Izzy was a modern-day Cyrano de Bergerac. "I'd introduce you two, but she already has a boyfriend."

"Isn't that always the case? But this clears up why you act so different in person than you did over IM. I wrote it off as you being shy or something. I thought we had a real connection, but you acted like you didn't know me at all. I guess that's because you didn't." He sighed. "And the escape room? Was that a ruse, too?"

"No, that's real," I admitted. "In fact, I'm heading there now. I'm running late."

"Mind if I tag along?"

Seriously? I told Raleigh that I wasn't at all who or what he thought, and he still wanted to spend time with me? Those must have been some spectacular conversations he'd had with Izzy.

"Odessa, wait up!" I turned to see Parker hurrying toward us. "I'm glad I caught you. Instead of waiting for Wednesday, how about we go get that coffee and Limoncello cake we talked about now?" He looked over at me and then back to Raleigh. "Am I interrupting something?"

"Nope," I replied. "Parker, this is Raleigh. We, um, kinda met on Tinder. Raleigh, this is my good friend Parker." They exchanged curt nods. "Sorry, Parker, I'm gonna have to take a rain check on that Limoncello cake. I am supposed to be meeting Izzy at the escape room in . . ." I glanced at the clock on the wall over the front desk. It was enormous, a custom piece with heavy hands in the middle ringed by number-themed books that we swapped out whenever we got bored. The long hand was almost pointing at *Twelve Years a Slave*. I could see that someone had removed my most recent contribution, *Life of Pi*, which I had hung just a tad bit lower than the previous "three" book had been. "Well, now, actually."

"I'll walk with you," Parker offered.

"I already Venmo'd you for my escape room ticket," Raleigh said. "So I might as well come along."

"Another escape room?" Parker asked. "This is your second in, what, a week? Next thing you know, you're gonna be one of those escape room junkies that goes every weekend."

"I doubt that," I said. "They're expensive. Why don't you and Hazel join us?" I had no idea how many people could participate in an escape room or how many people were already coming, but it was comforting to know that there would be at least another friendly face there.

Not that Raleigh wasn't friendly, I just didn't know him very well. Or at all.

"Hazel's got plans, but I'd love to tag along," Parker agreed. He was closer to the front door, so he opened it and gestured to Raleigh. "After you." I followed Raleigh out onto the sidewalk.

It was nearing sunset, and the sun was piercing between the Manhattan high-rise buildings on the other side of the river. It was still stifling outside, and I was glad I'd worn a breathable skirt. However, I'd forgotten to change out of my work shirt. I tugged at the stiff collar and willed myself not to sweat. I'd learned the hard way that these cheapo dyed polos were *not* color safe and unless I wanted to look like the Incredible Hulk, I'd do best to avoid sweaty skin coming into contact with the shirt until I'd had a chance to wash it a few times.

We arrived at the building on 5th Street, and I noticed a "For Sale" sign on the door below the "Verrazzano-Narrows Escape!" sign, along with a phone number and website address for the same company that Vickie Marsh and Marlie Robbinson worked for. I hadn't noticed the sign the last time we were here. Vickie's picture was on the sign as the listing agent. That was interesting. I wondered if the companies inside would soon be homeless or if they would continue to lease space from the new owner.

The idea that someone could own an entire building in New York City blew my mind. I couldn't even afford bus fare to get home to Piney Island. I couldn't fathom scraping up enough money to pay rent for a studio apartment in Williamsburg, much less the exorbitant real estate broker fee.

We approached the sign-in desk, and to my surprise, I instantly recognized a familiar face behind the counter. Yes, one of the two men was the same pimply-faced tuxedo-wearing man who had checked us in last time, but my attention was drawn to the *other* clerk. Standing there in a crisp white shirt and shiny black pants, with a sparkly red bow tie around his neck was Detective Vincent Castillo.

He narrowed his eyes at me and gave me a shake of the head so slight that if I wasn't focused completely on him, I would have missed it.

"Hi," I said. "Three more for the Clueless room. I see the rest of our party is already here."

"Aren't you . . ." Parker started to ask, and I stomped on his foot, cutting him off in midsentence. I'd forgotten that he had to have seen Castillo hanging around Untapped Books & Café before and likely recognized him.

"Everyone needs to sign in," I said, grabbing clipboards that I shoved at Parker and Raleigh. If the Game Master noticed Parker's gaffe, he didn't show any sign of it. I got another clipboard for myself and turned to wave at the assorted women assembled on the waiting room chairs. "Hey, y'all. This is Parker and Raleigh," I announced to the room.

Gennifer waved back. Marlie was there, too. She glanced at them without much interest. She was dressed as usual in business attire that had been probably been purchased in a store that had gone out of business a decade ago. Her clothes were in great condition for their age, but they were out of fashion. Then again, maybe there were clothing websites that catered exclusively to real estate agents permanently stuck in the nineties.

Amanda was taking selfies of herself, of course. She didn't

notice us. She was too busy reviewing her pictures and then trying again with a slightly different angle.

Finally, there was Izzy. She looked bored as she played with her phone, but then my phone buzzed. It was a text from her. Act cool! it said, followed by a winky-face emoji. I gave her a half grin. It would have been nicer if she had warned me before I noticed Castillo behind the counter.

"Excuse me, ma'am, I need a copy of your driver's license," Castillo said, holding out his hand when I turned back toward the counter.

"Yeah, alrighty, sure." As I dug for my wallet, Parker and Raleigh must have been in a race to see who could produce their driver's license first, and both slapped their ID cards down on the counter at the same time. I noticed that Raleigh's was an actual driver's license, whereas Parker's was a state ID. Considering how few native New Yorkers ever needed to learn how to drive a car, much less own one, it wasn't surprising.

"Follow me," Castillo said, indicating me. I gathered up the other IDs and followed him into an adjacent room where he lined up the IDs on a copier. "You don't know me," he said.

"I'm starting to think I really don't," I agreed.

"When Izzy told me your plan, I knew I couldn't talk you two out of it, but I wasn't about to let you get locked in a room with a bunch of potential murderers."

"You know the door isn't really locked, right?"

"Huh?" he asked.

"Ask the other guy, the Game Master. He'll explain."

"He is going to give me access to the cameras so I can watch

NO MEMES OF ESCAPE

your every move. Company policy is they only observe but never record, so I'm not taking my eyes off that screen."

"Oh yeah? That's inconvenient that they don't have a tape of Vickie's death."

"That's what I thought, too. Apparently, there was a legal kerfuffle a while back . . ." He shook his head to get himself back on track. "In any event, I'll be watching closely, and I'm just a scream away."

It was cute how overprotective he was of me and Izzy, but then again, he might be more worried about protecting his crime scene or his pool of suspects. With Castillo, it was hard to tell. "You interrogated everyone here, even me. Aren't you afraid they'll recognize you?"

"Who? Me?" He pointed to his name tag. "My name is Trainee. I'm invisible. Those ladies haven't so much as made eye contact with me. No one notices the help. I mean, tell me one thing about the last cabbie you met."

"His name was Raoul. He was born and raised in Jamaica, Queens. He has two daughters, nine and twelve, and raises angora bunny rabbits that his kids sell in Grand Central Terminal on the weekends. Should I go on?"

"Only you, Odessa," Castillo said, shaking his head, but he sounded grudgingly impressed.

"Problems?" The tuxedo-clad Game Master stuck his head in the room.

"Machine jammed," Castillo lied, and pushed the button. He took the copy and handed me the IDs, walking out of the room without so much as a backward glance at me.

"I'm so glad you were able to squeeze us in today," I told him. "Brandon, right?"

He looked impressed that I'd remembered. My little talent for remembering names sure did come in handy. "You guys got lucky. The cops released the room thirty seconds before your friend called to make a reservation. It's about time. It was one of our most popular rooms before, and now that, well, you know, requests have been flooding in."

Ew. "People specifically want that room *because* someone was murdered in it?" I asked as I followed him back to the waiting room. Maybe the landlord had made a mistake when he discounted the Williamsburg Slasher apartment. I hadn't realized that a gruesome murder scene might actually make it more attractive to some people.

He shrugged. "I mean, you guys were pretty adamant about wanting this room, weren't you?"

"That's just because we thought that finishing the room would be a fitting way to say goodbye to our friend." If only that were the real reason we were here. That would be a nice tribute, instead of searching for a killer.

"Whatever," he said. He raised his voice and addressed the rest of the assembled players. "If we're all ready? Welcome to Verrazzano-Narrows Escape!, Williamsburg's premier escape room experience. In a minute, your exciting experience will begin. Please follow me."

He led us to Door Three, the same room as we'd entered last time, and gave us the same speech, word for word. He went over safety and rules with about as much enthusiasm as someone might muster up to order a pizza over the phone if the website

NO MEMES OF ESCAPE

was down and they couldn't order online. I admit I wasn't paying much attention to him. Instead, I was watching the three suspects as closely as I could without being weird about it.

On either side of me, Parker and Raleigh listened to his every word as if there might be a quiz later. "Good luck," Brandon the Game Master intoned, and opened the door. We all crammed inside the dark room. I held my breath as the door clanged shut behind us.

"There's a switch on the wall somewhere," Izzy said, and everyone shuffled. A few seconds later, the lights clicked on, illuminating the glowing numbers on the far wall. "Anyone remember what number we pushed last time?"

"Four," I said, reasonably sure that was it. If I was wrong, we would have another chance, but I wasn't wrong. The door unlocked and swung open to reveal the library.

The last time we'd been in here, the room had seemed impressive with its attention to detail and the overwhelming number of objects. Add in the noise of everyone talking at once and the confusion of not knowing what to do next, it was downright mystical. Now the shine had worn off and it wasn't just because my last memory of this room had been Vickie lying facedown in a pool of blood just over there.

I forced myself to turn my attention elsewhere.

The room felt cheaper this time around. I was seeing painted plywood and sloppily constructed bookshelves where before it had been a magnificent library. Even the props looked faker. "*Moby-Dick* in the fish tank," I said, pointing to the table in the middle of the room. "And someone grab that flashlight, too."

There might be other clues that we were missing, vital to

solving puzzles farther down the road, but I wanted to be out of this room as quickly as humanly possible. Parker reached the book first and held it up. "What next?"

"It goes in that slot up there," Izzy said, pointing at the wall. "Hold the ladder still for me?"

"No need," Raleigh said, plucking the book out of Parker's hand. "I can reach." He had to stretch, but was able to settle the copy of *Moby-Dick* into place. I heard a click, and the secret passage swung open.

"Seriously, what's even the point?" Amanda asked as she turned on the flashlight app on her phone and entered the tunnel.

Izzy was immediately behind her. "Come on, Amanda, be a sport. Do you really want to leave this room unsolved?"

Marlie entered the tunnel, moving stiffly. It was her fault that she'd worn a long suit skirt and heels. She knew she'd have to crawl through this dark, narrow tunnel, and possibly worse. "I wasn't going to lose any sleep if we didn't," she grumbled.

"Just don't go wasting all of our time with stupid questions this time around, okay, Marlie?" Gennifer grinned at me before following her. "At least it's easier now that we know the solutions to some of the puzzles," she said, her voice nearly swallowed up by the tunnel.

"After you," Raleigh said to me.

"No, go ahead." I gestured for both of them to go. After a minute of hesitation, Parker entered the tunnel with Raleigh at his heels. Raleigh was tall enough that crawling through the narrow passage was awkward for him. Only when I was convinced that everyone in the group was through to the other side was I ready to follow them. That was the biggest mistake I'd made last time, not keeping track of everyone in the party.

I glanced around the library one last time, taking comfort in the fact that Castillo was back in the control room, watching our every move.

Or was he?

I couldn't see any cameras.

Yes, I knew that the whole point of hidden cameras was that they weren't supposed to be easy to spot, but the last time we were in here, they had been obvious. I took a step back, and sure enough, there was a white globe mounted to the ceiling with a lens pointing at me. I hadn't been able to see it before because when the secret passage door opened, it partially obscured the view.

Talk about unfortunate design.

Then again, it made sense to an extent. The Game Master wouldn't have been able to see inside of the library once we solved the *Moby-Dick* puzzle. He wouldn't have noticed that Vickie had either stayed behind or retraced her steps later. He couldn't have seen the killer, much less witness the murder. He would have watched this screen long enough to verify that we moved on to the next room, and by then he wouldn't have cared that his view was blocked because he assumed we were all in the billiard room like we were supposed to be.

I ducked into the tunnel and crawled as quickly as I could. I got there just in time to hear Amanda, on her back underneath one of the pool tables, call out the numbers written in invisible ink while Marlie punched them into the lock and opened the next door.

"It feels like we're cheating," Parker observed.

"Not really, because this is as far as we got last time," I told him. "Everything after this is totally new territory."

"Wait a second. It took you guys a full hour just to get this far?" Raleigh asked.

"It's harder than it looks." I protested, but he did have a point. The puzzles were challenging but not nearly as intricate or difficult as I had imagined they'd be. If we'd worked together a little better, we would have made it further. "Come on, let's see what's in store for us in the next room."

Parker gasped when he saw the kitchen. "Just look at the size of this place!" he exclaimed. "I could die happy if I had a kitchen this big."

"I cook a little, too," Raleigh added. "You should come over for breakfast sometime. I make a mean French toast with brioche bread."

"Oh yeah?" Parker asked, even though the invitation was clearly aimed at me. "But do you make your own brioche?"

"No, I buy it at the market like everyone else," Raleigh said, opening the top cabinets and pulling out anything that looked like it might be a clue.

"I bake my own brioche," Parker muttered.

"I know you do, Parker," I told him, patting him on the shoulder.

"I make a killer vegan brioche," Izzy added.

All this talk about bread was making me hungry. I returned my attention to the escape room to distract myself from the rumble in my stomach. "What are we looking for, guys?"

"Last time, the Game Master entered the room through the

fridge when our time ran out, but I've already tried and the door feels like it's sealed shut. Probably only opens from the outside for employees. But there's a padlock on this pantry door, and I think that's our way out," Izzy said, rattling the door for effect.

"Key or code?" I asked.

"Key," she replied. "Everyone keep their eyes peeled for a key."

"It's hot in here," Marlie said. "Is anyone else hot?" She walked over to a thermostat on the wall and started fiddling with the temperature. "I don't think this dial is working. It's set at fifty-six, and it's at least seventy in here."

"Wait a second." Gennifer came over to join her. "I did an escape room once where the thermostat was actually a puzzle. Start looking for anything with a temperature on it."

"Like this?" Raleigh asked, holding up a cookbook.

"Maybe." She joined him, and they started flipping through the pages to see if anything jumped out at them.

I walked over to Marlie, who was tugging at her elaborate necklace. A bead of sweat formed on her temple. Guilty conscience, maybe? Stress from returning to the scene of the crime? Fear of getting caught?

Either way, short of wearing an "I'm guilty, ask me how!" button on her scalloped collar, I couldn't think of a better sign that I was on the right track.

Was Marlie the killer?

23

Dizzy Izzy @IsabelleWilliamsburg · July 15
TFW you return to the scene of the crime
#innocentuntilprovenguilty

MARLIE LEANED AGAINST the wall and fanned herself.

"You all right?" I asked. It wasn't difficult to feign concern. I was plenty concerned. Just not for her. If I was being completely honest, I was more worried my friends and I might be in the same room as a murderer. I glanced up at the white camera mounted in the corner. Unlike in the library room, I was in plain view. Castillo was watching, and that gave me courage.

She sighed. "No. Hot flashes. They're the worst."

Oh. I hadn't considered that there might be another plausible explanation for her excessive sweat. Then again, even if it was just a hot flash, it didn't let her off the hook. She could be using that as an excuse.

"Can I get you something? Some water, maybe?"

"Thanks, but it'll pass." She pulled out one of the kitchen stools and sat down. "You're so sweet. Vickie used to make fun of me anytime I had a hot flash. Said I was old and out of touch. Said I might as well get out of the business before I needed a hip replacement or something. As if! I'm only in my fifties. Hardly ancient."

"Not at all," I agreed. I was struck again by how unkind Vickie had been to the people around her. "I saw the sign outside. Vickie was listing this building?"

Marlie nodded and dabbed sweat away from her upper lip. "It's a big deal, actually. If Vickie had managed to sell this place, it would have set her for the year."

"Who gets the listing now?" I asked.

"Who knows? Me, probably. I've been number two at the firm ever since Vickie came in, and I've inherited a lot of her listings now that she's gone."

"So you stand to make a lot of money when the building sells," I said.

"*When* the building sells?" she asked with a wry laugh. "Honey, this place has been on the market as long as I can remember. The owner's asking way too much. It's a hot neighborhood, but this block is zoned commercial only. Any developer with a lick of sense would do better off investing in a residential-zoned building in Bed-Stuy, or something cheaper in Queens."

"It was your idea to host Vickie's party here, wasn't it?" I asked, the answer dawning on me. "You wanted to rub it in. That she might be broker of the month, but even she couldn't sell this building."

She made an odd noise in the back of her throat, like she was suppressing a laugh. "You're a very astute young woman, aren't you? I think I like you. You know what? I'm gonna waive my commission if you want to reconsider that place on Bedford."

"You mean the murder apartment? No way," I said, shaking my head vehemently.

"You're missing out on the deal of a lifetime." She fished one of her business cards out of her purse and pressed it into my hand. "Give me a call tomorrow and I'll take you around to look at a couple of other places. Fee-free."

"Golly, I'd love to, but even without your fee, I can't afford anything in this neighborhood. Not on a waitress's salary. Not without five or six roommates."

"Probably not. But keep the card and call me if you change your mind."

"Sure," I said, tucking the card away into my bag. This time, I held on to my own messenger bag, thank you very much. I didn't want to set it down and risk it becoming part of a murder scene. Again.

Not like I thought there was going to be another murder. I had hoped that being here would shake something loose. So far, all I had was a swing and a miss. Marlie didn't have any reason to kill Vickie. It was a little mean-spirited to arrange for Vickie's party to be in a building that she'd failed to sell, but it was a far cry from murder.

Marlie was organized. She had to be to make a living in real estate. She was fastidiously neat, or her decades-old, unfashionable wardrobe would be riddled with signs of wear. She wasn't the type of person who would want blood on her hands, literally or figuratively. If Marlie was going to commit murder, she would pick a less messy method.

Marlie didn't kill Vickie. I would stake my boots on it.

That left only Amanda and Gennifer.

I wanted to interrogate them both, but Gennifer was busy vigilantly searching for clues to solve the escape room puzzle, whereas Amanda was checking her makeup in the reflection of the shiny range hood that hung over the oven. "Any luck?" I asked her.

"They've got this well in hand," Amanda said, flipping a hand toward where Gennifer, Izzy, and Raleigh huddled over the cookbook.

"Don't you want to contribute?"

"I *am* contributing," she insisted. "I got the numbers in the last room, didn't I?"

All right, technically she had, but that was only because she remembered me finding them under the pool table the first time around. Which I couldn't have done without the flashlight she'd picked up in the first room. In a way, we had solved that clue together. I begrudgingly gave her half credit. "You know, the game would go a lot quicker if we all cooperated with each other."

"What's with you and this silly game anyway?" she asked. For the first time, she put her phone away and concentrated her attention on me. "You tagged along the first time for what, a free escape room with a bunch of strangers? But what are you getting out of it now? You didn't even know Vickie, so don't give me that nonsense Izzy was spouting about doing this to honor her memory. I know you're not supposed to talk bad about the dead, but Vickie was a jerk. Frankly, if you'd known her half as good as I did, you'd be happy she was dead."

"And are you? Happy?"

"Do I look happy to you?"

I wasn't certain. Maybe? It was hard to tell under all that makeup and in the poses she held so carefully even when there wasn't a camera pointed at her. "Is it true that Vickie was spending a lot of time with your boyfriend?"

"Where did you hear that?" she asked.

"I don't remember," I lied. "So, it *is* true?"

"It most certainly is not," she insisted. "You're talking about Gary, right? *I* broke up with *him* last week because he was such a lousy Instagram boyfriend. I couldn't give two figs who he's seeing now."

"What's an Instagram boyfriend?"

She gave me an exasperated look. "Selfies are great and all, but sometimes I need a free hand to catch the perfect picture. That's where an Instagram boyfriend comes in. I was trying to get this perfect pic and Gary was supposed to climb up a fire escape so he could get the angle right, but he dropped my phone, if you can believe that!"

"You broke up with a guy because he dropped your phone?"

"Do you have any idea what the latest iPhone costs?" she asked, flipping her hair over her shoulder.

"Your phone seemed right as rain," I said, recalling navigating through it to recover the deleted photos. "It's not even cracked."

"The screen shattered," she said. "I had to trade it in for a refurb with half the memory. And I swear it's got gremlins or something."

"Gremlins?" I asked.

"It's always messing up. Logging me out of apps. I never get email notifications anymore. GPS insists I'm somewhere in Jersey. Plus, it keeps rearranging my icons."

"But it still tags your pictures correctly, right?"

"Hardly," she said, blowing out a sigh. "They're always out of order, and the metadata is all sorts of messed up. The numbering's off and the time stamp's always wrong." I was hardly a techie, but I knew that the metadata was the hidden information associated with a picture, like when it was taken and if location was turned on, where it was taken. "I swear, I've got thousands of followers on Insta. Would it kill Apple to give me a free iPhone? Imagine all that good publicity."

"Yeah, all right," I agreed. I hadn't checked lately, but Apple had a couple million more followers than Amanda. I doubted her influence would make a dent in their social media presence.

Far be it from me to direct Amanda's brand strategy. What did I know? I had only a handful of followers on my personal accounts. Sure, I managed the Untapped Books & Café's accounts, but it wasn't like people followed them to read my boring updates. They just wanted to know what was going on at Untapped and stay ahead of upcoming events and menu changes.

But Amanda had also inadvertently let herself off the hook. Vickie hadn't stolen her boyfriend. Plus, Amanda hadn't deleted photos to hide evidence. The gaps in the pictures I'd recovered were explained away by the operating system bugs in her phone.

"If you weren't mad at Vickie for stealing your boyfriend, again, then why were you arguing on your way to the escape room?"

"Aren't you the nosy one?" Amanda asked. "We weren't really arguing. Vickie was mad that I'd tagged her in an unflattering picture, so I took it down. Happy?"

That explained why there were no pictures of Vickie on

Amanda's feed from that day. All things considered, Amanda didn't seem to have a strong motive to kill Vickie, which left only one suspect.

"Bingo!" Gennifer called from across the room. "Try setting the thermostat to seven hundred and fifty degrees."

"You've got to be kidding me," Parker said as he headed toward the thermostat.

"Nope." She held the cookbook upside down and shook it so the pages flapped against one another. "There's got to be a hundred recipes in here, and not a single one of them lists a temperature setting."

"So where did you get seven hundred and fifty degrees from?" I asked as Parker fiddled with the dials. I scanned around like I'd done every five minutes or so since the game had started to make sure I knew exactly where everyone was at all times. I wasn't going to make the same mistake again and lose track of anyone.

"Look at the stove." Gennifer pointed and, sure enough, the stove was set to seven-fifty. Which I like to think I would have noticed if I hadn't been so busy interrogating Marlie and Amanda.

"That's it," Parker said, staring at the thermostat. "Nothing's happening."

"Try pushing 'run program,'" Gennifer suggested.

He did. There was a popping noise as a tile in the ceiling above us swung open. A key on a long string dropped out of the hole. The key swung like a pendulum. "Well, what do you know?"

Raleigh reached up and snatched the key. I was glad he'd come along, because if it had just been me alone in that room, I would have had to climb up on a barstool to reach it. "Heads up." He tossed the key to Izzy. She inserted it into the lock, opened the door, and a siren went off.

Everybody jumped backward as the Game Master stepped into the open doorway with a flourish. "Congratulations," he said with the enthusiasm of someone who had just stepped in gum. "You have managed to escape. Now, if you'll all follow me, we'll take a group photo. Check our Facebook page tomorrow to download or share your picture."

"Not for nothing, but the last time I did an escape room, we had to solve something like a dozen puzzles. This one had, what, four? Five? Hardly worth it, if you ask me," Gennifer said as we filed down the hall.

I blinked at her. "We barely solved this one, and it took us two tries."

"Yeah, but not everyone was contributing. Call me if you want to try a more challenging one with me later. We'll have a blast. There are a few on Staten Island that are real bears, but they're fun," Gennifer offered. I wasn't sure I wanted to take her up on that. This room had been plenty difficult enough for me.

We all picked through a box of silly hats. I selected an oversized tiara. Izzy grabbed a top hat and hung a sign around her neck that said "escaped prisoner." Parker put on a long sleeping cap, like the kind that might be featured in a Dickens novel. Not to be outdone, Raleigh found a pair of glasses with an integrated Groucho Marx–esque mustache and put that on over his real glasses. Marlie tossed a pink feather boa over her shoulders, Amanda went straight for the flapper girl headband, and Gennifer nabbed a pair of Christmassy reindeer horns.

It took a minute of arranging and rearranging until we were settled, with Raleigh behind me and Parker next to me with our arms looped at the elbows. Izzy was on my other side, with everyone else crammed in around the edges. At the last minute, Parker held up an "I'm with stupid" arrow, pointing at his own head.

"Great," Brandon intoned after snapping a few pictures. "That should be online by close of business tomorrow. Thank you for joining us, and we hope to see you at Verrazzano-Narrows Escape! again soon."

As we put away our silly hats, I tried to corner Gennifer, but she brushed past me. "I'd love to stay and chat more, but I'm gonna bounce. I hate leaving Penny for long."

"But . . ." I said, not even knowing how to finish that sentence. Izzy was a stellar judge of character. That should be good enough for me. Gennifer was uber competitive but also seemed super nice. I had no reason to mistrust her just because Vickie had bullied her when they were younger, but I had run out of suspects and I hadn't even had the chance to question her again.

"Text me if you want to try one of those escape rooms in Staten Island I told you about, 'kay?" Then she was gone.

I made eye contact with Izzy, and she shrugged. I returned the gesture. "Well, that was a blast," Raleigh said, coming up beside me. "Now how about we go grab a coffee somewhere? Or maybe a beer?"

"Or we can go try that Limoncello cake like you promised," Parker said, on my other side.

"Gee, those both sound great, but I think I left something behind in there. I'll see you guys later." I hurried back to the front desk and caught Castillo's attention.

I had to admit, it was a bit strange and flattering to have Parker and Raleigh vying for my attention, but in the end, it was just awkward. Raleigh was nice. And cute. And in a band. I wasn't sure what he saw in me, except maybe a few conversations I hadn't even taken part in. I had no idea what Izzy had told him about me, but I was at a definite disadvantage because I knew practically nothing about him at all.

I hadn't even looked his band up on YouTube yet.

It wasn't that Raleigh wasn't attractive. He was. He was also tall, humble, and had a genuine sense of humor. Plus he was in a popular band but didn't seem conceited.

Unfortunately, Raleigh wasn't actually interested in *me*. He was interested in the woman he'd met online. He was interested in Izzy. Who wasn't on the market, not that I was, either.

And then there was Parker.

Sweet, funny, talented Parker.

My dear friend Parker.

I'd known him for almost two months, and not once had either of us shown any kind of romantic interest in the other. Was he actually attracted to me, as more than just a friend? Or was he caught up in the idea of competing with another guy?

Not that it mattered. He had a girlfriend.

"See you tomorrow?" Parker asked, hesitating at the door.

"Of course," I said, waving him on his way. I held up one finger to get Castillo's attention. "I think you still have my ID."

"Sure, come this way."

"What did I tell you, man?" Brandon said. "Always check the copier when you're done. If people have to come back to get their

IDs or anything else they forgot, they give us nasty reviews on Yelp."

"Ten-four," Castillo replied without pausing. I followed him back to the copy room.

"So? Did you see anything suspicious?"

He shook his head. "Nothing out of the ordinary. You?"

"Nothing with a side of nothing. I didn't get a chance to talk to Gennifer, but I'm pretty much convinced that none of those women hurt Vickie. Which is impossible. *Someone* killed her."

"Which means we're back to you or Izzy."

"You know as well as I do . . ."

He interrupted me. "Yeah, yeah. You're both innocent. But you're also the only ones with fingerprints on the trophy."

"Wait, the only fingerprints? How is that even possible? There had to be a dozen people that handled it before we won it."

"There are several other partials from unidentified sources. We tested it against everyone in the escape room, and you and Izzy were the only matches. Ran the extras through the system, too, but nothing popped."

I sighed.

"Odessa, don't act so glum. I'll solve this."

"I know. I just feel like we're running out of time. It's fortunate that the room was released when it was, or Izzy never could have arranged this little reunion in the first place."

Castillo laughed. "You know, for a smart person, you can be so thick sometimes. You really think the police just up and decided to release a crime scene right before Izzy called to book it? Or I just happened to show up and announce I was the new guy, reporting for training, ten minutes before your reservation?" He tapped me on the forehead. "This is why you need to leave the detecting to the professionals."

Oh. Duh. I should have put that together sooner. It was encouraging that Castillo would go to so much trouble to not only allow us to set up the failed sting, but to actively help us. It gave me hope that he really did believe that Izzy was innocent and wasn't going to let his department railroad him into arresting her.

24

⸳∘∘∘◌∘∮⸳∮∮∮∘∘⸳∘∘∘◌∘∮∮∮∮◌∘∮⸳∘∘∘◌∘∮∮∮∮

Odessa Dean @OdessaWaiting · July 15
New York City isn't a place you live. It's a place you survive.
Unless you're stupid rich or super lucky. And I'm neither.
#GoFundMe #please

∮∮∮∮∮∘∘∘∘∘⸳∘∘◌∘∮∘∮∮∮∮∮∘∘∘∘∘∮∮∮∘∘∘∘◌∘∮∮∮∮∘∘

THE GAME MASTER stopped me on my way out. "Did you get your
ID?" he asked.

"Yep," I told him. "Silly me, it was in my wallet all along, I'd
just put it in the wrong pocket."

"Cool. Hey, I heard you were looking for an apartment,"
Brandon said.

How on earth did he know that? Izzy, probably. She never
met anyone she couldn't immediately befriend.

I nodded. "You got any leads?"

"All the nope. I'm the last person you would want to take
rental advice from."

"How so?" I asked. "I mean, you have to live somewhere,
right? How'd you find your place?"

Brandon grimaced. "I paid Vickie Marsh a small fortune to

get the apartment of my dreams. Apartment of my nightmares is more like it."

"Small world," I said. Not only did Vickie end up celebrating her big day in a building that she couldn't sell, but then she happened to get stuck with a Game Master who was an unhappy client. Talk about adding insult to injury.

"Tell me about it."

"What makes your apartment so horrible?" I asked. "Is it rats?" I shuddered. Louisiana had rats, but New York City had *rats*. I'm talking enormous crazed critters almost as big as the nutria back home, with absolutely no fear and big, beady eyes that belonged on a creature out of a bad horror movie. I'd rather face a swamp full of alligators and water moccasins than come face-to-face with a Brooklyn rat in my apartment.

"No rats, thankfully. But the building has a high-tech fire alarm and water sprinklers everywhere, which is great. Until the system malfunctions three, four times a month. I can't begin to tell you how many times I've been jolted awake at two in the morning to wailing sirens and streams of cold water driving me, soaking wet and with ringing ears, into the street. Everything I own that isn't already ruined is covered in roofing tarps because I don't know the next time the sprinklers will randomly go off."

"That sounds horrific!" After hearing everyone's housing horror stories, I was actually starting to miss Piney Island. Louisiana might be a swamp, but I didn't have to worry about cockroaches the size of my fist, apartments with broken appliances, or random fire alarms triggering a sprinkler flood. The more I heard, the more I wondered if New York City wasn't the epicenter of some kind of biblical plague.

"Even my underwear drawer is growing mold. And that's not even the worst," he said, flexing his fingers as if he wanted to hit someone.

"How is that even possible?" I asked.

"I live on the top floor. Great view, right? Sure. Except there's a malfunctioning air handler on the roof mounted right above my unit. Doesn't even belong to the building, it belongs to the salmonella factory on the first floor, a cheap take-out joint that the city should have shut down ages ago. Randomly throughout the day this AC unit makes a noise like an air horn going off and shakes my whole apartment. Sometimes it's quiet for hours at a time, then other times it blows every twenty minutes, usually in the dead of the night. I haven't had a single night of uninter-rupted sleep since I moved in."

"Why don't you move?"

"Wow, wish I would have thought about that," he growled.

I held my hands up in mock surrender. "Sorry, I'm not from around here."

He scowled and continued. "Problem is, every penny I had went into that ridiculous broker's fee and I'm in an iron-clad sixteen-month lease. I'm reduced to popping sleeping pills each night and huddling under a shower curtain, hoping to get two, maybe three hours of sleep before the sprinkler goes hay-wire or the HVAC unit erupts." He held his hand out. It twitched. "See this? The tremors started a few weeks after I moved in. Between too little sleep, the pills, and the gallons of caffeine I down every day just to function . . . well, let's just say if I could afford health care, I'd probably be hooked up to a pacemaker by now."

"Isn't there something you can do?" I knew he was between a rock and a concrete bunker, but there had to be a better way.

"About the tremors? Probably not."

"I mean about the apartment," I clarified.

"I wish. I've lodged complaints with the city, with the housing board, with the super, with the building, and—of course—with my broker. And have gotten exactly zero for my troubles. Honestly, there were a few times I was ready to take a walk off the roof just to get it to all stop, you know?"

"That sounds horrific." And here I thought Izzy's and Parker's experiences were bad, but this really took the cake. I made a promise to myself then and there that when I was ready to move back home, I would never complain about living with my parents ever again.

Their house wasn't haunted with the victims of a murder spree's ghosts. There wasn't a bug infestation. I wasn't hiding out illegally in a windowless basement or paying thousands of dollars a month to rent a shoebox studio apartment. I certainly didn't have to worry about sprinkler floods and random cacophonies driving me up the wall.

Then something he said clicked. "Wait a second, didn't you say that Vickie Marsh was the broker who found you the nightmare apartment?"

Brandon let out a snort. "The one and only. Out of all the escape rooms in all the cities in all the world, little Miss Broker of the Month had to walk into mine. It's bad enough I have to see her face on the 'For Sale' sign outside every time I come to work, but now I have to deal with listening to her brag about her killer deals and huge commissions right in front of me, too?"

I took a step backward, suddenly aware that the participants—Marlie, Amanda, Gennifer, Izzy, and myself—hadn't been the only people in the escape room. As the Game Master, Brandon would have had full access. If his apartment was half as bad as he claimed, he certainly had motive to hate Vickie Marsh. And if he hadn't been getting any sleep, he might not be in the best frame of mind.

I was fairly certain I didn't want to be in the same room as him anymore. "Sorry, that sucks," I said, turning and heading toward the door.

"You in a hurry or something?" he asked. I turned to face him. "You sure do ask a lot of questions. I was watching you on the monitors, you know. You didn't seem half as interested in solving the escape room as you were backing people into corners and interrogating them. I figure you only booked this room as an excuse to talk to me, so ask away. Don't you want to know?"

"Know what?" I asked, but I had a sinking feeling I already knew the answer. Brandon blamed Vickie for his unlivable living situation. We had discovered one employees-only door into the kitchen, and there might be other ways for employees to access the rooms that we hadn't found.

"You ever have one of those dreams that's so real it's hard to tell if you're awake or not?" Brandon asked, instead of answering.

I nodded, slowly. In fact, I felt like I was trapped in a nightmare right now.

"That's how I've felt ever since I moved into that dump. Like I'm never really awake but I'm never asleep, either. Then I saw Vickie Marsh all alone in the library, and I realized I finally had a chance to talk to her."

"Only Vickie didn't want to talk," I guessed, unable to stop myself. My head spun as I realized that Brandon couldn't have possibly seen that Vickie was in the library alone once the hidden passageway door opened and blocked the camera's view. The only time he'd been alone with Vickie was for a few minutes after our timer ran down.

Gennifer, Amanda, Marlie, Izzy, and I were already in the kitchen when Brandon killed Vickie.

"She had the nerve to tell me to call her office on Monday and we'd work something out. I've been calling and emailing her for months! She never once returned a call. Now that I was in the same room as her—finally—I guess I lost it."

It all made perfect sense when I thought about it. I was kicking myself for not figuring it out sooner, and now I was just buying time until I figured out a way to get far, far away from Brandon before I met the same fate as Vickie had. "I mean, I sorta understand that. You're upset, and you're not getting enough sleep, so you weren't thinking straight. But why'd you have to hit her with my trophy?" I asked.

"I should be thanking you, really," Brandon said. "Pretty much everything that isn't nailed down in the escape room is a cheap prop. Plastic. Foam. Cardboard. I could have bashed little Miss Broker of the Month over the head with anything in the room, and it would have bounced right off. It was just sheer dumb luck that the first thing I grabbed was your trophy."

I found myself wishing that Izzy and I had won a gift certificate instead of that heavy cornhole trophy.

Brandon muffled a yawn. I knew he hadn't been getting much sleep lately, but there was something immeasurably creepy

NO MEMES OF ESCAPE

about someone who could yawn in the middle of a murder confession. "The whole thing was like I was sleepwalking," he continued. "One minute she was standing there, lecturing me about how I should have read the contract better, and the next thing I knew, I was swinging the trophy."

I flinched. I really did *not* want to know the details.

"She screamed, so I hit her again to get her to shut up."

My mouth was suddenly dry as I realized that the scream we'd heard wasn't Brandon discovering the dead body, as we'd originally assumed. It was Vickie. She'd still be alive if one of us had followed the Game Master back into the library.

"She fell down that time. I kept swinging that trophy until I heard you and your friend crawling back through the tunnel, and, well, you know the rest."

I swallowed, hard.

Brandon's eyes seemed to come back into focus. He backed away from the desk without breaking eye contact. If he'd had a full night's sleep last night, he might never have spilled his guts like that but somehow, something had cut through his haze and the Game Master realized he'd made a mistake. A huge one.

"I get it," I babbled. "You did what you had to do. After all she put you through, it was, like, justified."

"It was," he said, nodding.

"Plus, with the sleeping pills and all, you were technically under the influence. Any judge could see that."

"Yup," he agreed. He moved around the edge of the desk as I inched backward toward the door.

"Besides, sounds to me like Vickie had it coming," I said. I felt something hit the back of my knees and steadied myself before I could trip over one of the waiting room chairs. If I could reach the door before he did, I would be home free.

"Exactly," Brandon agreed.

I scooted closer to the door, feeling along the wall behind me for the door handle. When my hand brushed it, I practically doubled over in relief. I was safe.

I turned the doorknob.

Nothing happened.

"Going somewhere?" Brandon asked, sounding closer than I'd realized. While I'd been searching for the door, he'd managed to close the distance between us. I noticed something metallic glinting in his hands. I hoped it was just his enormous key chain, but I had a sinking feeling it was worse. I didn't want to look down and risk breaking eye contact again. "I don't think that's a great idea."

"My friends are waiting for me outside," I told him.

He replied with a dry laugh, brandishing a box cutter. He slid a button forward and a sharp-looking blade appeared. "No, they're not. You forget, I've got cameras all over this place. Even outside. I checked before I locked the door, and there's no one out there."

"But you're forgetting one thing," I said, pressed against the door as he crept closer.

"Oh yeah?" he sneered. "What am I forgetting? You're so full of questions. What are you, some sort of undercover cop?"

"Nope," I said, trying to keep my voice from shaking. "I'm really not. But he is."

Detective Vincent Castillo stepped into the room, gun drawn. "Brandon Reaves, drop the knife. You're under arrest for the murder of Victoria Marsh."

The box cutter clattered to the ground. The Game Master slowly raised his arms in the air, palms out toward me. He looked over his shoulder. "New guy?"

"Wrong," Castillo said, approaching the other man. With practiced, efficient motions, he wrenched Brandon's arms behind his back and clasped handcuffs on his wrists. "I can't believe I showed up out of the blue and said you were supposed to train me, and you never even questioned it." He smiled at me over Brandon's shoulder. "What did I tell you, Odessa? No one ever notices the help."

I nodded stiffly. When the effects of the shock wore off, I would probably collapse into a puddle of jelly, but right now, it was all I could do to breathe and wait for my pulse to resume a normal rhythm. "You got all that, right?"

"Yup," Castillo replied. He frog-marched Brandon over to the waiting room chairs and forced him to sit. "Not only did I hear everything, I recorded the whole confession on my phone. More than enough to put him away for murder. People never learn, do they?"

I shook my head slightly. "Nope."

He turned his attention back to Brandon. "Now, you sit there all quiet-like until transport comes to take you back to the station." He pulled a card out of his wallet and recited Brandon's Miranda rights. "Do you understand your rights as I've explained them to you?" he asked.

Brandon nodded.

"I need a yes or no," Castillo prodded.

"Yes. I understand. But there were, like, extenuating circumstances, man. You heard her. It was completely justified. I haven't had more than a few hours' sleep in months, not counting when I was doped up on over-the-counter sleeping aids. I was out of my mind when I killed that broker lady. There's not a jury in New York City that wouldn't sympathize. Heck, they might even give me a medal!"

"You've got a point," Castillo agreed. "And the DA might not have even chosen to prosecute, based on those circumstances. Until you came after my friend here with a deadly weapon."

Brandon slumped in his chair, all the fight escaping him like a deflating balloon.

Castillo continued. "Defense can produce a parade of witnesses that the victim ripped off, but once Odessa takes the stand, you're going away for life. Because there's no one quite as sympathetic as a kindhearted waitress with a Southern accent."

25

Untapped Books & Café @untappedwilliamsburg · July 16
Closing early tonight for a private event, but come on in tomorrow to check out the best selection of books & cold craft brews in Williamsburg! #books #craftbeer #privateparty

PARKER SURVEYED THE crowded café. "I can't believe you pulled this off," he said. It was extremely late on Tuesday night—or more accurately, very early on Wednesday morning. Untapped Books & Café had three times as many people crammed inside as it normally had on a busy Saturday night. We were all there to celebrate Parker's twenty-fifth birthday.

I didn't know how Izzy managed it all. She'd thrown a hugely successful surprise party for Parker with only a few days to set everything up. She'd handled everything, from convincing Todd to close early and let us have the space to tracking down Parker's roommates and friends who were scattered as far away as Jersey. She even ordered a Limoncello cake, just like he wanted.

Todd had brought his new girlfriend, the woman with the Irish accent he'd met on Tinder. She was glued to his side all night. I'd accidentally walked in on them making out in the hall when I'd stepped out to use the bathroom. I retreated hastily, considering using the emergency eye wash station in the kitchen to scrub that scene out of my brain.

The birthday boy in question had a cold bottle of Pour Williamsburg in one hand and his other arm looped over Hazel's shoulders. "I helped," she said, grinning. Izzy had roped her in on the surprise party plan, and she'd made sure to get Parker back to the café without him ever suspecting a thing.

I think I was gonna like Hazel. I still wasn't convinced that she was good enough for my friend Parker—I wasn't sure any woman was—but she laughed at his corny jokes and praised his culinary genius, so she couldn't be all bad. Plus, she made him happy.

Speaking of happy couples, even though they'd worked out their problems, Izzy had gone to the party stag. "It's a shame Vincent couldn't come. He should be with us, celebrating closing Vickie's case."

"He wanted to be here, he did. But, you know, paperwork. Apparently that's the reward for bringing in a murderer. Frankly, I don't see why Vince gets to take all the credit when we did all the work!"

"I know, right?" I said, but she could tell I was joking. I was perfectly happy with Castillo getting the credit. I wasn't comfortable being in the spotlight.

"Are you sure you have to leave?" Parker asked me. "It's early."

"It's past three in the morning," I protested. But I knew he wasn't really talking about the party anymore.

While I'd been busy trying to solve Vickie's murder and help

Izzy plan Parker's surprise party, I'd run out of time to find alternative living arrangements. I'd worn out my welcome at my aunt's apartment. She'd even taken the liberty of printing out a Greyhound ticket and leaving it on the counter where I'd be sure to see it. Maybe if I had another week or two, Izzy could have found us an apartment, but that ship had sailed. It was time to go back home to Piney Island. "And I've got a bus to catch in a few hours."

At least I'd spent my last night in Williamsburg surrounded by friends. I couldn't ask for much more than that.

"Odessa . . ." Parker said, but I stopped him.

"Dude, don't make this any harder than it has to be. Besides, we have internet in Louisiana. We can FaceTime anytime you want."

It wouldn't be the same, of course. But now that I'd gotten a taste of New York, no place else would ever be quite enough for me. I'd go back to Louisiana and get my old job back at the Crawdad Shack. I'd save every penny until I could afford to return to Williamsburg and move in with Izzy. It might take me a few months, but I'd be back.

I took one last look around the room. Silvia and Emilie had pushed three tables together for beer pong and were currently beating Parker's roommates, Suz and Tony. Kim, Betty, and Nan were cheering them on.

Todd and his date were nowhere to be seen. I didn't want to think about what that meant.

Gennifer and her husband, Pete, were there, too. His mom was watching the baby, which was probably a good thing because it was very late and the music was loud enough that the tenants that lived above the café would be well within their rights to complain. Adding a screaming baby into the mix wouldn't have been good. It turned out that Pete and Parker were distant cousins or something. Small world.

Gennifer saw me staring and waved. I waved back.

"Yo!" Andre called as I started up the stairs toward the bookstore section of Untapped. Tonight, after all this time, I'd *finally* gotten to meet his boyfriend, Trey. He was Andre's polar opposite—a quiet, reserved wallflower. Then again, it was hard to get a word in edgewise while Andre was around, so they were a perfect match. "Where do you think you're going, young lady?"

"Home," I said. My heart sank a little when I realized I meant Piney Island.

He thrust his phone at me. "Have you seen this?"

On the screen was Huckleberry, flopped over on his back, surrounded by a mess of books. The caption read, "When you've had one too many."

"Wait, there's more," Andre said, and scrolled down. The same picture appeared, but this time it said, "Mondays be like." He scrolled through picture after picture of Huckleberry, each with a pithy caption. "You did it, Odessa. You created a meme. And you even managed to get the Untapped logo in the window. Good job, girl." He pulled me into a hug. "Gonna miss you."

"Me, too," I said. I had to get out of here before I made a fool of myself and ruined Parker's birthday with a waterworks display. "I'll be back," I promised.

I hoped I meant it.

"Come on, Odessa. It's late. I'll walk you home," Izzy offered.

I waved at everyone and hurried out into the night. The door closed behind us with a tinkle of bells.

"I wish you would have let me invite Raleigh," Izzy said as we walked.

"Thanks, but that would have been weird. It was Parker's birthday party, and the two of them don't even really know each other."

"Duh, I wasn't inviting him for Parker. I would have invited him for you."

I shook my head. "Raleigh's a nice guy, but I'm not interested in him. I'm glad I got to be with y'all tonight instead of making awkward small talk with a guy I barely know." We paused at the corner, waiting for a break in traffic or the crosswalk light, whichever came first. "You really do throw an amazing party," I told her, a little too loudly. I'd been shouting all night to be heard over the crowd and the music, and I hadn't yet adjusted my volume.

"I couldn't let my best friend leave Williamsburg without a proper send-off, could I?" she asked.

"Tonight was supposed to be Parker's night," I reminded her.

"He didn't mind sharing."

"You really don't have to walk me home, you know."

"I know that." Izzy linked her arm with mine as we crossed the street.

A man in a gorilla suit jogged past us from the other direction. "Man, he's gotta be hot," I mused. Then I realized I wasn't even startled at seeing a grown man dressed like a gorilla running down a sidewalk at three in the morning.

That's my Williamsburg.

The short walk—I'd been in New York long enough to consider three quarters of a mile a *short* walk, I realized with amazement—was over too quickly and we soon found ourselves looking up at my aunt's apartment building. Like many of the buildings in Williamsburg, it had started out as a warehouse before it was gutted and converted to high-end apartment units. The lobby was dim. Earl the grumpy concierge had gone home hours ago.

I unlocked the front door and stood there awkwardly, one foot propping it open. I didn't know how to say goodbye to Izzy. It might be a while before I could save enough money to move back to Brooklyn. At least I had Brandon the Game Master's trial to look forward to, since I had to return to New York to testify against him.

"Well? What are you waiting for?" Izzy asked, pulling the door all the way open and squeezing past me into the building.

"You don't have to walk me all the way to my door," I protested.

"Might as well," she said, crossing the lobby and punching the button to call the elevator.

"You staying at Vincent's tonight?" I asked her. The last time I'd assumed she had a place to stay, she'd actually been crashing in the stockroom. Which, technically, was a place to stay. Just not a very good one. I'd feel better if I knew she had someplace safe to live until I got back, and I couldn't think of anyplace safer than a cop's apartment.

"Yeah, but I don't know when he'll be home. Between his full-time job and moonlighting as security, I hardly ever see him even when I'm not dodging him."

"What's his apartment like?" I asked, bracing myself for another horror story.

"Not bad. Small. Really small. There's almost always someone couch-surfing in his living room, so he's got, like, zero privacy. This week, it's that giant guy Myke. He got evicted when his building went condo, and he's staying with Vince until something permanent comes along."

I dug through my bag and pulled out Marlie's card. "Tell him to call Marlie and have her pass along my discount to him."

"Discount?" she asked.

"She said she'd waive her broker's fee. Unless you want it?"

"No thanks. I'm sure something will pan out soon."

I nodded. I wish something had come up sooner, but I guess it wasn't mean to be. That was okay. Williamsburg wasn't going anywhere. "You should talk to Silvia, see if she's looking for a roommate. Commuting from Queens every day is wearing her down."

"I might do that," Izzy said, waiting for me to unlock the door.

"I'm surprised you don't want to stay with Vincent permanently."

Izzy shrugged. "I like him, but it's way too early in our relationship to talk about moving in together. Besides, he snores."

"Out of all the things you've put up with in the past, having a cute roommate that snores is hardly a blip on your radar."

"Tell me about it," she said. "When I was little, before we moved out to Staten Island, my parents had an apartment above a pet store in Jersey City. All night long, those puppies would bark and howl and the birds would squawk. But that wasn't the worst of it. A fourteen-foot-long albino boa constrictor escaped one day and somehow ended up in our bathroom. I've never heard my dad scream so loud in my entire life." She giggled at the memory. "But at least the snake didn't snore."

I had assumed that my aunt's apartment would be dark and

quiet, but to my surprise, when I opened the door, the lights were on in the tiny kitchen and the overcrowded living room. Rufus ran to greet me, purring loudly as he made a figure eight between my legs, begging to be picked up. I obliged, burying my hands in his curly fur.

Aunt Melanie was awake, reading a book with a glass of wine in her hand as she sat on the couch in her robe. "You're home early," she said. "I wasn't expecting you until later."

"Later?" I asked. "It's well past three in the morning." I pried off my cowboy boots and sank down onto the couch next to her.

I knew Aunt Melanie wasn't the typical aunt. She never retired to bed before midnight unless she was sick, she was fiercely independent even when her foot was in a cast, and she was extraordinarily gracious to have put me up for so long. I thought she'd asked me to come watch her cat and her apartment as a favor to her, but I'd since come to realize that this had been for my benefit all along. She'd used her trip as a chance for me to get out of Louisiana for a while and see a part of the world I'd never elsewise have a chance to experience.

Aunt Melanie laughed at my answer and set her wineglass on the coffee table in front of her, next to a statue I hadn't seen before. "You're young and in New York City. Enjoy every minute while you can."

"Good advice. Is this new?" I asked, picking up the statue to get a better look at it. It was heavy, a two-foot-high ceramic piece depicting a three-headed monster covered in emerald and teal green scales. Its eyes—nine of them in total—glittered like rubies and its two tails had suction cups on the underside like an octopus's tentacles.

"Actually, it's old. I made this when I was about your age, I think. It's been buried in my studio for decades. Found it while I was cleaning."

"I'm glad you found it and dusted it off," I said, being careful to place it back in exactly the same position that I had found it. I relaxed back on the couch next to my aunt. "It's cool. Hey, why are you cleaning your studio? Starting a new project? Wanna talk about it?"

Aunt Melanie glanced over my shoulder at Izzy before looking back at me. "Actually, I haven't worked on anything new in a while. I thought this trip to Europe would inspire me, shake something free, but all I brought back was . . ." She motioned to her walking boot. "I think I need a change of scenery."

"What? You're not moving out of Williamsburg, are you?" I asked. It was hard enough leaving tomorrow knowing that I'd always have a place to stay if I needed to when I scraped up enough money to return, but if my aunt moved, what would I do then?

She chuckled. "No, not that. But I think it might be good to relocate my studio. There's a great shared space overlooking the river where I can work surrounded by other artists, and we can inspire and encourage each other every day."

"That sounds amazing," I said. "I can't wait to see what you create next. You'll have to send me photos. Or we can always Skype."

"About that." My aunt glanced at Izzy again. "Once I move my studio, I'm going to have a spare bedroom. The new space is wonderful, but it's an added expense every month. I might have to take on a roommate just to make fiscal sense. And it wouldn't hurt to have an extra pair of hands around here." She winked at Izzy.

My face lit up and I turned to Izzy. "*This* is your new apartment? How wonderful!"

I couldn't have been happier for Izzy if she'd won the lotto. She deserved a nice, safe place to live. A real place to call her own, that wasn't overrun with mice or accessed only by a broken fire escape. A place where she could have a real bed—not some ratty old sleeping bag—and hang up her own curtains. A place where she didn't have to fear eviction or worry about some horrible roommate beating her up in the middle of the night and stealing all her stuff. A place with a working elevator.

Izzy nodded, and I jumped up and gave her a big bear hug. "This is so extra!" I continued to gush. I turned to my aunt. "You're going to love living with Izzy. She's an amazing cook, and she always picks up after herself. Rufus adores her, and she's the ideal roommate."

"I'm glad you think so," my aunt said. "Because you'll be sharing the room with her."

Goose bumps sprouted on my arms. "Wait, what?"

"Man, Odessa, you can be so dense sometimes. I told you to trust me, didn't I?"

"Wait, this was your plan all along?" Izzy nodded. I turned to Aunt Melanie. "But the bus ticket? You made it pretty clear that you wanted me to leave."

My aunt flapped a dismissive hand in my direction. "If we're going to live together, we need to learn how to communicate better. I thought you *wanted* to leave. I'd hoped you'd stay, especially when Izzy came to me with her idea, but this had to be your decision. The bus ticket was there to give you an option so you didn't feel like you were trapped here."

"Trapped? In Williamsburg? Don't be ridiculous!" I exclaimed. My head was dizzy with the possibilities.

"What do you say, roomie?" Izzy asked. "You and me, splitting everything down the middle. We could build a shelf for our cornhole trophy, once the police release it from evidence. I'll print out our photo from the escape room, and we can frame it and hang it on our wall."

I couldn't help myself, I jumped up and down in place for a minute before realizing it was incredibly late and the downstairs neighbors were probably trying to sleep. "Yes!" I screeched.

"I don't know," Izzy said, shaking her head sadly as she addressed my aunt. "I was legit hoping she would be more enthusiastic."

I punched her playfully in the arm. "Are you kidding? I'm so happy, I could kiss the cat!" Then I scooped up Rufus and proceeded to place a big wet smooch on the end of his nose. "I have to call my mom!" I whipped out my cell phone and started dialing.

My mother answered the phone, sounding frantic. "Odessa? What is it? What's wrong?"

"Nothing's wrong, Ma."

"Do you have any idea what time it is?"

Yikes. "Oh, sorry about waking you." After two months in New York, I'd already adjusted to the city's habit of going to bed late and sleeping in late, but I had to admit that it was way too early—or too late, depending on how I looked at it—to be making phone calls. "I just have the best news!"

"You can tell me all about it when you get home," my mother insisted. In the background, I could hear my father's sleepy voice asking what was wrong.

"But I'm not going back to Piney Island." A huge grin broke out on my face. "I'm staying right here, in Williamsburg."

My mother sighed on the other end of the phone. I heard her bedsprings squeak as she sat up. "Odessa, don't be silly. Your family's waiting for you."

"That's just it, Ma," I said. I squeezed Izzy's hand.

Tomorrow, instead of traipsing to the bus stop in the wee hours of the morning boarding the first Greyhound heading south, I was going to sleep until noon, then walk the eleven blocks to Untapped Books & Café and beg Todd to give me my job back. Then I was gonna eat breakfast in the café, utilizing my employee discount to treat myself to whatever Parker was cooking. I'd take a coffee to go and wander through Domino Park until it got too warm, and then I'd come back to my aunt's apartment—*my* apartment, I corrected myself—and take a dip in the rooftop pool. "I've found a wonderful family here, and I *am* home."

#TheEnd

Acknowledgments

A very special thanks goes out to the friends, family (family don't end with blood!), and total strangers who bought *Killer Content* so I could write *No Memes of Escape*. Y'all put up with a lot from me in exchange for Odessa adventures and puggle pictures, and I'm grateful for all of you—especially Potassium, Liz, La, Ris, and Dare, who are always there for me, 24-7, "whether you like it or not." Whether you boosted me on social media, texted me supportive messages in the middle of the night, or bought ten copies to give out to everyone (thanks Toni <3), you wonderful weirdos are the real heroes.

There's a huge team behind this book—my very patient agent, James McGowan, at the BookEnds Literary Agency; my fantastic editor, Kristine Swartz; and the entire magnificent Berkley team. This includes cover design, page layout, meticulous correcting of my less-than-stellar grammar, the wonderfully talented audiobook production team, marketing, publicity, and a million other moving pieces from the distribution centers (hi, Stewy!!!) to the booksellers.

Last, but never least, for the absolutely amazing authors in the #Berkletes 2021 debut group that supported, entertained, enlightened, and encouraged me and Odessa—through a pandemic nonetheless!—here's a very special :heart_eyes: emoji. #ILY

Photo courtesy of the author

Brooklyn Murder Mysteries author OLIVIA BLACKE writes quirky, unconventional, character-driven cozy mysteries. After shuffling around the USA from Hawaii to Maine, she currently resides with her husband and their roly-poly rescue puggle, but is forever home-sick for NYC. In addition to writing, disappearing into a good book, and spending *way* too much time on social media, she enjoys scuba diving, crocheting, collecting tattoos, and baking dog cookies.

CONNECT ONLINE
OliviaBlacke.com
🐦 OliviaBlacke
📷 OliviaBlackeAuthor
📘 AuthorOliviaBlacke

Ready to find
your next great read?

Let us help.

Visit prh.com/nextread

Penguin
Random
House